D1636258

BROILER

ALSO BY ELI CRANOR

Don't Know Tough
Ozark Dogs

BROILER

ELI CRANOR

Published by
Soho Press, Inc.
227 W 17th Street
New York, NY 10011

Library of Congress Cataloging-in-Publication Data

Cranor, Eli, 1988– author.
Broiler / Eli Cranor.
Identifiers: LCCN 2023045381

ISBN 978-1-64129-590-1
eISBN 978-1-64129-591-8
Subjects: LCGFT: Noir fiction. | Thrillers (Fiction) | Novels.

LCC PS3603.R38565 B76 2024 | DDC 813'.6—dc23/eng/20231011
LC record available at https://lccn.loc.gov/2023045381

Interior design by Janine Agro

Printed in the United States of America

10 9 8 7 6 5 4 3 2 1

For Mom, and every other mom out there.

For the two we lost between Emmy and Fin.

And for my first-block students who couldn't stay awake; now I know why.

I fell for you like a child,

Oh, but the fire went wild.

—Johnny Cash, "Ring of Fire"

Now and then a visitor wept, to be sure; but this slaughtering machine ran on, visitors or no visitors. It was like some horrible crime committed in a dungeon, all unseen and unheeded, buried out of sight and of memory.

—Upton Sinclair, *The Jungle*

BROILER

1.

Despite all that Mimi Jackson knew, the chicken fajitas still looked good. Smelled good, too. She watched the dark-haired waiter balance three plates on one arm as he hustled past her table and the five other women she'd invited to La Huerta. They were wives of Detmer Foods plant managers. They played bunco and were members of local Junior League chapters. And just recently, they'd all performed a miracle.

"Really appreciate everyone making the time," Mimi said, reaching for her glass of water, wishing it was a margarita. It'd been almost a year. "Know you're busy. I'm busy, busier now than ever, but it's important for us to get together, to share things and express our—"

"Hold up," Gina Brashears said, the only woman at the table with an alcoholic beverage. Gina was older than the others by at least ten years. "Sounds like we're about to have some sorta AA meeting."

Mimi was afraid of this, or something like it. There was a good chance she was alone in her fear. Maybe the other women didn't feel like she felt. Maybe they didn't want to be there at all. A ranchera tune played from a speaker hidden behind the fake fern in the corner. A group of Mexican men perched along the bar stared up at a television with solemn faces as other men kicked a ball around on the screen. Mimi watched them, thinking her husband should get a soccer league going at the plant. Then thinking, no, it'd just be another thing he'd have to keep up with.

"I went to AA with my sister's husband once," Gina said. "Read the Big Book. Recited the Serenity Prayer." She paused to chug the rest of her margarita. "Ain't nothing but a bunch of old drunks, slurping coffee and chain-smoking Pall Malls."

The women flinched.

"Well, I don't see any Pall Malls," Mimi said and forced a smile. "But yes, I was thinking we could all get together about once a month and run this kind of like an AA meeting."

"Ain't following you, hon," Gina said, waving a waiter down and pointing to her empty glass. "Nobody here's a alcoholic, at least not the obvious kind."

"No," Mimi said, cheeks aching from holding the fake smile. "I don't see any alcoholics, but I do see a tableful of new moms."

There it was. The common denominator. The responsibility, the *burden*, they all shared. The other young mothers—Trish, Whitney, Nina, and Lilly—seemed more restless now than ever, acrylic nails tapping at cell phone screens, checking on their babies, trying to come up with an excuse so they could leave.

The meeting wasn't supposed to go like this. Mimi had been planning it for weeks, rehearsing her lines in the bathroom mirror, preparing the perfect message for the other new mothers, a slightly veiled cry for help, or at least comfort. Misery loves company, right? Wasn't that what motherhood was? *Misery.* It wasn't all sunshine and rainbows. Of that much, Mimi was certain. Being a mom was the hardest job on the planet, but nobody had ever told her that. Had the other women been warned?

"I go to Walmart . . ." Mimi paused and picked at a cuticle, waiting until the women looked up from their phones. They were all so well-manicured, every last one of them, even Gina. Perfectly put together young mothers, that's what Mimi saw. It's what she saw every morning in the mirror after she put her face on, a touch of color here, a simple gloss there. Nothing crazy. The other women were looking at her now. What did they see? "It's about a fifteen-minute drive in from the farm. I like to go early Saturday mornings. There's barely any traffic, but the whole time I'm driving, you know what I'm thinking about?"

Gina put a hand over her mouth and whispered to the waiter: "*I ordered sugar on the rim, José, not salt . . .*"

"What, Mimi?" Nina Ferguson said. "What are you thinking about?"

"Car wrecks."

"*Car wrecks?*" Gina took the first sip of her second margarita. "Y'all live off 412 just west of Sonora? I'm out that way all the time. Never see any wrecks."

"I never see any real wrecks, either, but I can't stop thinking about them," Mimi said.

Gina snorted and glanced back at the rest of the table. Nobody returned her gaze.

Whitney Blackburn said, "I see gas fires, everywhere."

"Anytime we go to the pool," Trish Jameson said, a beige bra strap peeking out from under the sleeve of her burgundy blouse, "I count beats in my head. You know, like for CPR? Thirty chest compressions then two breaths. The compressions time up with that song, 'Stayin' Alive.'"

"The *Bee* Gees? Chest compressions?" Gina stirred her drink and sucked from the straw at the same time. "The hell's all this about?"

"Postpartum anxiety affects close to ninety percent of new mothers," Mimi said, pulling statistics from the 3 A.M. Google searches she used to fill the time between Tuck's feedings. "For me it's worse at night, especially if Luke's not home. Right before I fall asleep, my mind starts racing through a checklist of horrible stuff—carbon monoxide poisoning, SIDS, anaphylactic reactions. It's like I have OCD."

"I was diagnosed with OCD when I was twelve," Lilly Taylor said, "and now I have a three-month-old daughter."

Mimi said, "I'm so sorry," and leaned back in her chair far enough that the waiter could place a basket of chips and six small bowls of salsa on the table. "Each one of you has your own story to tell, and *that's* why I called you. That's why I wanted us to get together. Something outside of bunco or Junior League, something where it was just us new moms. I thought if we talked about all the crazy crap in our heads, then maybe we'd feel a little better."

A chip crunched loud enough for Mimi to hear it over the ranchera music and the soccer game. Gina took another bite, chewing as she said, "You know I got three boys, Mimi? Shit. Blaine just turned nine."

Mimi said, "Yeah, but Dax is still in diapers, right? I thought—"

"Oh, *now* I get it. Thought you'd get ol' Gin-Gin in your little club, let her tell the girls everything'll get easier? It all works out eventually? That it?"

Mimi studied Gina, her inverted bob hairdo, shorter in the back than it was in the front, the forty-something mother of three going for the youthful, edgy look. Maybe Mimi had made a mistake. Maybe this whole idea was bullshit, just like her husband, Luke, had said. The same thing he'd said when she'd come home with the Xanax prescription. *Luke.* What was she thinking leaving Tucker—her six-month-old baby boy—home alone with Luke? All he ever thought about was that stinking chicken plant.

That's how it always started. Mimi could be doing fine, making it through another day with Tuck, this whole new life she knew nothing about, and then, in the very next instant, she might notice a warning label on a jar of peanut butter, or read a childhood cancer post on Facebook. One thought led to another, then another, and before long, Mimi was gone. It felt like going over a big hill too fast, or driving through a storm and the tires slip, two tons of metal floating down the interstate and nothing can stop it.

Mimi pushed back and stood. "No," she said, answering Gina's question without looking at her. "That's not it. This is something different. Something worse." Mimi waited, hoping one of the other women would stop her. No such luck. They were all leaned forward on their elbows, eyes sleepover wide. "Just last month . . ." Mimi had come there to confess, to get the bad stuff out, and this was the worst of it. "I was driving through the Bobby Hopper Tunnel. Tuck was in the back, in his car seat, asleep." He wasn't asleep. He was screaming like he always did when his refluxes flared. The sound he made, it was like a goat bleating. It split Mimi in two, separated the woman she'd been from the woman she was. Only a mother could withstand such torture. She should've pulled over. She should've stopped. "I could hear him breathing, making this wet, sucking sound, when the wheel started to turn toward the wall and—"

Gina slapped the table. Chips rattled free of the basket. Drinks spilled. "It don't get any easier." Gina paused long enough for Mimi to realize the woman had saved her, stopped her before she went too far, said too much. "But a ice-cold marg every now and then don't hurt none. Y'all ever heard of the pump and dump?"

Ferg said, "The pump and—"

"—*dump*. Yeah," Gina barked. "When you're breast-feeding and you wanna get your drink on? All you got to do is pump when you get home. Ain't never easy pouring all that milk down the drain, but the last thing anybody wants is a drunk baby."

Ferg was the first to laugh, letting out a high-pitched squeal that brought Mimi back from the tunnel, back from the concrete wall and just how close her 4Runner's driver-side headlight had come to it. A moment later, the whole table was cackling, so hard, so loud the group of Mexican men turned from the game, watching as the table of white women ordered two pitchers of margaritas, three plates of chicken fajitas, and chimichangas with extra cheese.

GABRIELA MENCHACA WAS still wearing the diaper when Edwin came home. She barely heard the trailer door open, lost in the dream that carried her through her ten-hour shifts. The one where they lived in a three-bedroom house outside of town with a washing machine and Gabriela had time to prepare real meals instead of just microwaving noodles. Edwin was lost in his own dream, the one he kept returning to lately. Tequila breath and glassy eyes on a Thursday night, knowing his shift at the chicken plant started in less than six hours. Knowing he wouldn't get a single break, not even to go to the bathroom.

Gabriela slid the diaper down around her ankles, stepped out, and said, "That was the last one."

"The last what?"

She looked down at the wadded diaper on the floor.

Edwin said, "I'll go get more," and jingled the car keys in his pocket.

"With what?"

"Tomorrow is payday."

"You'll need one for in the morning, for your next shift."

Edwin fell back into the sofa they'd bought secondhand from the Goodwill in Fayetteville. Their trailer was a dumping ground for forgotten things: a boxy television set Edwin had salvaged from a coworker, a microwave with a splintered glass door. Posterboard signs were folding in on themselves beneath the window, all that remained of

Edwin's failed attempt to stage a walkout at the plant. The Mexican flag tacked above the sofa also came from the Goodwill. There was an inscription on the back written in black Magic Marker: *Hot Chicks and Big Dicks, Cancún '06*. The kitchen stunk of propane, always, a problem with the stove's pilot light.

Edwin said, "We've worked so hard, Gabby," and ran his index finger and thumb over his thin mustache, the one he'd been growing for months and couldn't go five minutes without touching.

"I know."

"Seven years ago, when I graduated and walked across that stage—Principal Buckley, remember him? He passed me my diploma and you know what he said?"

Gabby knew. Every time Edwin got drunk he told the same story. She let him play it out anyway.

"He said to me, 'You're going places, Saucy.' Remember that? How they started calling me 'Saucy' when I scored those three goals in—"

"—the state championship our junior year." Gabby loved him, but she didn't want to hear the whole thing again. "Yes, Edwin Saucedo, I know your story. I know it because it's my story, too."

"Seven years," Edwin said. "In some ways it seems like yesterday. When I think about where we are now, though, it feels like the life of another man."

"You've been drinking."

"No," Edwin said. "I've been *thinking*." He pulled his face out from his hands and tapped the side of his head. The look in his eyes, Gabby could almost see the boy they'd called "Saucy" all those years ago.

"At the bar tonight," he said.

"Where you were drinking our money away."

"It's the bar in that restaurant. You know the one?"

"La Huerta."

"Yeah. We were trying to watch the game, Chivas versus Cruz Azul, but these women behind us, they were acting so crazy."

"It was someone's birthday?"

Edwin shook his head. "No, no. You'll never guess what it was."

Standing barefoot on the kitchen's linoleum floor—a place Gabby Menchaca had stood for most of the seven years after high school, except for the hours she spent in line at the plant—she could feel something catch and bite in her stomach, off to the side a little. Like her body knew what was coming.

"*Babies*," Edwin said and leaned back, putting his feet on the piece of plywood held up by four plastic crates, a makeshift coffee table. "I could barely watch the game."

Gabby reached out, steadying herself on the kitchen cabinets. Her legs were bare. She'd forgotten she wasn't wearing any pants. Right there on the floor by her feet was the diaper, the one she had to wear to work because there were no breaks, just broiler after broiler. She said to Edwin, "Would you like to eat?" and felt her shirttail rise as she took a pack of ramen noodles down from a shelf above the stove.

"These women . . ." Edwin said, ignoring the question. "At first, it was like they were scared."

"Scared of babies?" Gabby dumped the noodles into a pink plastic bowl and turned on the faucet.

"Yeah, that was it. They were scared of their babies. They were young. Not much older than you or me. It was pretty dark inside the restaurant, but I could still see them."

Edwin made circles with his fingers and pressed them to his eyes, an imaginary pair of goggles. *Night-vision* goggles, if Gabby had to guess. Some sort of joke. She set the microwave for three minutes.

"The one sitting at the head of the table, Gabriela, I saw her face and thought, *I know you.*"

"A friend?"

"No, no," Edwin said, still with his fingers wrapped around his eyes. "Mr. Jackson's wife."

Edwin stood and walked the five steps from the sofa to the kitchen. Gabby kept her back to him, still facing the microwave. His hands were rough at the palms from seven years spent cutting the left leg off broiler chickens. His calluses scraped across her bare thighs as he moved in behind her and rested his chin on her shoulder.

Edwin said, "Mr. *Jack*son. The man who ups the birds per minute from one-forty to one seventy-five and now we can't even take a piss? That was his *wife* at the restaurant, complaining about her six-month-old child. Talking crazy. Like you wouldn't believe."

"What was she complaining about?"

"I don't know. Her words, her worries, none of it made sense to me. Not after what we've been through."

Gabby struggled under his weight. She lifted her finger to the microwave and pushed a button. The pink plastic bowl, spinning as it heated up, was distorted through the microwave's cracked glass door.

"It wasn't our time, Edwin. We weren't ready. That's all."

"And these women at La Huerta? They were ready? They're not even *thankful*."

Gabby watched the green glowing numbers across the top of the microwave tick down, thinking of the long hours at the plant, the antibacterial sprays coating everything. Stuck in her hair, on her skin, so thick she would taste it on the noodles when it was finally time to eat. The worst part—the point Edwin would've made if he hadn't gone to the restaurant and come home with his beer goggles on—was the lack of bathroom breaks. That's why Gabby had stopped drinking water. She'd go a whole day and drink nothing, terrified of standing there in her soaked-through panties for hours like she had that one time, early on, but never again. This was back before Edwin talked to Luis and learned about the diapers. Before he knew she was pregnant, and then she wasn't. Edwin in the living room saying to her one night, "You *knew*? You knew and still you would drink nothing? *Gabriela?*" In the weeks that followed, Edwin printed off articles from the internet, citing the importance of water consumption during pregnancy, something about the amniotic fluid.

Gabby felt Edwin's hands fall away from her thighs, his chin heavy on her shoulder. She watched the green numbers change, trying not to think of Mr. Jackson's wife in a Mexican restaurant complaining about her baby, and then the microwave dinged.

GINA SAID, "YOU think the other girls'll be okay?" sitting behind the wheel of her GMC Denali, Luke Bryan's "Knockin' Boots" going strong over the stereo.

"After a night like this?" Mimi said. "It's their husbands you should be worried about."

Mimi was small-framed, thinner now than she'd been in high school. With her clothes on, she looked exactly like she had during her Kappa Kappa Gamma days, long legs, tanned skin—a figure most women would kill for—but things were different underneath. Parts were missing. The pieces that had come together to form her son. Every new varicose vein, all those stretch marks, led straight back to her beautiful baby boy. When Tuck cried, she could still feel it in her gut, the place where he had grown from a pea-sized fetus into a full-blown baby boy.

Mimi touched the spot and realized Gina had been right; the margaritas made her feel better. She could still feel the tequila in her cheeks as she reached for the radio dial, spinning through the SiriusXM stations before finally coming to a stop on "Willie's Roadhouse." She wasn't sure who was singing, but she knew the song, her lips moving in time with the words, "*Looking for love in all the wrong places . . .*"

"Johnny Lee," Gina said, tapping the wheel. "Now, that's more like it."

"New country music isn't really even country."

"There's some of it I like. You ever heard that song 'The Joke'? Think a lesbian sings it."

"Brandi Carlile. Yeah," Mimi said, "that's a good one. You see where she teamed up with Tanya Tucker?"

"I saw 'em on the TV a while back. Tanya looked like she'd had a stroke—or maybe like she was having one, right there on stage—but damn, she could still sing."

Mimi laughed. She hadn't laughed so much in one

night since she'd been a student at the University of Arkansas, just a few miles down I-49 in Fayetteville. Sam Walton had opened the first Walmart in nearby Rogers, and William H. Detmer started farming chickens just outside the Springdale city limits. Northwest Arkansas boomed, leaving the rest of the state behind, either lost in the meth-infested hills or rusting away down in the sticky Delta heat. Mimi had met her future husband, Luke, at a sorority function her sophomore year. He was a senior, darting around the Galaxy Skateway on rollerblades, the other guys wearing blocky skates and busting their asses, probably drunk already. Not Luke Jackson, the blue-eyed senior up from Arkadelphia, Arkansas, a town of less than ten thousand. Mimi remembered saying, "Ark-a-del-phi-*a*? You're serious?" Luke was always serious, and that's what Mimi liked about him. He had a plan—he already had a job lined up at Detmer for after graduation. One year later, they were married.

The SUV turned left off 412 onto a dirt road, Mimi singing over Johnny Lee still going strong on the satellite radio. Gina nodded down the long, dark road. "All that worrying you were talking about earlier, but you don't mind living way out here in the boonies?"

Mimi's mouth had gone dry. She licked her lips. "Luke keeps a couple chicken houses."

"A manager *and* a grower?" Gina said as the Johnny Lee song ended and one by Waylon came on. "Me and Brett been in this business going on twenty years. Never heard of a plant manager growing his own broilers."

"Ferg's husband, Steve?" Mimi said. "He has two chicken houses out near Harmon. They do pretty good."

"How many your man got?"

Mimi said, "Seven," and shrugged.

"Seven chicken houses *and* he runs the biggest plant in Arkansas?" Gina took the wheel with both hands and leaned forward. "No wonder you're such a mess."

"*Hey.*"

"The first step is admitting you got a problem, like you said earlier, talking all that AA shit."

"I don't remember what I said, but the other girls got it. They knew what I was talking about."

The pine trees on either side of the dirt road were trimmed so no branches stuck out too far, no chance of a vehicle getting scratched. Luke's doing. Mimi thought of her husband, how he was always going on about the other plant managers, making everything into a competition, like they weren't all on the same team already. *The Detmer Team.* Mimi wondered what Luke would say when Gina Brashears's Denali pulled up in their front drive.

"'Course they got it, hon. They're just as screwed up as you are," Gina said. "That story Lilly Taylor told about watching her daughter sleep? Now that gave me the willies. How many times she say she went in there at night?"

Mimi said, "A lot," abandoning any thoughts of Luke, her mind moving to Tuck now, imagining her son fast asleep in his crib, hoping he'd had his one milliliter of famotidine for his reflux and the single drop of vitamin D solution. Mimi wasn't sure what the vitamin D drops were for. His skin? Maybe she'd forgotten to mention the drops to Luke at all. Maybe . . .

"Think it was seventeen times," Gina said. "What

weirded me out most was the fact Lilly counted. Probably all that OCD stuff she's talking about."

Gina took the wheel in both hands. Her wrists were as thick as Mimi's ankles.

"And that phone app," Gina said. "What'd she call it?"

Mimi said, "SpyMe," remembering the look on all the other women's faces as Lilly explained how she'd installed an application on her husband's phone that allowed her to read his text messages and trace his calls.

"That's it," Gina said and shook her head. "Poor girl. You remember what Ferg said to her?"

Mimi remembered. Of all the women, Nina Ferguson was the only one Mimi didn't like. Ferg had red hair and played up the feisty ginger stereotype every chance she got, always going on about her wild days down in Florida. Made Mimi cringe just thinking about it, the same way she'd winced when Ferg told Lilly there was only one way to keep a man from cheating.

Mimi shook her head. "You've never thought about it?"

"Honestly, Mimi, there's some things I'd just as soon not know."

Mimi's mind was on her husband again when the pruned pines gave way to an open field. A looming structure rose in the distance, towering over a few freshly planted maples. A security light clicked on above the garage, revealing the two-story mansion Luke had had built the year before he'd been promoted to manager of the Springdale plant.

Gina said, "Your husband's been a manager for how long?"

"Four years."

"Hot damn. Maybe Brett needs to get us a few chicken houses," Gina said, turning "Willie's Roadhouse" down. The Denali rolled into the Jacksons' front drive and Gina eased off the gas, ogling the whitewashed brick, the board-and-batter shutters, the wraparound porch, the wall-sized window offering a straight shot through the kitchen—past the exposed overhead beams and ten-foot farmhouse table—to the L-shaped pool in the back, complete with a fountain made of local limestone. There was only one thing missing.

Luke's truck.

The Denali's passenger-side door was still open when Mimi clamored up the front porch steps. The tequila in her blood boiled as she jabbed the key into the lock. The door swung open and Mimi shouted, "Luke? *Lucas!*" breathing so fast, so hard, she could barely hear the house alarm, a robotic voice coming out of the far wall, saying, "*Front door ajar. Front door ajar. Front door a—*"

Mimi rushed over to the keypad she'd had installed the week before Tuck was born, her pointer finger pecking at the glowing buttons until the monotone voice was gone, leaving only silence in the five-thousand-square-foot house.

"Hate them damn things," Gina said, standing in the doorway, fighting to catch her breath. "Hope it didn't wake your kid up."

Mimi let out a single syllable—"*Tuck*"—and took off down the hallway. The nursery was dark, but the sound machine wasn't on. Still, Mimi refrained from hitting the lights for fear of waking her son. Despite the shadows, Mimi could see the crib was empty. She walked toward it anyway and pressed the backs of both hands flat against the firm mattress.

Cell phone to her ear, Mimi hissed her husband's name. Five rings then straight to Luke's voicemail. She tried him again, and this time she heard a song she recognized— "Traveller" by Chris Stapleton—coming from somewhere inside the house.

Gina said, "*Hey*," as Mimi burst back into the hallway, heels clacking over the hardwood floors. Luke's ringtone grew louder, clearer, as she started down the steps to the basement. The song ended before Mimi could find his phone. She knew it was coming from somewhere in the basement, though. And then it settled on her, the realization that her husband's phone was downstairs, but he wasn't, and neither was her son.

The sugar from the margarita—not to mention all that Jose Cuervo Gold—mingled with the hot cheese, ground beef, and refried beans in Mimi's stomach, burning as it started up her throat. Mimi tried swallowing it down, but the bile kept rising, along with a bitter pang of guilt. If she hadn't gone out with the girls, Tuck would've been in his crib, asleep already. He would've been right where he was supposed to be, instead of pawing through the cabinet under the kitchen sink, or floating face down in the swimming pool out back. Tuck couldn't swim. He couldn't even crawl.

Mimi made it to the base of the stairs before saliva spurted from her gums. The sudden gush was strong enough to change her course. She was almost to the toilet when Gina laughed upstairs.

Head suspended over the toilet, Mimi held it down

long enough to hear a man's voice now, too, a confident, smirking tone she recognized.

"Yeah, took little man to check the chickens," Luke said as Mimi gathered her hair and lowered her head into the bowl. "Don't tell his momma."

2.

The clock by the bed read a quarter to six in the morning. Gabby lay on her back, listening to Edwin breathing beside her. Ragged, wet sounds. The kind of sleep that did no good. She knew she would have to wake him. His shift started at seven. The plant was a ten-minute drive across town. There wouldn't be much traffic, not this early. Gabby nuzzled Edwin's arm, holding out hope he could make it.

"Gab-*by*," he said and rolled away.

"Look at the time."

Edwin's right arm flopped out from under the covers. His hand groped around on the nightstand until his fingers found the clock. Gabby knew what he would do before he did it, but the sound still surprised her: the sharp crack the plastic made as it splintered against the wall nearest the bed. Then Edwin's arm recoiled, drawing into his body as he made smacking sounds with his lips.

Gabby spoke his name again, her voice as flat and cool as the threadbare sheet, then looked to the place on the nightstand where the clock had been. She began counting in her head, wanting to be sure about her next move. When she'd made it to ten, she slid sideways out of the bed, taking the covers with her. All of them.

Edwin sat straight up in his boxer shorts. "Gabby. *Jesus.* What time is it?"

She glanced at the shattered remains of the bedside clock but said nothing. It was Friday, her only day off.

"Gabriela?" Edwin brought his knees into his chest and wrapped his arms around them. "I can't go to work, not today."

"You're sick?"

"What does it matter? It's not like we get sick days."

"If you're sick, you can go to the infirmary at the plant. Maybe you could get a note."

Edwin rubbed his face with both hands. "I'd get a packet of ibuprofen, and that's if I'm lucky."

"What's wrong with you?"

"I'm tired. That's all. Just tired."

One of Edwin's T-shirts from high school hung loose past Gabby's waist, covering the tan panties she always wore to bed. Edwin would find them in the bathroom sometimes, laid across the hamper or dangling from the door, and say, "Look at the *size* of these things. *Granny* panties!" And Gabby would laugh. She wasn't laughing now.

"You're tired?" she said. "I don't understand."

"Everything I told you last night, I meant it." Edwin still had his knees pulled into his chest, sitting in the center of the bed, as far away from the edges as he could get. "I feel fine. I feel great, you know? You can see? Look at my eyes."

She'd already seen his eyes. Last night when he came

home talking about the women at La Huerta, there was that same glassy expression she'd been noticing more and more lately, like a lens between the boy she'd fastened herself to all those years ago and the man he had become. They'd met almost by accident. Springdale High was huge, one of the largest high schools in Arkansas. Of the hundreds of other boys in Gabriela's graduating class, she'd never expected Edwin Saucedo to be the one, but there he was, in the same bed where her parents had slept, moping around the same trailer where she'd been raised but not born.

Gabriela Menchaca was born in Celaya, Mexico, just like her older twin sisters, Yesina and Yasmin. Before the moment when Gabby's memories began, her family had fled to America. She didn't remember the heat, the hunger, or the coyote her father revered as a sort of desert demigod. She'd just heard the stories, different versions of the truth, all those miles her mother had carried her. Her mother was gone now. Her father and sisters, too. Almost eight years had passed since they packed their bags and drove back to Mexico the summer before Gabby's senior year.

"Put your feet on the ground," Gabby said, still holding the bedding in her arms. "That's what I tell myself in the morning. Just put your feet on the ground. That's the hardest part. Then you'll be ready to go."

"What if I don't want to go?"

Gabby dropped the blankets and the sheets on the floor. "Not even for me? For our plan?" She was in the bed beside him now, fingers working up his arm, feeling the cords of muscle there, stringy and tight. She had to rub him the right way some mornings to get him out of bed, redirect him toward the plant and the life they'd been dreaming of forever. "Edwin, I will keep my promise to you, but you have to keep working. It's the only way."

He rolled his head around, popping his neck. "Mr. Levon came by yesterday, before I went out."

Mr. Levon owned and operated Wink-Land Trailer Park, a nod to his ridiculous last name. *Levon Wink.* Gabby wanted to spit just thinking about the gristly white man whose slack face reminded her of the gooey chicken parts she fingered every day. Mr. Levon only rented to people who looked like Gabby and Edwin, people like their parents who worked two, sometimes three jobs. People who had money but were still scared. All the time scared of everything, everyone, even men with droopy faces and thin hair like Mr. Levon.

"He came here?" Gabby said.

"It's not the first time."

"No?"

The way Edwin looked at her, the way his eyes were squinting like they hurt, it told Gabby just how far gone he was. How far she'd let him get without saying anything about the nights at La Huerta or wherever the hell it was he went, drinking their money away. And now this. The thought made Gabby squint like Edwin but different, no shame in her eyes, just anger, pure hot hate aimed straight at the man she loved above all others.

She loved Edwin because she had to, like a sister loves a brother, like her family back in Celaya. Her mother had wailed for weeks before they left, but Gabby wasn't budging. She was a straight-A student her junior year and had just received the reading list for AP Senior English.

Gabby might not have been an American citizen, she might not have had the proper paperwork, but she'd read *Their Eyes Were Watching God* and understood most of it, especially Janie and Tea Cake. She begged her parents to stay. Said she'd do anything, not realizing that there was a limit to what a person could do. Getting a job at the plant was easy, which Gabby forgot sometimes when the supervisors yelled about how many applications they had, how many people were out there, waiting to take her job. Gabby worked nights at the plant and shuffled into school an hour or so after her shift ended, just barely enough time to shower, if she was lucky. She rented the same trailer her parents had rented, the home where she'd grown up. The same kitchen where her sisters had shouted, "Mordida!" after they'd pressed her nose into cake after cake, year after year. Once they were gone, there were no more cakes, no more parties. Only work then school then work again, a vicious cycle like the line at the plant.

"Why did Mr. Levon come here, Edwin?"

He leaned over and put his chest on her back like he had the night before. Gabby felt his arms slide in around her waist and wanted to punch his nose. She wanted to scream. She said his name instead, softly, slowly, drawing out both syllables.

"He was saying something about the rent," Edwin said, finally. "I'm not sure."

"You're not sure?"

"I just told you. I said—"

"How much?"

His shoulders moved up and down. "I told you—"

"Yes. You told me. You just told me you don't want to

go to work, like we don't need the money? Like you can *afford* to stay home?"

"I'll get a new job."

"You know we can't take that risk."

"I'll cook at the Taco Bell. I don't care."

"And lose everything we've built already?" She felt his chin digging into her left shoulder blade, the full weight of him, pinning her down. "We had a plan, Edwin. We still have it. The plan is all we have."

"Tell me again," he said. "Tell me about our plan. How long it will take?"

Gabby knew. She'd calculated everything already—the dates, how much they would have to save before she would be willing to try again, every penny budgeted and tallied in a black-and-white composition notebook she kept in a cabinet above the microwave.

"Five years," she said.

Edwin mumbled, "That's right. Five years," and Gabby squeezed his arm, holding tight to the plan they'd made, even if her heart feared it was pointless.

"And twenty thousand dollars, Edwin. Then we will be out of this place."

"Twenty?" he said, his voice sounding upbeat now, childish. "Why not more?"

"More?"

"What was it you were telling me about the overtime? Maybe I should go talk with Mr. Jackson, show him those numbers you showed me."

The numbers were in the same notebook as Gabby's budget. It was just something she'd been thinking more and more about lately. They didn't receive pay stubs at the plant. They didn't clock in or out. They stayed until all the broilers had been processed and the truck was empty. Gabby and Edwin worked days now. They never got home before five. Usually, it was after six. The result was a lot of overtime pay they'd never received, an average of two hours a day. Multiply that out over the two thousand one hundred and ninety-one days they'd worked over the last seven years, and the number was staggering.

"The less we talk with Mr. Jackson," Gabby said, "the better. Okay? Forget my silly numbers. I just like to play."

"Why don't we leave, then? We could make more," he said. "We could make twice that in half the time if we left the plant."

Maybe there were other jobs, but who has time to look for a job? A new job meant change, and for those who lived month to month, day to day, change was never easy. Change meant paperwork and sideways glances. Change was scarier than hard work. In the plant, at least, Gabby knew what to expect. The same way a prisoner grows accustomed to his wretched routine. After seven years, the world outside Detmer's concrete walls was unimaginable. There were so many ways things could go wrong. Edwin had a cousin who was always flashing money around, money he hadn't earned. Gabby wouldn't even think his name, much less speak it. Instead, she said, "We've already waited seven years. What's five more? I'll only be thirty when it is time to try again. That's not too old."

"The women at La Huerta," Edwin said and lifted his chin from her shoulder, "they might've been thirty, maybe younger."

Gabby had almost forgotten about the women. Mr. Jackson's wife drinking and complaining about her baby.

"Yes," Edwin said, sitting behind her, fingering his mustache as Gabby held tight to his arm. "They were young, like us. Do you think they waited? Saved up their money just to get married and have a child?"

Gabby said, "In my mind we are married already."

"But in the eyes of others, Gabriela, we are nothing."

The muscles in Edwin's forearms twitched beneath her fingers, but Gabby would not let go. She'd held onto him for so long. For so long, they'd held onto each other. She met Edwin in her senior English class, the regular class she'd been moved to after sleeping through the smart one. There was only so much she could do alone. Edwin was alone, too, but in a different way. He buried his mother, the woman who had brought him to America all by herself, the same summer Gabby's parents went back to Mexico. He wanted to put it all behind him, wanted to move into Gabby's trailer, said he'd get a job at the plant too and help pay the rent. Gabby needed help, so she let him. The money was more real than a diploma, something they could actually use. It wasn't much, but when you've had nothing for so long even the smallest allowance feels like enough. With money in her pocket and a man in her bed, Gabby no longer dreamed of college. She dropped out of Springdale High before Christmas break and settled into her new life with Edwin, the plant, the line, the ten-hour shifts with the extra, unpaid hours at the end. Add it all up, and this was the result.

"We're together, Edwin. Please just put your feet on

the ground," Gabby said. "Everything will be easier after that."

He jerked away from her, a violent shudder like something inside him had snapped. Then his feet were on the floor, head pushing through the long-sleeved work shirt that would need washing tomorrow. He bent to pick up his brown Carhartt jacket and white tennis shoes. Gabby sat in the center of the bed listening to the sounds Edwin made. She would not look at his face or his eyes, afraid she would see the part of him that was broken.

The bedroom door opened. "Five years, Edwin, and—"

"—twenty thousand dollars," he said. "Yes, I know. I *know*. That is when our life begins."

TUCKER WAYNE JACKSON had his daddy's eyes. A cobalt blue Mimi couldn't look at too long without feeling like she'd had one too many margaritas. At six months old, Tuck had his momma wrapped around his chubby little finger. All she had to do was smell his hair—Johnson's Baby Shampoo, pure innocence in a bottle—and her whole world would melt. Tuck was a good baby, too. Easy to love with his chunky cheeks and budding personality. There was nothing for Mimi to worry about, but she did.

All night she'd worried.

Tuck had never stayed up past midnight. Not even close. What was Luke thinking? Taking him into those stinking, musty chicken houses? Mimi had only been in there once, back before the first truckload of broilers arrived. The smell alone had shocked her. Tuck coughed a lot already. A tiny, helpless sound, like something a bird might make. Were the chicken houses to blame? There were huge fans at the south end, blades the size of aircraft wings, chopping up all that rancid air and pushing it out over their property.

What *was* Luke thinking?

He wasn't; he was moving, looking for his next project, the next chore on his checklist. Mimi had never—not once in their nine years of marriage—seen her husband sit down and watch the television. Not even an Arkansas Razorbacks football game. Luke only drank on the weekends, and even then, he never had more than a couple beers. He couldn't afford to waste time on a hangover. Which was exactly why he'd taken Tuck with him to check the chickens at midnight—there was work to be done.

Mimi was standing in the kitchen, getting the blender down from the cabinets, when she noticed a shadow darkening the granite countertops. Tuck bounced in his baby chair and made a happy sound. It softened Mimi enough for her to turn and face her husband. They'd slept in the same bed, spent the whole night together, but she hadn't really looked at Luke. Not until now.

He was bent forward, doing what Mimi had told him at least a hundred times not to do: touching Tuck's hands. Playing with his fingers. Which would've been fine, if sick season wasn't just around the corner. Mimi dumped half a bag of spinach into the blender and pushed the red "mince" button, remembering the year they'd spent in quarantine, the way the whole country had shut down, but not the plant. Never the plant. Not even when the workers started getting sick. So many cases the local news parked a van across the street. Mimi had worried about Luke then, worried he'd bring the virus home and it would keep her from getting pregnant. Luke wasn't worried, though. He was on a mission. America still needed to eat, even if they were coughing their guts up. They needed meat, and chicken was by far the most cost-effective source of protein.

Luke waited until Mimi was done with the blender then said, "You had fun last night," not asking her anything, informing her of a conclusion he'd come to, maybe because her 4Runner was still in the back of the La Huerta parking lot, or maybe because he'd heard her puking in the basement. It had taken her a while to get Tuck down, so long Luke was already asleep when Mimi came to bed, which was fine. She didn't feel like talking. She still didn't.

Mimi dropped a banana in the blender and said, "Sanitizer," nodding toward the two-liter bottle of Purell on the kitchen counter before she pushed the blender's red button again.

The pump on the sanitizer bottle went up and down. Luke rubbed his hands together, barely, then snatched his truck keys from the bowl on the counter as he started for the door.

Mimi let the blender chug to a stop before she said, "I need to go into town, and you need to eat breakfast."

"Got to get to the plant."

"It's not even six thirty."

"Need to get there early."

"Why?"

"Christ, Amelia. How many margaritas did you have last night?"

Mimi said, "Three," and cut her eyes at Tuck, his pacifier going in and out, unaware of his parents' argument. "Maybe four. You want to see the receipt?"

"Three margaritas on top of those pills you take?"

"*Those pills* were prescribed by Dr. Dunaway."

"Yeah, and I bet he'd prescribe me some too, if I asked. Medicine's not supposed to make you feel good, Mimi—it's supposed to make you better."

It was an old argument, one that just kept resurfacing soon after Tuck was born and Mimi started taking Xanax. She didn't take it every day. Just when she needed it. When things inside her head went sideways and thoughts slipped through that were not her own. Like when she'd been driving through the Bobby Hopper Tunnel and the wheel started turning toward the wall. A fraction of an inch. Nothing more. But far enough for Mimi to give Dr. Dunaway a call.

"I didn't take it last night," Mimi said. "I didn't need it, but the margaritas were nice. And now, I'm asking you for a ride, to pick up my car. That's all."

Luke took a step toward the door to the garage and Mimi pictured him leaving, another Friday where he would only see his son for the first ten minutes of the day. With him standing like that, Mimi could see a spot on the back of his head a shade lighter than the rest of his close-cropped crew cut.

Mimi took two glasses down from the cabinet, surprised she hadn't noticed the spot before. The contents of the blender—a slimy green concoction chock-full of vitamins and protein, enough juice to get Luke through even the busiest morning—slid out of the spout and into the glasses. She liked how long it was taking her husband to respond, thinking maybe she'd won this time, until he said, "God, Mimi. I don't have time to take you into town. Don't you remember what today—"

Tuck whimpered and Mimi's world condensed, tunnel

vision as she turned in time to see his bottom lip curl. Luke's sharp tone had scared him. Mimi felt a hot red rash working its way up her neck, spreading out beneath her blond hair.

"I need to pick up his prescription," Mimi said, standing beside her son, trying to work the pacifier back into his toothless mouth. He wouldn't take it, too busy screaming. "Famotidine, for his reflux." She waited a beat. "The medicine you were supposed to give him last night? If he doesn't get it, he'll be coughing and cranky all day."

From the front, Luke showed no signs of aging. Strong jawed with a perfect hairline. He looked like a quarterback, but he'd never played ball. "*Not even when you were little?*" Mimi remembered asking him during the nine short months before they were married. "*Never,*" Luke said. "*My father wouldn't let me. Too much work to be done.*" Looking at her husband now in his tan Detmer work shirt buttoned all the way to the top, his tight Wrangler jeans and three-hundred-dollar Lucchese boots, it was hard to imagine Luke growing up poor, but he had. All those southern Arkansas summers spent in the soybean fields, the winters in the barn cleaning and sharpening the combine blades—they'd shaped him. Made him tougher than most men and their high school football trophies. In many ways, Mimi wanted her son to turn out just like his daddy. The look Luke was giving her now, though, hands on his hips, eyebrows raised—this was not one of those ways.

"Fine," Luke said. "I'll take you to get your car. Let's go."

Mimi took a drink of her shake. Tuck kept crying as Luke started for the door. A moment later, she heard her husband's Ford come to life. She had Tuck out of his baby chair, tears and drool staining the fabric of her Patagonia pullover, when she noticed Luke's satchel, the leather one he kept his laptop in, sitting in a chair beside the kitchen table. The truck's horn honked from the garage and Mimi thought about leaving it. Make Luke drive all the way home after he realized what he'd forgotten. It might've been a fun trick to play, but there wasn't enough time.

The leather satchel dangled from her shoulder as she found her purse, got Tuck strapped into his infant car seat, the diaper bag packed and secured on her back—all in under ninety seconds.

When she made it to the garage, Luke's truck was gone. He'd reversed it out into the driveway and pulled around so the passenger-side door was facing the house, an asshole way of telling Mimi to hurry the hell up.

EVEN THOUGH IT was Gabby's only day off, there was still work to be done. Different from the work at the plant, but similar in its monotony. The chores that lay ahead of her now were the same chores she'd done last week, and the week before that, repeated every Friday morning.

Vacuum the trailer. Wash the plastic plates. Scrub the toilet and the sinks. Gather the laundry then haul it down to the washateria. Gabby hated the laundry because of how hard Edwin made it on her, leaving his clothes out everywhere. Gabby tried not to let her hatred for the laundry bleed into her love, but it was hard. There were ways Edwin could help. Simple tasks like putting his boxers into the bin instead of just throwing them down outside the shower.

Edwin hadn't always been that way. Things changed after Gabby lost the child. Better for a moment, then worse. So much worse. The baby had been reason enough for Edwin to try again. He brought Gabby flowers they could not afford. He started doing push-ups in the morning, drinking one cup of coffee instead of four. The prospect of fatherhood gave him hope. The child was something new, something to get him out of bed. Edwin was always looking for the next big thing, and nothing was bigger to him than the idea of having a son. "A daughter, even. I don't care, Gabriela. A kid!" That's what he'd said, over and over again.

As much as Gabby wanted a child of her own one day, there was a part of her that was thankful for the extra time to prepare. A baby would've compounded her load. She had trouble enough staying ahead of the chores as it was. There was also a chance the pregnancy would've cost her her job. Without proper documentation, nothing was for certain, not even maternity leave. Edwin had somehow seemed to sense this relief in Gabby, wagging a finger in her face and droning on about the water she'd refused to drink, but he didn't know the whole story.

Gabby had gone to see the medical provider at the plant infirmary after it was over, the same man who handled all the workers' ailments. He'd rolled Gabby's shirt up to her bra and tapped her belly with two well-lotioned fingers. "These things happen, you know?" He said other things too, but what he never said was anything about dehydration, nothing about water at all. That came from Edwin. The articles he found online at the Springdale Public Library. The words he'd underlined and highlighted like he'd never done back in Mrs. Hubbard's senior English class.

The drinking started sometime after those printed-off articles had been balled up and thrown away, but not forgotten. Never forgotten. Edwin made sure of that. Every pair of boxers left out on the bathroom floor, every dirty plate, was a message sent, a reminder.

Gabby snatched a sock from the kitchen counter and wadded it into her fist, letting her mind drift ahead to the only Friday task she enjoyed. The bills. The result of the work they'd done that week, outlined in figures she could understand, everything laid out in front of her. Gabby handled all of their money—or so she'd thought, until Edwin had mentioned Mr. Levon coming by and asking for the rent.

She didn't want to think what that meant, but an image formed in her mind, a moving picture of Edwin taking the money, the crinkled bills Gabby always flattened down and slipped into Ziploc baggies. The baggies were stupid. She saw that now. Like a mother packing a sandwich for her son. "It's something I should do. Man to man, you know?" That's all Edwin ever said when Gabby asked him why she couldn't just take the cash to Mr. Levon. The payments were always made in cash. That part of the deal never changed, but Edwin did. Somewhere along the way he'd started taking the cash out of the bags she'd sealed. He'd used their hard-earned money to buy more beer, the tequila she'd smelled on his breath the night before, the real reason he didn't want to get out of bed. He'd been drinking their rent away. The *bastard*. He'd—

Three solid knocks shook the trailer and the ugly thoughts from Gabby's mind.

Nobody came around this early in the morning. All the other Wink-Land tenants were already at work, or asleep after a long night shift. Gabby moved toward the door but did not open it, not yet, peering through the dust-covered blinds, yellowed by sun and time. She groaned when she spotted the shriveled man standing at her doorstep, pinching a stack of papers in one hand.

"Mr. Levon," Gabby said, playing up her white-girl accent, the voice she'd honed in the halls of Springdale High. "Good morning. How are you?"

"Cut the shit, Menchaca." The top of the little man's head was liver spotted and brown like the wild mushrooms Gabby had picked with her mother as a child. "Where's Edwin?"

"I'm sorry. Edwin's at work."

"Work, huh?" Mr. Levon pinched the papers tighter. "Could've fooled me."

"Is there a problem?"

"Yeah, there's a problem." He lifted the papers and shook them. "You suckers owe me damn near three months' rent."

Gabby clamped a hand over her mouth before she remembered taking the work sock from the counter. The sock smelled just like the plant. She dropped it and watched Mr. Levon's eyes follow it down.

"Three months?" Gabby said. "How can that be?"

"You got me, duck."

"What?"

Mr. Levon swatted the air. The papers in his hand made

an angry, flapping sound. "Y'all owe me damn near two grand."

"Two *thousand* dollars?"

"That's right. And don't come at me with a wad of pesos, neither. Like some of your cousins around here." Mr. Levon lifted his free hand and pointed toward the rest of his property.

Gabby blinked. "My family is in Celaya."

"Yeah, well, mine are all right here in Arkansas. Got sixteen grandkids. Couple great-grands, too. And damn near all of 'em are still on the tit." The man paused, as if he were waiting to see if Gabby understood his meaning. She did, but could think of no way to respond. "What I'm saying," Mr. Levon continued, "I got a lot of mouths to feed. My own people. This ain't a charity. It's a trailer park."

Gabby said, "Yes, I know," because she feared what he was about to say next. It did not stop him, though.

"And if y'all don't get me that money by Sunday, then you're out of here. You got me? *Gone.*"

Gabby brought her hand to her mouth again. The sock was gone, but she could still smell the plant on her fingers.

"You hear, Menchaca? Next time I come here, I ain't coming alone."

Gabby nodded once and stepped back, letting the door swing shut as the first warm tear rolled down her cheek.

THE WHOLE TWENTY-MINUTE drive into town, Tuck never stopped screaming. Mimi couldn't believe it, sitting in the truck's backseat, right there next to him, trying to shove his pacifier in his mouth again and again.

She was unaware of the fall foliage on full display through the windows of Luke's gray Ford, the Ozarks on fire with death, Arkansas at its best, its brightest, the rolling hills blazing in the early-morning, October sky—Mimi missed it all. Too busy blaming her husband for Tuck's tantrum. He didn't get a full-night's sleep, she thought. Of course Tuck was cranky. Mimi was thinking how Luke hadn't given their son his one milliliter of famotidine the night before, when the truck pulled into the La Huerta parking lot and stopped.

She popped open the back door, had the car seat hooked in the crook of her left arm, her purse and the diaper bag draped over her right, standing in the lot where she'd laughed and drank less than twelve hours before, and then it hit her. This was Friday, an important day for her husband, the plant, the day of the—

"*Inspection,*" Mimi said.

"Yeah." Luke gave her one corner of a smile. "The plant passes this one, and it's ten straight. They'll *have* to promote me to Executive Officer of Poultry. I don't give a damn how many years Steve Ferguson's been at it. His plant's never passed ten straight government inspections."

Standing in the La Huerta parking lot with her still-screaming son and twenty pounds of bags, diapers, and sensitive-skin baby wipes strapped to her back, Mimi Jackson said, "I forgot." She remembered now how Luke hadn't wanted her to go out the night before the big inspection because he had a few final preparations to make, some sort of plant diagnostics he had to run on his laptop.

"Luke," Mimi said. "I'm sorry."

He was out of the truck now, squatted down beside

Mimi, saying to his son, "Don't give your momma too much trouble today. Okay, little man?" He kissed Tuck on the forehead. A moment later, Luke was sitting in the driver's seat, running his fingers over the wheel. "We pass this inspection today, Mimi, our life will change forever."

"Listen, I shouldn't have . . . I mean, I just get so worried, I can't—"

"I know."

"You *know*?" A knot formed in Mimi's throat, the words she wanted to say getting hung up like always.

"Sometimes," Luke said and glanced at his watch, "I don't think you know how good you've got it."

The window started up and the truck eased forward. Luke had his cell phone in his hands, steering with his wrists. The Ford hooked a left onto Main.

Mimi's blood boomed in her ears, so loud she could barely hear Tuck's whimpering voice, worn out now but with too much of his daddy in him to quit. She finally felt the weight of the junk in her arms, the fun she'd had the night before a lifetime away as Mimi surveyed the diaper bag, the car seat, going over a checklist in her mind of the things she'd need to make it through the day.

She'd need Tuck's insurance card to pick up the prescription. She kept it in the second flap of her wallet. Mimi kept her wallet in her purse, and her purse was right there, dangling from her arm, but it was heavier than she remembered, the leather a different shade of brown. An image formed in her brain: Luke waltzing into the plant for the government-issued inspection with her purse draped over his shoulder instead of his laptop bag.

The hint of a smile creased Mimi's lips—thankful for the weight now, the burden she carried for her husband, her son—and then she started to run.

THE FIVE MILES between Wink-Land Trailer Park and the Detmer Foods plant were marred by construction. Bulldozers and excavators tearing up sidewalks. Cranes with jibs that extended out over the mountains. All that heavy machinery hard at work erasing Edwin's hometown. *All that money*, he thought, running the numbers in his head. The millions of dollars that surrounded him. A yellow dump truck beeped as it backed out in front of Edwin's Dodge. The black ribbed tires rose up higher than he could see through the windshield, each one costing more than he would make in a month at the plant.

Edwin drummed his fingers over the wheel, checking his time on the dash. Six more minutes and he'd be late. Again. Late for the only job he'd ever had. The one that Gabriela had gotten for him at the start of their senior year, the best year of Edwin's life. The plant was even fun back then, fun because it was new and Edwin was making real money. No worries about the other stuff, the big stuff, yet. Just giddy about getting paid, living alone with a girl inside a trailer they rented together. There was beauty in the simplicity of their lives, a certain kind of sweetness that sours over time, the same way the knives at the plant went dull after the first couple of hours. Single, quick slices replaced by sawing and tearing, work that wears your muscles away, muscles Edwin did not know he had until he'd cut into a hundred thousand chickens or more. Always more. Too many to count.

Gabriela Menchaca was the same. No way to keep up with her. She was out of Edwin's league from the start. On a whole different level. So, when she asked him to move in with her, what could he say?

Edwin had spent the better part of his childhood inside the Econo Lodge on 48th Street where his mother was a housekeeper. When Edwin thought of Carmen Saucedo, he pictured her in her uniform, black slacks and a company shirt with the navy-blue logo over the left breast. No hat. Nothing fancy like that. It was just the Econo Lodge, but to a boy from Tepic, a farming town on the western coast of Mexico, the hotel was the manifestation of the American Dream.

Mr. Khoury, the Lebanese man who owned the hotel, lived on the first floor. He rented rooms out to his workers sometimes, women like Carmen with dirt under their fingernails and desperation-rimmed eyes. Women without proper documentation. It was a trap, but Carmen didn't see it that way, not at first, and neither did Edwin. He was five when they moved into room 116. The room had a wall unit that churned out cool damp air. The continental breakfasts were a perk. Free toilet paper and shampoo, too. Edwin loved the pool the best. The late-night swims when all the lights were out and no other guests were around. He started using the fitness center in high school, training to be a star striker for the Springdale soccer team. He helped his mother clean sometimes too, or at least went into the dirty rooms with her and sat on the bed. Edwin would peel the sheets from the mattress and watch cartoons until his mother finished with the rest. Each room taught him something about the people who'd stayed there, something about America. All the soiled towels wadded on the floor. The half-used bottles of lotion. The spilled coffee. So much waste.

Growing up in the hotel provided Edwin with a particular kind of education. He saw, firsthand, what it took other immigrants longer to see. He knew his place. He learned to stay out of the way, always taking the stairs or the industrial elevators. He ate his breakfast late, in that window of time when last night's guests had checked out and the new ones had yet to arrive. The Econo Lodge had its own class system. The workers stayed on the bottom floor, crammed two, sometimes three families into one room, while the guests came and went above, leaving behind Styrofoam containers full of food they did not eat and thermostats set as low as they would go.

As much as the hotel taught him, Edwin's mother taught him more. He knew his father only by the stories Carmen told on the weekends. The look in her eyes, Edwin didn't know what to make of it. Love? Hate? Or something in between? He studied his mother's face in the bathroom mirrors. They had the same nose, but where had his lips come from? His eyes, always watching. He didn't fully comprehend everything he'd learned from her until after she was gone.

Her death came like every other tragedy in Edwin's young life, swift and without warning. It wasn't like Carmen to sleep in. For seventeen years she'd been the one to get him up in the mornings, and then, one day, she didn't.

Twenty-one rooms were left dirty that day. Carmen was transported from the hotel to the morgue in a windowless minivan. The medical examiner offered no explanation outside of natural causes. *Natural to her line of work,* Edwin had thought but not said. A week later his mother was cremated and Edwin was on his own, back at school for the start of his senior year, wearing the same clothes he'd worn the day before, hoping nobody noticed. That's how Gabby found him. How she always saw him, he feared. A poor boy who needed her help. Gabby was already working for Detmer. Edwin asked if he could work there too. He didn't know any better, didn't realize he was falling victim to the same trap that had ensnared his mother. Edwin just knew he liked Gabby, liked the amber color of her eyes, the mole in the crease of her left cheek, a beauty mark like the ones he'd seen on the hotel televisions. Gabby took over where Carmen left off. She cared for him, cooked and cleaned for him. She had a plan, and Edwin was just happy to be a part of it. Gabby was dead set on college. They were going to go together. Then, it was just Gabby, and that was fine. Edwin wasn't a good student. He was so bad at schoolwork Gabby started tutoring him in her free time, whatever moments she could spare between the plant, her own after-hours studies, and keeping the trailer up. Then, in the same sudden way his mother had departed, Gabby left Edwin to fend for himself in the uncharted waters of polynomial functions and expository texts. The memory of that night stayed lodged in his mind forever. The way the trigonometry textbook splayed open on the makeshift plywood coffee table had seemed to mock him, a book full of factors he would never use, not even if he had passed the class. It wasn't until after they'd both dropped out of high school that Edwin realized the college part of Gabby's plan had only been a dream, a delusion, the first of many to come.

Without a degree, they were nothing. Not in Springdale. Men with degrees rode bicycles to work. There were mountain bike trails everywhere now, and bearded white men wearing spandex shorts and neon helmets, using the debris on the sidewalk like ramps to jump ahead of Edwin.

The dump truck finally lurched forward and Edwin jammed the gas pedal all the way down. The Dodge's tires squealed, propelling him to the same place he'd been yesterday, the same place he'd be tomorrow, and the day after that. But he still couldn't afford one of Mr. Levon's trailers? The numbers got mixed up in Edwin's head. Nothing worked out like it was supposed to. All the rules Gabby had made him follow since high school—where had that gotten them?

Edwin knew, but wouldn't let himself think of the ten hours that lay ahead of him. It didn't matter. In three more miles, he'd be back there again.

3.

What Luke enjoyed most about his plant—any plant, really—was how it worked. Everything had a purpose, everything followed the same schedule, which was exactly what Luke would tell the government inspectors as soon as they arrived. The schedule was simple. It went like this:

After forty-five days, broiler chickens are of proper weight and ready for harvest. They arrive at the plant in modular bins, specifically designed for maximum comfort and proper ventilation. From there, workers trained in humane handling carefully suspend the birds by their feet, strapping them into a moving line. Next, the chickens enter a dim-lit room where they are subdued with "rub bars," which provide a relaxing sensation and encourage neck extension. Luke always made sure the inspectors noticed how the broilers closed their eyes when the bars touched their chests. The birds' necks are cut a few moments later. Then they're run through a scalding bath designed to loosen the feathers, and finally the broilers are eviscerated, the part where a machine guts the chickens and cuts off their feet. Luke's plant processed 175 broiler chickens every minute—a rate not allowed in most states, not even some counties in Arkansas—and Luke was damn proud of that, especially when things ran on time.

As he steered his Ford into the parking space marked PLANT MANAGER, Luke thought maybe he should tell the government inspectors nothing was wasted; they shipped the chicken feet to China. He checked the clock on the dash. He was two minutes late. It took less time than that to mess up a factory line. Workers scratched their noses and cut off their pinky fingers. It was always something. These days, dependable employees were getting harder and harder to find. Even the Mexicans were getting lazy.

From the outside, the plant looked similar to a prison, a concrete structure with security gates and a chain-link fence running all the way around. A yellow sign out front read, 298 DAYS WITHOUT AN ACCIDENT. The numbers were displayed digitally like a scoreboard. Luke grabbed his leather satchel from the backseat, threw the strap over his shoulder, and hustled toward the plant's office doors.

He was halfway there when a blacked-out Suburban pulled through the front gate.

Luke kept walking, hoping these were new inspectors. Ones he'd never met before. If he could just get inside, get things situated in his office, then maybe they wouldn't recognize him. Maybe they wouldn't realize he was late.

The doors opened and Luke stepped inside, recalling his first days on the job when they'd stored all the guts and chicken blood onsite, sometimes for up to a week. Back then, the whole plant smelled like a busted nose.

Not anymore. The memory made Luke feel better about the inspectors in the parking lot. He had nothing to hide.

Luke had just entered the lobby when he heard someone shout his name.

"Mr. Jackson?"

Luke took a step back without turning, catching the door with his foot.

"Excuse me, Mr. Jackson?"

The voice didn't sound like any inspector Luke had ever known.

"Mr. Jackson, I know I'm late, but listen, please . . ."

An employee Luke recognized was sitting behind the wheel of a ratty Dodge Neon pulled up sideways on the curb. A Mexican the other workers called "Saucy" sometimes. He had his left arm dangling out the driver-side window, talking louder now, saying, "My girlfriend, Mr. Jackson, she's sick. I know I'm late, but she's sick. You know? Can you hear me? Mr. Jackson?"

Luke could hear him, and he remembered the guy's full name now: Edwin Saucedo, a habitual excuse maker, always had some story about his wife—no, his "girlfriend"—who was also an employee at the plant. Edwin had been a real thorn in Luke's side as of late. It all started when he'd tried to file a claim the year before, something about that girlfriend of his and a failed pregnancy. It grew from there to a half-assed form of activism. Luke heard from another worker that Edwin had even tried organizing a walkout a few months back. Some sort of strike. And now, there the guy was in his rusted-out Dodge pulled up on the plant's front drive, the two government inspectors, all black suits and briefcases, coming up behind him.

"Mr. Jackson?" Edwin said, opening the car door and stepping out, wearing white Converse sneakers, the kind that weren't allowed at the plant. "Do you hear me, sir? I want you to know I am—"

Luke raised his hand, cutting Edwin off. He looked rough, rougher even than the plant's newest batch of workers, men with matted hair and women with whiskers thicker than Edwin's. There was a smell Luke couldn't place coming off him too, a stomach-clenching stench like he'd spent the night curled up in a Porta Potti.

"Come over here, Edwin," Luke said and held his breath. "Yeah, right here up close. Let me tell you what you are."

MIMI PARKED HER 4Runner behind the rusty Dodge in time to see two guys who had to be the inspectors disappear through the lobby's glass doors.

She hissed, "Shh," but thought, *Shit*, trying to ignore the screeching still coming from the backseat. It was only a fifty-foot walk to the front doors, but there was no way she could take Tuck inside the plant without causing a scene.

She reached for Luke's satchel, holding tight to the advice Gina Brashears had given all the young mothers the night before: "*Don't make it harder than it's got to be, girls.*" Mimi was out of the car now, satchel in hand, but she could still hear her son screaming. She ducked back inside the 4Runner's cab, reaching for the volume nob, the satellite radio tuned to "Willie's Roadhouse" as Johnny Cash sang, "*Love is a burning thing . . .*" And then she was back out again, running for the lobby doors as "Ring of Fire" thumped along behind her, the mariachi horns blocking out the cries of her only son.

Twenty feet from the doors, Mimi stopped and jabbed a hand into her pocket, going for the 4Runner's smart key. She pushed the "Lock" button twice and waited, expecting to hear the horn honk, signaling a completely secure vehicle, but it didn't.

In the distance, Johnny Cash's voice died away, replaced by trumpets. The horns were the only sounds coming out of the vehicle. Maybe Tuck had finally given up and gone to sleep? The thought was enough to get Mimi moving again, all the way up to the plant's front doors where she stopped and stared at her reflection in the glass. A worried mother in a rush. That's what Mimi saw. That and her 4Runner parked behind that junky-looking Dodge pulled way up on the curb. Something about the angle, the way the car was leaning to one side, off balance, like whoever had been driving it was in an even bigger rush than she was—it made Mimi stop. Made her turn.

Glancing back over her shoulder, Mimi felt a waft of cool air on her neck, the lobby door opening. Her eyes never made it all the way around to see her vehicle. Not before a voice said, "Hola. Good morning."

A man held the door open for her, a wiry Mexican man with a thin black mustache, smiling back at Mimi like he knew her. She didn't know him, but the way he just kept standing there, grinning back at her . . .

Mimi gripped Luke's satchel with both hands and stepped into the lobby. She didn't know if the guy was still standing there or not. She didn't look back, too focused on the men in their black suits talking to the receptionist, a woman named Terri sitting behind a pane of smudged glass. Luke's office was the first one on the right. The door was open. Mimi kept both hands on her husband's satchel and started past the inspectors, the Johnny Cash song still going in her head, "*And it burns, burns, burns . . . the ring of fire . . . the ring of fire.*"

THE MARIACHI HORNS were the first thing Edwin heard as he exited the plant. Sometimes, after a shift, the parking lot came alive with banda and ranchera tunes. Maybe even a Latin pop-rock song or two. But mariachi?

It took Edwin five steps down the walkway to realize the music was coming from the white 4Runner parked behind his Dodge. Two more steps and he recognized the voice, Johnny Cash singing words to match his heart: "*I fell for you like a child, oh, but the fire went wild.*"

Wild, *yes*, Edwin said in his mind, thinking many things at once: of Gabriela probably still lying in their bed, trying to recover for the shift she would work Saturday; of Johnny Cash singing songs for Mexican people instead of just stealing their trumpets, how the message of country music and ranchera music was one and the same: drug addiction, loneliness and death, love turned good or bad, working-class problems. Maybe, if Mr. Cash was still around to tell Edwin's story, things would've gone differently this morning. Maybe Edwin would still have his job. Maybe Mr. Jackson would've understood why Edwin was wearing the same salty diaper Gabriela had worn the day before. Did he tell the man this? No. Edwin knew better when he heard his boss's tone of voice, speaking loud enough for the other men—the ones wearing black suits into a chicken plant—to hear him and know he meant business. There was no point talking to Mr. Jackson when he was like that, no point in Edwin trying to tell him his story, but if Johnny Cash—a white man from Arkansas—had ever decided to sing about a Mexican losing his job with a couple months' rent already past due, then maybe Mr. Jackson would've understood. Yes, Edwin thought, it sounded like a country song.

"Ring of Fire" was over by the time Edwin made it back to his Dodge. A surprising silence hung thick over the parking lot, the morning shift already at work inside the plant, nobody coming in or out. Edwin noticed three crows sitting on the chain-link fence and stared at them until he could see the blacks of their eyes, anything to keep his mind off Mr. Jackson and the seven pointless years he'd spent working for the man.

His life didn't feel like his life anymore. It wasn't a new feeling, but this latest exchange had shown Edwin how detached he'd become. He'd just sat and stared at Mr. Jackson. Didn't say a single word when he'd brought him into his office. Didn't even nod his head. He just sat there like he did at the bar most nights, waiting for whatever came next. The problem, though, was that it was always the same thing. The child Gabby lost would've changed that. Edwin would've changed for his son. He could've kept going for him, but now?

Now things were worse than they had been. The last thing Mr. Jackson had told Edwin was the reason he'd fired him. It didn't have anything to do with the OSHA signs Edwin had been scribbling on, translating the words into Spanish for the other workers. It didn't have anything to do with complaints Edwin had filed, or even the strike he'd failed to organize. Oh, no. Mr. Jackson fired Edwin because of the papers he'd signed when he was seventeen. The "false documents" that had allowed him to get a job on the line back at the start of his senior year. The same sort of documents that could cost Gabriela her job, too.

The next song began and startled the crows, sending them flying. Edwin followed them with his eyes. This song was different, painful, a high-pitched wail coming from the speakers now instead of the mariachi horns.

Edwin sat down in the driver's seat of his Neon. He pulled the car off the curb, up almost even with the SUV, the song's bassline thumping in time with his heart. It was when the tiny hand slapped against the back window that Edwin realized the music was not what had sent the crows flying.

Mrs. Jackson, the pretty blond lady rushing through the plant's front doors, the one he'd seen at La Huerta the night before, it was her baby—Mr. Jackson's *son*—making that crazy sound.

Edwin pushed open the driver-side door and started for the 4Runner, glancing back at the plant's windows. There was no one outside the lobby. No one in sight. When he looked down, what he saw didn't seem real. The child was locked into a car seat, red faced, screaming, all pink gums and quivering tongue. A lanyard was clipped to the boy's shirt. A blue pacifier dangled from the other end. Edwin's hand went to the SUV's door handle, pulling it before he realized what he was doing. The door opened and the cries of the child drowned out the twangy country song, washing over Edwin, reminding him of his pain.

Gabriela's pain.

The way she'd stood from their sofa one morning and

walked to the trailer's only bathroom. Like it was nothing. Like she had to go pee. Leaving Edwin alone with the voices on the television like his mother had done while she cleaned the hotel rooms. What was taking her so long? Ten minutes passed. A lifetime. Edwin's mind spun as the toilet flushed and Gabriela walked into the living room again, her eyes altered somehow, empty. Edwin remembered the look she'd given him, different from the contorted, gnashing expression of the Jacksons' crying child but also similar in a way Edwin could not explain.

Three days later, Gabriela told Edwin their baby was gone. That's when he started going to La Huerta or Crossroads Bar and Grill to watch the games with other men who had lost something. Cheap shots of tequila washed down with cheaper beer—it was never enough. All of those hazy nights had somehow led Edwin here, to this very moment, standing in the parking lot of the plant that had taken seven good years from him, looking down on a screaming child who had no reason to cry.

THE LOOK ON Luke's face, God, it was worth it. Mimi had never seen her husband smile like that. Not even on their honeymoon, those six beautiful nights at the Excellence La Plaza, a five-star, all-inclusive resort in Cancún. The way Luke had smiled at her when she'd handed him his satchel—when she'd saved the day—it was a mixture of gratitude and joy, the same face Tuck made at the end of a warm bottle, or sometimes in the middle of a nice long bath.

"If you don't pass the inspection now," Mimi had said, one finger tracing her mouth, the place where her husband's lips had just been, "you can't blame me."

The inspectors were still chatting it up with Terri the receptionist, probably already digging for dirt, as Mimi slipped past them and pushed open the lobby doors.

The cool morning air felt good on her face, the first nip of fall settling in. A song she liked played from inside the 4Runner, catching the breeze and drifting up the walkway. Mimi's mouth moved along with the words as she walked.

It was perfect. The ratty Dodge was even gone, and Tuck had finally stopped crying. Gina Brashears was right. There was no sense making motherhood any harder than it had to be.

Mimi eased the vehicle into gear and glanced at her rearview, hoping to catch a glimpse of her little angel fast asleep in his car seat. Except, the baby mirror attached to the headrest was pointed in a funny direction, almost straight up. Mimi guessed Tuck must have kicked it when he was pitching his fit. She steered the SUV out of the parking lot and headed for the Walgreens on the corner of Oak Street and Main.

Three songs later, the 4Runner rolled into the pharmacy's drive-thru lane, the music still cranked as loud as it would go. Tuck hadn't made a peep since they'd left the plant. There weren't any cars in front of Mimi as she reached for the volume knob and braced herself for another one of Tuck's screaming fits.

Mimi spun the knob counterclockwise as she pulled up next to the pharmacy's window. A grainy voice said, "Name on the prescription?" and Mimi blinked. There were no cries coming from the backseat. No whimpers. Not even the snotty, sucking sounds Tuck made sometimes when he breathed.

A red-hot wire of fear uncoiled in Mimi's chest as she lurched over the center console toward the backseat. She was almost there when the seat belt caught, leaving her dangling in between. Visions of Tuck in the trunk of that dirty-looking Dodge flashed through her brain, sending a one-way message through every cell in her body.

When Mimi's fingers finally found the seat belt buckle, she clicked the button and catapulted herself headfirst into the backseat just as the pharmacy's outdoor speaker crackled and a woman's voice said, "Mighty cute kid you got there."

Mimi was eye level with the car seat now, that red wire still on fire inside her heart, watching as Tucker Wayne Jackson grinned around the baby-blue pacifier in his mouth, a smile that reminded Mimi of his father.

4.

On Friday nights in high school Gabriela would cruise the strip with Edwin and his cousin Chito, Chito behind the wheel of his customized '77 Chevelle, Gabby and Edwin in the backseat sipping from a bottle of anything they could get their hands on but mainly just getting their hands on each other, learning new moves that would grow old in seven years.

Edwin had been Gabby's first and only. He always said she was his first too, but Gabby didn't believe him. It was fine. She'd been all he'd had for long enough. She'd opened herself to him on the same bed where her mother and father had slept throughout her childhood, the same bed where she and Edwin slept still. The springs were louder now than they had been in high school, creaking as they tossed and turned. The same was true of Gabby. Her joints ached, her fingers, her wrists. It got so bad so fast Gabby couldn't even write a full page without stopping and popping her knuckles. Gone were the days of A+ papers, replaced by checks and bills.

Gabby didn't miss high school but she did miss Friday

night. The thrill of it. A week's worth of schoolwork in the books and two days of complete freedom lying out ahead of her like the quarter-mile stretch from Kroger to Walmart, the open road of her youth. Edwin had made a promise to her in those days, an offhand remark that Gabby never forgot. He said he was going to save her. "You stick with me, Menchaca, and I'll get you out of here. Deal?" She'd believed him, even though Edwin was the one who'd needed saving. Gabby had believed him.

She wasn't so sure anymore.

Not after the day she'd had. The things she'd learned while Edwin was away. It was all she could think about. How he'd lied to her. Stolen from her in some ways. *Yes.* He'd stolen from her. The kitchen counter, the toilet bowl, the shower—they were all cleaner than ever because of how angry Gabby had been, gritting her teeth as she scrubbed, grinding away like Edwin had worn her down over the years, mistake after mistake, excuse after excuse, but still, she loved him. She couldn't help but love him. After what they'd been through, Edwin was more than just her boyfriend, he was her family, the only one she'd had for so long.

A low rattling sound brought Gabriela back to the trailer, the Dodge pulling up out front. A door slammed, followed by footsteps, and then nothing for a moment but silence.

Gabriela was curled up on the sofa under a blanket, the same place she'd been since she'd finished her last chore only a couple of hours before. The clock on the microwave displayed the time. Well past midnight and Edwin was just now getting home? Probably swaying around on the third cinder-block step, trying to think up some bullshit excuse. Gabby pulled the blanket over her head as the trailer door opened.

His footsteps were light, softer than she'd expected, like maybe Edwin hadn't noticed her on the sofa. She peeked out from under the blanket and asked where he'd been, what he was doing getting in so late?

Edwin said, "Gabriela," and right away she knew he was drunk. He drank almost every night but when he said her name like that—"Gab-*rella*"—nothing good followed.

Her elbow twitched, remembering how hard she'd scrubbed. She threw the blanket back and said, "What, Edwin? What?"

"I need a marker," he said, "a pen, or something."

The blanket fell to the floor as Gabriela stood. Between the suspended cabinets and the kitchen countertops, she could see his hands shoved down in the drawer, pawing at all the small bits of paper she worked hard to keep organized.

"A pen. Edwin?"

"Something to write with."

"That explains it."

His hands went still. "Do not sass me, Gab-rella."

There was only one pen in the trailer Gabby was aware of, a felt-tip Paper Mate she used to write in her composition notebook. Gabby knew where it was, but she wouldn't tell Edwin, not until she understood which Edwin she was talking to.

"And one clean sheet of paper," Edwin said, twirling his mustache tips. "A single piece without your scribbles everywhere. What is all this?"

It was their life, receipts from the bars that weren't even bars, just Mexican restaurants that served beer and margaritas but not any real Mexican food. Gabby had each receipt paperclipped and tallied.

"Gab-*rella*," Edwin said, chewing her name as he lifted his hands from the drawer. He stumbled backward, a quick misstep that made her think of high school again. The first Friday night she'd ever seen him like this, tugging at her bra straps in the backseat of Chito's Chevelle. Gabby remembered the sound her hand made as it smacked against his cheek, the way he took her by the chin and laughed. Then, the very next morning, he was her Edwin again.

His hands were pushed into the cabinet above the microwave when Gabby came around the kitchen bar and Edwin said, "Look what I found."

Her eyes fell to the linoleum floor. She did not have to look to know that he was holding her black-and-white composition notebook, the one she used to keep up with their money.

"Mr. Levon came by today. He told me how much we owe," she said. "Three months, Edwin? *Three months?* What have you done?"

He ripped the first page from the notebook, their first year together in the trailer where they were able to save over a thousand dollars. After Edwin started drinking, they had never saved that much again.

"Ah, look." Edwin tapped the notebook with a single raised knuckle. "My little mathematician, hard at work."

Gabby saw the equation from where she was standing, the one she'd come up with, trying to figure out how much Mr. Jackson had stiffed them in overtime pay.

"Was this the number you told me the other day?" Edwin brought the paper closer to his face. "No, this says *fifty* grand. That's how much the plant owes us?"

Gabby said, "Seven years is a long time," thinking maybe the bad part was over. Maybe she'd be able to talk to him now. "A lot of days. So many extra hours."

"Fifty thousand bucks," Edwin said and tore the page from the notebook, then the next one too, and the next. When he finally stopped tearing, piles of paper lay crumpled on the floor. The few blank pages that were left represented the years that were ahead of them. Edwin brushed past her without another word, Gabby's good pen dangling from his lips like a cigarette, the dismantled notebook tucked under one arm.

Gabby watched Edwin walk through the door, down the steps, and back out to his car, the engine still chugging along on idle, wasting their gas and their money.

It was a straight shot from the kitchen to the Dodge, but the night sky closed in around Edwin, making it hard for Gabby to see him. The only light was a blue glow coming from a bug zapper hanging from the trailer's awning.

"Gabby?"

In the darkness, the voice almost sounded like her Edwin again.

"Gab-*rella*, can you hear me?"

"I don't know you, Edwin Saucedo."

The Dodge's driver-side door squeaked as he opened it and got in. The window rolled down. "You're right, Gabrella. You don't know nothing," Edwin said, his face cast in the bug zapper's fizzling light, "but you will."

THE BABY MONITOR on the nightstand cost close to five hundred dollars. It had a six-inch, high-definition screen, two-way audio, and a range of up to one thousand feet. All that money—all those fancy specs—and the damn thing kept cutting in and out, beeping all hours of the night, a safety feature to alert sleeping parents of a lost signal.

A grayscale image of Tuck, asleep in his crib, disappeared from the screen, then reappeared a moment later. Mimi lay on the opposite side of the bed from the nightstand, trying to stay focused as Luke gave a recap of the plant's big inspection.

"The satchel, my laptop . . ." Luke had his back against the headrest, still too excited to lie down. "It was perfect. *You* were perfect."

It had been such a good day. As soon as Tuck had his reflux medicine, he was like a different kid. After Walgreens, Mimi took him to the park. She strapped him to her chest in a baby carrier and went for a walk. The leaves were beautiful.

"The plant didn't get a single write-up. Nothing," Luke said. "We didn't just pass the inspection, babe, we *killed* it."

Mimi smiled because Luke was smiling. He'd even gotten home at a decent hour. A little past five o'clock. The first thing Luke said every time he saw his son was, "My *boy*." Something about the way he said it—those two simple words coming out easy in his south Arkansas drawl—melted Mimi's heart. Luke played with Tuck all the way up until bedtime. He even asked to feed him his bottle and put him down for the night. Mimi couldn't believe it.

She'd stood outside the nursery door, back pressed to the wall, holding her heart with both hands.

"And there's the other thing, the *big* thing," Luke said, turning and facing Mimi. "I got a call this afternoon and—"

The baby monitor beeped, the steady churn of the noise machine in Tuck's room—waves lapping against a distant shore—gone for a moment, then back again.

Mimi's eyes were on the monitor when Luke said, "Amelia Jane Jackson . . ." and pushed a strand of blond hair behind her left ear, getting his wife's attention in a gentle way that wasn't like him at all. "I've been waiting all day to tell you about this call."

Luke's hand slid along the inside of Mimi's thigh, sending a ripple of goose bumps up her leg, a feeling she hadn't experienced since Tuck was born, not once in the last six months. After eight straight hours of labor, Mimi wasn't sure she'd ever feel anything down there again. All the pregnancy books she'd read, and not a single one of them ever mentioned anything about hemorrhoids. She had to be careful when she sat down on the toilet, extra cautious about everything. But now, in this moment—with Luke's hand still moving up her leg, his fingers slipping under her silk sleeping shorts—all the pains and horrors of pregnancy seemed far away. Like it wasn't her body that had split open and given birth to an eight-pound-seven-ounce baby boy. Mimi's body felt fine. Better than fine. It felt good.

"You were saying something about a phone call?" Mimi said, her voice breathy, hot. She walked her hand across the bed, her index finger and middle finger alternating like tiny legs until they were standing on Luke's belly, ready to start down his happy trail.

Luke said, "The call . . ." running the back of his hand around the place Mimi wanted him to touch most of all. "Yeah, it can wait."

They came together, kissing and squeezing in a way that only comes from waiting, their six-month delay finally over. Mimi had Luke's whole left ear in her mouth, climbing on top of him, when the monitor beeped and the electric waves cut out again.

Mimi went through the motions a few seconds longer, waiting for the monitor to find the signal. Another beep then Mimi rolled away, reaching for the nightstand as Luke groaned.

"Sometimes, I feel sorry for you."

Her hand stopped short of the monitor, still silent, no grayscale image of Tuck on the six-inch screen. Luke was on his side now, elbow pressed into a pillow, scratching himself beneath the covers.

"I'm serious," he said. "Our parents didn't have high-def baby monitors. How'd we survive?"

"My mom kept me in her bedroom until I was six."

"That explains a lot."

The monitor still hadn't clicked back on. It never took this long. Sometimes, if Mimi turned it off then on again, it'd reboot or something, like a computer.

Mimi was reaching for the nightstand when Luke said, "I got the promotion," his tone flat, pouty. "Mr. Detmer said it wasn't official, not until the board voted me in. But as long as nothing crazy happened, it shouldn't be a problem."

Mimi sat on the edge of her bed, caught between her husband and her son, waiting for the moment when those waves would come rolling out of the monitor's tiny speaker and she'd see Tuck lying flat on his back with his hands above his head, mouth open, his favorite way to sleep.

The monitor beeped, but there were still no waves. Only the silence of a marriage after six months spent waiting for a moment that had passed them by. Luke placed his hands on Mimi's back, working his fingertips up her neck and over her shoulders. It felt good, but not good enough to turn off her mind. That would take some doing.

A friend had shared an article on Facebook recently about the power of cold water, a shock to the system or something, a metabolism boost. It was supposedly great for you, but that didn't make it easy. The water was just so damn *cold*. No matter how many times Mimi had turned the shower handle all the way to the right, she always had to convince herself to do it again. Just squeeze her eyes shut and twist until the water ran like freezing rain across her chest.

That's how this was. Like eating a broccoli salad or completing a set of a hundred hip thrusts. It was tough, uncomfortable even, but it would be good for her. For them. Mimi squeezed her eyes shut and leaned into her husband.

There was nothing at first.

Then, slowly, a warmth blossomed up from the numbness inside her, all the parts she'd lost bringing Tuck into the world coming alive again somehow. Mimi's toes tingled as she broke free of the monitor's pull and spun to face her husband, both hands going to his chest, sliding down his stomach.

In one quick twist, Luke was on top of her. Mimi

grimaced and thought she heard the soft roar of rolling waves timing up with the rhythm already going in the bed. Then the waves were gone, replaced by her husband's stuttering breath. For the first time in six months, Mimi wasn't thinking about her son. It was surprising, but nice, like the buzz that comes after the third margarita, a cheap high that never lasts.

EDWIN KNEW WHAT he would do the moment he stuck the blue pacifier back in the baby boy's mouth and watched the child smile up at him. He went straight for La Huerta, waited in the parking lot for the doors to open, then went inside to think. He knew what he would do; he just didn't know *how* he would do it.

Four tequila shots and six Dos Equis later, a thought slipped through. The answer to all of Edwin's problems was right there, waiting for him at the bottom of the bottle. The way Gabriela had thrown the rent in his face, the thousands of dollars they owed Mr. Levon, that had sealed the deal. Edwin needed a pen, paper, and not much else.

The gravel road leading up to the Jacksons' house was twisty and long, hard to follow with the headlights off, but he'd made it. He scribbled the note in the dark with a drunken hand, and then he started walking.

Edwin's feet were still moving now, heart thumping like the small, spinning drums he'd played with as a child. He kept waiting for an alarm to sound, or blue lights to start up behind him. That would've been better than going home to Gabby and telling her he'd been fired. Was that the reason he was there? The way Luke Jackson had talked to him, putting on a show for the men in the black jackets? That was part of it. The other part was everything else, the bad cards Edwin had been dealt for twenty-five straight years. He'd come to the Jacksons' house expecting another bad hand, a way out, but there was only the child asleep in his crib and the window Edwin couldn't believe had been left open. Just a crack to let in the cool fall air, wide enough Edwin could get his fingers in there and pull.

It didn't make a sound.

The note in Edwin's jacket pocket—a torn-out page from Gabriela's stupid book—had creases running all over it like crosshairs. Edwin had folded the note in a special way he'd learned from his mother, seven times for luck, shaped like a star. The points poked into Edwin's palm.

A fog hung eye level in the nursery. It freaked Edwin out until he saw the humidifier chugging along in the corner of the room, a dim green light blinking midway up on the wall behind it. A camera of some sort.

Shit.

What was he doing there?

Edwin shook his head and stepped through the humidifier smoke. He yanked the camera from the wall and liked the sound it made, the way the cord dangled limp in his fingers like a broiler's neck. From the Econo Lodge to Detmer Foods, Edwin had received an American education no classroom could provide, and now he would take Luke Jackson to school.

The best part? Nobody had to get hurt. In two days—less than forty-eight hours—the Jacksons would have their child back and Edwin would be halfway down to Mexico, a place he couldn't remember but still sounded better, so much better, than Arkansas. In Mexico, Edwin would start calling Gabby "Tica" and looking for ways to spend all his new money. Fifty grand. Yes. A big fat number. More than twice the amount Gabby had said they could save in five years.

Five years, Edwin thought and started toward the crib.

5.

They were at a water park, or maybe it was just the pool out back. Mimi couldn't tell. Her legs kicked and her arms flailed, fighting the waves that crashed around her. A red Old Town canoe floated by. Luke sat in the back holding Tuck instead of a paddle. Another wave crashed and Mimi went under. Gina Brashears swam up from the darkness wearing scuba gear and handed Mimi a frozen margarita. She tried to drink it but couldn't get her mouth around the straw. By the time Mimi made it to the surface again, the margarita was gone and Luke had Tuck dangling over the edge of the canoe, shouting, *"Is sink or swim!"* His voice all wrong, sounding more like one of the waiters at La Huerta than her husband.

Mimi's head went under the water, watching as Luke lowered Tuck down into the ocean—it was definitely the ocean now; no land in sight for miles—and said in that strange voice, "This will be good for him, Amelia. It will make him strong."

Tuck made a small splash, a wave crashed, and Mimi awoke.

The bedroom was silent. Sunlight tore through the Venetian blinds in sideways rays, creeping across the hardwood floors as a new day began. Mimi watched the light climb the bed skirt, recalling broken pieces of her disheveled ocean dream. The light played across her fingers, warm and alive.

Mimi sat up, fully aware of the silence now, the absence of waves in the bedroom. The sunlight. The clock beside the bed that read: 7:45 A.M. The monitor was still sitting on Luke's nightstand, the screen dark, the speakers noiseless, no beeps or chimes. Luke grunted as Mimi leaned over him, clicking the monitor's power button twice before her feet hit the floor.

"You checked it?" Mimi hissed, halfway to the door. "Last night, Luke, before we went to bed. You said you checked it."

Luke was sitting up on his elbows, blinking himself awake as Mimi stared back at him, her ocean dream floating somewhere on the rim of her subconscious, alongside all the possible reasons Tuck's cries weren't filling the house at almost eight in the fucking morning.

Luke said, "Checked what?" and Mimi started running, her footfalls like waves crashing through the quiet house.

LUKE WAS STILL in bed, holding the dead baby monitor in both hands, when the screaming began. It almost made sense, a sound like that to start the morning.

The wood floors were cold on Luke's feet as he hustled toward the nursery. The room was still dark when he got there. He blinked, waiting for his eyes to adjust, and then he saw her, Mimi kneeling on the floor, one hand clinging to the crib rail. Luke stepped inside the brightly colored room, looking past Mimi to the window he'd cracked the night before.

The weather had been perfect, too perfect, Luke thought. His eyes went to the crib. There was a softball-sized indention on the left side of the baby mattress, the place where Tuck's head had been but wasn't anymore.

6.

Gabriela heard a dog bark and opened her eyes. She was alone, the side of the bed closest to the door—the space where Edwin slept—empty.

Good, Gabby thought as she checked the time. There were still fifteen minutes before her alarm would sound. The extra sleep wasn't worth waking up again. Gabby rolled over and put both feet on the floor. Saturday shift started at eight. She and Edwin both worked Saturdays and brought home twice the money. They didn't need to be late, especially not Edwin. There was no way he had made it to the plant on time yesterday. He would never tell her this, though. Gabby stretched then started out of the bedroom, wondering, what, exactly, Edwin would say when he saw her.

The dog barked again.

A small one, Gabby thought, examining the kitchen where her mother had once stood, the pages from the notebook still scattered across the floor. She had almost forgotten Edwin coming to the trailer in the night, his desperate search for pen and paper. What had that been about?

The little dog was still barking, making yipping sounds like it was hungry, when Gabby came around the kitchen bar and saw Edwin sitting on the sofa with the blanket in his lap.

Gabby rubbed her eyes. "We barely have enough money to feed our own mouths," she said, pausing to yawn, "and now you bring home a dog?"

"No, Gabriela." Edwin spoke without looking at her, both eyes on the blanket as he pulled it back. "Not a dog."

The child was screaming. He'd been screaming, the sound louder now that the baby's mouth was free. So loud, Gabriela could barely hear Edwin's voice.

"Sit down and let me explain."

The way the baby was writhing, flailing its little head around and pawing at the air—it didn't seem real. Gabby told herself it wasn't real and sat down. She feared she might never get back up again. That this last blow, whatever Edwin was about to tell her, what he was trying to tell her now, would be the end.

"Do you understand?" Edwin wrapped the blanket back over the child's face, muffling its cries. "Listen to me."

Gabby's chin began to tremble like it did when her family left for Celaya. The tears that followed had changed nothing. The same was true now. She said, "Give him here," and extended her hands. "You don't know how to hold him."

"I'll learn."

"No," Gabby said, taking the child and cradling him in her arms. "Whose child is this? Where did you—" The tiny boy worked his mouth toward her breast, stealing her words. "He's hungry."

Edwin stood. "Then feed him, Gabriela."

The child took hold of Gabby's finger and pulled it to his mouth, his gums spit-slick and warm.

"Mr. Jackson's wife . . . The woman from the other night who was complaining about her baby?" Edwin paused like he was waiting for Gabby to answer him. "This is her kid. But she was doing more than just complaining, Gabby. I didn't tell you everything she said. All the crazy stuff."

The child still had hold of Gabby's finger. She stared down at him, noticing his light blue eyes, the way they skittered behind his hands. He was heavy, like Edwin, weighing her down as far back as she could remember, sucking her under.

"You stole him?"

"I'll give him back."

"Yes, right now."

"No," Edwin said. "I'll give him back after they do like I said."

A low humming sound began buzzing in Gabby's ears, like the barking dog from earlier, a noise to mask a truth she already knew: there would be no getting out of this without misery. The feeling she had—that buzzing in her ears moving down her neck now and spreading across her chest—it was familiar. Similar to how she'd felt sitting on the sofa with Edwin that day when she'd gotten up to go to the bathroom. Her whole body pulsing, quick tremors she'd learn later were contractions. Gabby had to bite the meat of her hand so Edwin wouldn't hear her cries, so he wouldn't know. And all of that would've been okay. She could've withstood the pain if there had been something good waiting for her at the end. Instead, Gabriela had given birth sitting on the toilet in her single-wide trailer, and then she'd flushed the child away.

She looked up at Edwin without seeing him, remembering how Mr. Jackson had only given her two days off after the miscarriage. Mr. Jackson was like Edwin in many ways, brash and impulsive. A thought came to her, strong enough to become words, her lips barely moving as she said, "He fired you."

Gabby wasn't sure if she had heard Edwin say this earlier, or if it was just something she felt, something her heart knew already. "That's why you did this? Why you took his child. Because you were late yesterday and Mr. Jackson fired you."

"I did this for us, Gabriela. For you."

"For me? For *me*!" The child jerked back from Gabby's finger.

"For your job. The papers, that's why Mr. Jackson fired me."

"What papers?"

The posterboard in the corner with Edwin's writing on it flapped beneath the ceiling fan. Gabby hoped that was the paper Edwin was talking about, prayed it was something as simple as a strike that had never happened.

"The ones we gave him seven years ago. All those forms we filled out to get the job at the plant? *That's* why Luke said he fired me. He said your name too, Gabriela. He brought you up. He didn't say anything else. He didn't have to."

The fan spun a crooked circle above Gabby's head. "So you brought his child here to get your job back? To make sure I kept mine?"

The thin hair of Edwin's mustache crinkled between his fingers. "I brought him here for money, ransom money." He pronounced the words like a high school student stumbling through a read-aloud, like he'd never spoken that exact phrase before, only thought it, dreaming up this ridiculous plan.

"Take him back," Gabby said. "Take this child back to his parents. Do it for me, Edwin."

"Take him back and say what?" Edwin still had the same clothes on he'd worn to the plant the day before. He was standing farther away now, over by the kitchen bar with both arms out, as if the crying child scared him. "Just walk up to the plant for morning shift and say, 'Mr. Jackson, is this your child? I found him last night.' You know what he would do, Gabriela. He would call the police."

"He's called them already. How can you be so stupid?"

The child was screaming again, getting louder with every step Edwin took toward the sofa. He squatted down, leaning in so close Gabby could still smell the tequila on his breath, the fuel that had started this fire. "¿Estúpido?" he hissed. "That's what you think?"

Gabby rocked the child like she'd rocked her nieces and nephews once, but it wasn't the same.

"Let me tell you how *stupid* I am." Edwin took his jacket off and tossed it on the sofa, talking over the cries of the child. "The Jacksons didn't call the police because I told them not to."

The baby clamped down on Gabby's finger again but continued to cry around it. Gabby knew the child was hungry, but there was nothing she could do. Maybe he's cold, she thought, and reached for Edwin's jacket.

"All of the notes you made in your little book." Edwin nodded toward the kitchen. "All the money you said he owed us for the overtime? In two days, we'll have it. We'll have enough to pay the rent. No. *Wait* . . ." Edwin's arms sprung wide, all ten fingers flexed. "I'll have enough to get you out of here, out of Arkansas for good, just like I promised."

As she draped the jacket over the child, Gabby's hand slipped into one of the front pockets. The Dodge keys poked at her fingers. A candy wrapper crinkled.

"After what Mr. Jackson took from us?" Edwin said. "After the way he's treated you and me? This is fair, Gabriela, and he'll do exactly what I told him to do. He will pay."

There was something else in the jacket pocket, something Gabby's fingers didn't recognize. She had it in her hand, the cries of the child going quiet in her mind as she said, "The Jacksons will call the police. That's the first thing they'll do."

Edwin said, "I left a note. It says everything I just said. The two days. The money. Everything. I even told them where to leave the cash. And if they tell anyone about it, if they call the police?" Edwin paused, catching his breath. There was a crumb of something in his mustache. Dried salsa, maybe. "Then they'll never see their little boy again. I wrote it all down, Gabriela, in the note."

"Ah, the *note*." Gabby's fingers formed a fist around the folded piece of paper in Edwin's jacket pocket. "How could I forget the note?"

7.

The crib was empty. That was the hardest part to stomach. How someone could take a six-month-old child without any reason. No ransom note. No ultimatum. Nothing.

Mimi was on her back, palms flat on the ground, unaware of Luke pacing around the nursery. For all she knew, he'd rolled over and gone back to bed. For all she knew, Luke was dead.

The ocean rose around her and Mimi started to sink again. There was no Gina Brashears in scuba gear to save her this time. Falling fast, the water growing colder the deeper she went. Mimi closed her eyes and welcomed the bottom.

Except, there was no bottom, only some deep ocean current that swept her back to the nursery again. Mimi floated above it, looking down as a woman bent over the crib and took Tuck into her arms. The woman had blond hair and a faint scar that matched the one in Mimi's left eyebrow, the result of a bike wreck when she was ten. The woman placed the baby on the changing table and began unbuttoning his onesie, blowing on his belly the way Mimi liked to do.

Was this the woman who had stolen her child?

Mimi pushed off from the ceiling, swimming toward the woman, wanting to look her in the face and shriek obscenities. Mimi was right there, suspended beside the stranger, trying to make sense of the face that looked so much like her own, singing the same song Mimi sang her son every night:

> Bye-o baby bunting.
> Daddy's gone a hunting,
> to find a little rabbit skin,
> to wrap the baby Tucker in.
> Bye-o. Bye-o. Bye-o.
> Bye . . .

The woman rotated her head and said, "Get up," but her voice was all wrong, rough and low like a man's. Mimi blinked and saw Luke kneeling before the crib, tugging at her hand. "Please, Mimi," he said. "Get up."

Mimi flattened both palms out on the floor and dug her heels into the carpet. Her hips writhed. The morning light through the nursery window played tricks on her mind. Turned everything upside down, backward. She mumbled the only thing that made any sense. The only possible answer.

"The police?" Luke said, echoing her. He said it like the thought hadn't crossed his mind, and then the phone rang.

THE NOTE WAS lying on the plywood table, still folded in the shape of a star. Edwin stared down at it, thinking of his mother, a woman who believed wholeheartedly in luck. "*Sí. Sí, Edwin. You fold a paper seven times—like this—make a wish, and it will come true.*"

Edwin bent down, keeping the phone pressed to his ear, and picked up the ransom note he'd forgotten to leave in the crib, on the floor, anywhere other than in his jacket pocket. As soon as Edwin saw the folded paper, he knew what he had to do. He had to call and read the note to Mr. Jackson. It was the only way to keep the police out of it. Maybe ask to speak to Mrs. Jackson and let her hear the child crying in the background. Yes, Edwin thought. That was it.

Mr. Jackson's number was saved in his phone from when Edwin had talked to the labor justice organization, trying to organize the strike. He'd called his boss then, several times, and Mr. Jackson never answered. But *now*? Edwin thought. Luke Jackson would answer his call now.

The phone rang for the fifth time and Edwin unfolded the note. He squinted, scanning his drunken scrawl with morning eyes. The note didn't make sense. It was barely legible, the letters jumbled together, trailing sideways off the page. Edwin began to crumple the paper, ashamed until a new thought came to him. Maybe his mother had been right. Maybe the seven folds were lucky.

Edwin heard a soft click on the other end of the line then a robot voice saying, "The voicemail box for—"

Gabby said, "I told you," as Edwin lowered the phone. "They already called the police. They're talking to them now."

"No."

"*No?*"

"I know Luke Jackson. The type of man he is." Edwin rolled his hand over and looked down at the crumpled note in his palm, thinking again of his mother's superstitions. "His wife. I heard her talking about how much she worries."

"That's right," Gabby said. "That's why she will make him call the police. She'll call them if he won't."

THE NAME ON the cell phone's screen read, PRIVATE.

Luke had run from the nursery to the master bedroom in time to hear the fifth, and final, ring. He had the phone in his hands now, looking down at it, waiting to see if the caller would leave a voicemail. That would make sense. The private call was the first thing that had made sense all morning. Some meth-head takes your kid, Luke thought, they want something. Money, probably. How much money? Luke could only imagine. He gripped the phone tighter and walked back to the nursery.

Mimi was still flattened out on the floor, toes pointed toward the window. Luke stared down at the top of his wife's head, noticing dark roots and a few flakes of dandruff exposed in her part. Mimi had changed after Tuck was born. Other guys had told Luke this would happen, but none properly expressed just how drastic the transformation would be. The girl he'd married nine years ago—the one he'd met at the Galaxy Skateway, scooting backward around the rink, her long, blond hair whipping around her face like she didn't notice or care, a girl who wasn't aware of herself at all, beautiful in a way that was

effortless—that girl was gone. The day Tuck was born
Mimi Jackson died. From that day forward, she would
only ever be Tuck's mother.

That gray, dry strip of Mimi's scalp glared up at Luke, a
part of his wife he was never meant to see. Like when they
were in the delivery room and he'd watched all of that stuff
come out of her. Not Tuck. The other stuff. How could
a person bleed like that—scream like that—and not die?

Luke squeezed the phone, squeezed the life right out of
it. He was waiting for it to buzz again when Mimi's head
jerked back, exposing the cords in her neck and pale blue
veins like week-old crayon smears beneath her skin. The
way she moved, it was like Mimi was in the middle of
some strange new metamorphosis. Luke watched as her
hand rose, slow and limp, a marionette's limb, inching
toward him.

The phone buzzed.

PRIVATE flashed across the screen again and a sharp ring
filled the stuffy bedroom. Luke watched Mimi's hand fall
to her chest, all five fingers flexed as if she were holding
Tuck's head, feeding him.

Luke pressed the phone to an ear and said, "Hello?"

IT WAS LIKE the child knew who Edwin was speaking
to, squirming more than ever in Gabriela's arms. Gabby
didn't want to hear it. She stood and began bouncing the
baby, humming in his ear, doing her best not to ignore
Edwin using his white-boy voice, the one he'd been prac-
ticing since before he scored those three goals and became
"Saucy," back when Edwin told the teachers his name
was Ed.

"No, *you* listen," Edwin said, spinning the folded ransom note around with his fingers. "If you want to see your son again, you will do exactly as I say . . ."

Edwin named his price, fifty thousand dollars paid in cash. The figure was familiar, but Gabby couldn't place it. Edwin added, "No marked bills, nothing funny like that, okay?" Losing his white-boy accent for a moment then getting back to business, telling the man he had two days to make "the drop." Gabby shook her head and rocked the baby.

"*Where?*" Edwin said. "Where what?"

Where do you want the money, stupid. Gabby thought the line in her head but said nothing. Edwin wasn't saying anything either, and Gabby knew why. He didn't know where. He hadn't thought that far ahead. She watched him spin the star-shaped ransom note, the same type of fold he'd used in Mrs. Hubbard's class their senior year at Springdale High, passing notes and holding Gabby's hand beneath the table.

Edwin surprised her when he said, "Put half the money in the yellow dumpster behind the Walmart. The new one coming in off 412. Yes, just half." The child whimpered and Gabby realized she'd stopped rocking him, too caught up in Edwin's master plan. "The other half," Edwin said, "leave it in the baby's crib. When you get back from Walmart, the money will be gone and you will have your son again."

Gabby's lips parted. She fought the urge to spit. That's how stupid Edwin's plan was. All those moving parts? Different locations? There were so many ways it could go wrong, like a trap he'd set for himself, like his life. Gabby

bounced the child and hummed louder. Did she want
Edwin's plan to fail? What if they really could get that
much money and get out of there for good?

"And don't forget, I'll be watching you," Edwin said,
moving his hands as he spoke. "You try anything funny,
you call the police, get anybody else involved—you will
never see your son again." Edwin stared down at the boy
as he said, "Midnight, Sunday, Luke. Don't be late."

Edwin ended the call and threw the phone on the sofa.
He ran both hands through his dark, curly hair, and walked
a quick lap around the living room. A framed picture of
Gabriela's family hung on the far wall, the only shot from
her quinceañera. Both sisters, her mother and father too,
all outfitted in clothes from Variedades Garcia, a dress and
tuxedo rental store next to the Vape and Glass Emporium
on Thompson Street. Two more years, they'd be gone, back
to Celaya where things were bad but no worse than what
Gabby was up against now. She did not recognize the girl
in the middle of the picture, a child in a baby-blue ball
gown, blue like Cinderella's, Gabby's favorite fairy tale.

"Fifty *thousand* dollars?" Gabby said.

"That's what Mr. Jackson owes us. That's what you
said. All those overtime hours you added up?"

The papers Edwin had ripped from her notebook were
in a Walmart sack at the bottom of the trash can now.
Gabby had swept them all up between calls. She should've
never told him about the overtime pay. The smallest thing
could send him spiraling in the wrong direction, but he'd
never been this lost before.

"Why'd you tell him to split the money?" Gabby said.
The child found his left foot and brought it to his

mouth. Edwin didn't notice. "That way we don't have to see them," he said. "You'll go to the Walmart, make sure they put the money in the dumpster. I'll go to the house with the child. If there's money in the crib, and money in the dumpster, then their boy will be waiting for them when they get home."

"Not me, Edwin. I'm not going anywhere."

"It's the only way. A man like Luke Jackson plays by his own rules," Edwin said. "What if he brings a gun to the drop, like a cowboy, and messes everything up?"

Even with three toes in his mouth, the child was still crying.

"He's hungry, Edwin."

"I'll feed him."

"*You?*" Gabby said. "Listen to him. Do you want to stay here with him like this? You go get formula. I'll stay and—"

"It's almost eight," Edwin snapped. "You need to get dressed."

"I have to stay here." Gabby couldn't believe what she was saying, agreeing to Edwin's plan. What else could she do? The trailer, at least, was safe. It had once held her family. It had protected her, hidden her, ever since they left. "I know how to take care of a baby," she said. "You don't."

Edwin's hands came down from his hair to his face, kneading his eyes and his cheeks together. "You say it like you have a choice. You're holding a stolen child. If you don't go to the plant and work your shift today, what will Mr. Jackson think?"

"My shift . . ." Gabby said. "I won't be back until tonight. What will you do with this baby for that long?"

Edwin stepped around the plywood table. The child's head bobbed as he tracked the movement. A smattering of thin blond hair covered his scalp. Gabby felt it on her cheek, soft like nothing was in the plant or the trailer, and then it was gone. Edwin had the baby in his arms, rocking him awkwardly. One tiny hand emerged, sticking straight up, five fingers curled in defiance. Edwin started humming a tune Gabriela recognized but couldn't place. A moment later, the boy was still.

"Johnny Cash," Edwin said, his tone as soft as the sleeping child's hair. "That song is like his lullaby."

An image formed in Gabby's mind of the father Edwin would've been if things had gone differently.

"How will you feed him?" Gabby said.

"I'll get milk from the store, like you said."

"You mean formula. Baby formula."

"Yes, I'll get it."

"You can't go into a store with that child in your arms," Gabby said, "a baby boy who looks nothing like you."

Edwin stared back at her a moment then down at the child. "Please, Gabriela. Just go," he said, his shoulders swaying gently side to side. "You can't be late. Not today."

8.

The conversation played like an old radio program in the recesses of Mimi's mind, the words garbled, staticky, each one tugging at her heart, pulling her back to reality. When she opened her eyes, everything in the nursery was like it should've been, everything except the thing for which the room had been constructed. Luke's voice was gone now, too. He wasn't talking anymore. He was just standing there, over her, holding a mug in one hand, his phone in the other.

Mimi licked her lips. "What did he sound like?"

"Kind of like a Mexican, or maybe a Mexican trying not to talk like a Mexican? I don't know."

"He wanted money?"

Luke nodded. "Fifty grand."

"That's it?"

"That's *it?* God, Mimi. We don't have fifty fucking grand. Not in cash."

Luke rarely cursed. He'd stub his toe walking to the bathroom in the middle of the night and holler, "Shoot." This last outburst scared Mimi as much as anything else.

Whatever that man had said on the phone, it rattled her husband, and Luke didn't rattle easily.

"We don't have the money? What does that mean?"

"We took a loan out to pay for the house. My truck, your 4Runner—we're still paying those off. Most of our money is tied up in the mortgage and car payments." The words rolled out of Luke's mouth, disjointed and hurried. "Anything we have left at the end of the month, I put it into IRAs. My 401(k). Maybe I could liquidate some of the money I have in the market, but not by tomorrow night. Tomorrow's Sunday, for Christ's sake."

"Sunday?"

He nodded but didn't say anything. That was more like it. More like Luke. He never said anything when it came to their money. He was the breadwinner. Luke worked hard to provide for Mimi, always had, and she trusted him. Even after he'd first been promoted to plant manager and decided to create a separate checking account, depositing exactly fifteen hundred dollars into it each month, money Mimi used to buy the groceries and get her hair done, any other shopping she wanted to do—Mimi still trusted him. She hadn't asked questions. She was thankful she didn't have to work. But now they needed fifty thousand dollars. Needed it more than they'd ever needed anything in their lives, and Luke couldn't get it.

Mimi pushed up from the floor. It took every cell inside her, but she did it. And then thought immediately of the big green John Deere tractor—like something straight out of a country-music video—Luke had purchased only last month, saying he needed it for work around the farm. Luke owned seven chicken houses and the fifty acres that surrounded their house. He had a tractor, a hundred-thousand-dollar Ford, but he didn't have fifty grand?

Mimi spoke her husband's name and waited until he looked at her. "You're sure this man really has . . ." The water rose inside her again. She swallowed it down. "You're sure Tuck's okay?"

"Yeah, I could hear him. The guy wanted me to hear him."

"And you're sure it was him?"

"I know my own son's voice."

"Do you?"

Luke stared into the coffee mug a moment then held it out for his wife. "Here," he said. "Get this in you."

Mimi said, "I don't want coffee," but took it anyway. "What about the police?"

"No police. The guy was clear about that."

"What'd he say?"

The way Luke looked at her, Mimi knew what the guy had said, the same line every abductor said, the same threat, but people still called the police, didn't they?

"If the police get involved, and this guy realizes it . . ." Luke's hesitation confirmed Mimi's fear from before. "We can't do anything other than exactly what he told us to do. Do you understand? You can't call the cops. Not yet, at least."

The way he said that last line was familiar. It was a game they played, the same one they'd been playing since they'd first gotten married. Luke kept things from her. Little secrets made the best surprises. Made Mimi see him as her protector, her provider. Like Luke was always one step ahead, making plans for their life that she wasn't capable of understanding. The thought gave Mimi the strength to finally reach out for him. His forearms were tight. They felt strong.

"You've got a plan?" she said, rolling over on her side, staring up at him. "The money. There's got to be some way you can get it, right?"

"I've got an idea about the money, but don't you worry about it. Okay? Just drink your coffee, Mimi. Get some rest, and when you wake up, I'll bring Tuck back to you. I'll bring our son home."

Mimi brought the mug to her lips. Wavy lines like the ones that hovered over highways in the summer rose up from the coffee and blurred her vision. A thousand questions charred the edges of her mind, but she didn't ask them. Mimi sipped the coffee instead. It was good and strong, just like her husband, like she needed him to be now.

HIGHWAY 412 CAME down out of the Ozark Mountains winding and blue, hidden beneath the fog hanging thick over Saturday morning. A pair of headlights cut through the haze, Luke's Ford heading west along the highway. From the outside, there was no way to tell what was going on inside the cab. Any eastbound driver glancing through the windshield would've seen a white man in a tan shirt, leaned over the center console with one hand on the wheel. A plant manager on his way to work.

Except, nobody really saw Luke Jackson. Not the man he truly was. Not even his wife of nine years, the one he'd chosen out of all the other girls at the University of Arkansas. With his light blue eyes, muscular physique, and down-home charm, Luke had had his pick. He never boasted about it. Never told Mimi, either. Not even when she'd asked him about his previous girlfriends a month or so before they were married. What good would it have done for her to know his past?

Secrets were the secret to a happy marriage. How well each spouse hid the truth, their hearts, their inner lives— that's what mattered. Luke had been told so many things before tying the knot with Mimi, so many maxims and clichés. But he'd come up with that line about secrets on his own, after a year of sharing the same bed with the same woman, night after night. A man had to keep things from his wife in order to make it work, small things, big things, pieces of the boy he'd been that allowed him to be a halfway decent husband, a loving father.

Luke was the strong, silent type, through and through. So quiet, so reserved, he was sometimes able to think of himself as the man all the other plant managers and their Junior League wives, the members of the First Baptist Church and the Rotary Club—the entire town of Springdale—believed him to be.

Luke glanced into the rearview mirror as he pulled off 412. The highway lay long and twisted behind him. He didn't look at his eyes as they flashed across the glass. He rarely looked at himself. Other men, guys like Steve Ferguson, were always checking themselves out in every reflective surface they passed. Not Luke. He was too smart for that, too cool, always focused on what's next. What lay ahead of him now was the chicken plant, a rectangular structure waiting less than a half mile down the road.

Luke's knuckles flexed chalky as he gripped the wheel,

thinking about the situation from every angle. There was the other thing, too. The part of himself Luke might have seen if he ever looked in the mirror for more than a couple seconds at a time. The woman who was more than just some college fling. The one he'd met at the Junior League fundraiser, of all the damn places, a week or so after Tuck was born and Mimi had already begun her transformation. The woman who reminded Luke of the girl Mimi used to be.

Her name was Nina Ferguson, but Mimi and most of the other managers' wives called her "Ferg." That was the first thing Luke liked about her. A woman who let other women call her *Ferg*? Yeah, that got his attention. Her red hair and curves didn't hurt, either. Skin like whole milk, so pure and white, nothing like the chunky yellow stuff Mimi had pumped into all those plastic baggies.

Ferg was just someone to talk to. She was cool. Aware of herself in a way that made her unaware of herself, like Mimi had been once. Ferg had a one-year-old daughter who went to day care five days a week, even though Ferg didn't work. The kid hadn't seemed to change her at all, or maybe it was just that Luke didn't know Ferg from before, back when she was tending bars down at the Flora-Bama line.

They'd met a couple times over the last few months. Always late at night. All Luke had to do was mumble some excuse about the plant or the chicken houses and Mimi would just nod, too consumed by Tuck to even look at her husband as he walked out the door. Ferg's husband, Steve, ran the plant in Fayetteville and golfed so much she didn't have to say anything when she left at night. They'd meet in the back lot of the plant where there weren't any cameras. Ferg would pull up in her Audi and hop into Luke's Ford. They'd cruise the back roads and drink a six-pack of Bud Light. When all the bottles were empty, Luke would park the Ford behind a thicket down by Clear Creek and watch Ferg crawl over the center console, cracking jokes about the .30-06 Springfield deer rifle Luke had stuffed under the backseat. "That gun's got a mighty *long* barrel," she'd say and grin, tugging at the zipper on his jeans. It was always good until it was over and a strange new silence filled the cab for the ride home, miles away from the anticipation that had led them to the water.

The Ford rolled into the PLANT MANAGER parking space. Luke killed the engine but didn't get out, still thinking about the fifty grand and Ferg, trying to decide which problem he wanted to tackle first. Tonight was supposed to be a Clear Creek night. They were set to meet in the back of the plant, like always. Luke knew he wouldn't go, not after what had happened, but he'd never backed out on Ferg before. He pulled the keys from the ignition and caught his eyes in the rearview mirror. "Your kid's missing," he said to the man in the glass, a pair of pale blue eyes he barely recognized. "Your *son*." Luke slapped himself with both hands on both cheeks. He kept staring at the mirror until the welts turned from red to pink.

Luke slid out of the truck, thinking over the idea that had come to him earlier, the "plan" he'd mentioned to Mimi. It seemed like a long shot now. He kept some side money in his office. Nothing crazy. Just enough cash to get stuff done quick. Like if there was a softball tournament at Rotary Park and somebody called the front office asking if Detmer could help. Luke would dip into the little slush fund he kept in an ammo box on his desk. Take out just enough to buy a hundred hot dogs, some charcoal, maybe a couple cases of Coke.

The money came from dead-on-arrival chickens. Crates full. Even though all the broilers came to die at the plant, the ones that died in transit were of no use to Luke. Nobody processed dead meat, and the trucks killed the chickens by the hundreds. In an attempt to reduce splatter, the broilers aren't fed or watered hours before they're loaded onto the trucks. Some die of starvation, others heat stress. Luke had a driver quit on the spot when he went to unload his crates and saw half his load was dead already. This was just last summer, a boil-an-egg-on-the-sidewalk kind of day. The driver swore he'd heard the birds crying, screeching over the roar of his big rig's six-cylinder diesel. The man was shook, but Luke still made him pay, just like everybody else. Luke made the drivers pay him for the damaged goods right there on the spot. It was country math, no clear percentages or calculations, just enough of a refund for Luke to make his point; he wouldn't take shit off anybody.

Luke had been stockpiling the money in his ammo box for going on four years now, only using it when he needed quick cash. It'd take a week's worth of company paperwork to get the tiny dab of money Luke needed to help with stuff like hot dogs and Coke. It wasn't exactly legal, but neither were half the Detmer line workers. The only other person at the plant who knew about the money was Terri, the big-boned country girl sitting behind the front desk as Luke walked through the lobby doors.

"Morning, Mr. Jackson," Terri said, gnawing a wad of pink bubble gum. "Know you're probably excited and all about your big promotion, but I want you to know this place ain't gonna be the same without you."

Luke's boots clicked to a stop on the lobby's tile floors. He could hear the man's voice on the phone again, William H. Detmer—the company's largest shareholder and CEO—calling to tell Luke he was next in line for the Executive Officer of Poultry position, the job he'd been gunning for since the start of his career. Luke remembered what Mr. Detmer had said about the board meeting and how Luke needed to just sit tight and not do anything stupid, adding, *"Don't get caught with your hand in the cookie jar, son. Catch my drift?"*

A small flame flickered in Luke's belly as he nodded at the receptionist and said, "Appreciate it, Terri. You get the pack of Bubblicious I left in your box?"

"I got it, boss." Terri blew a fat pink bubble and popped it with her teeth. "You ain't got a clue how much I'm gonna miss you."

WITH LUKE GONE and the rest of the morning, the afternoon—however long it would take him to collect the money and get back home—waiting out in front of her, Mimi wished for dirt.

She wanted to clean the dishes, or mop the floors, a task she could complete, something to take her mind off the other thing—the only thing—but there wasn't a smidgen of dust anywhere, not even a few stray strands of Mimi's hair coiled around the shower drain. The house was spotless, just like always, and *that* was the problem.

It was Luke's idea to hire the cleaning service. Mimi didn't like it at first. She was a stay-at-home mom and felt like keeping the house clean was her duty. Four sleepless nights and a trash can full of soiled diapers later, Mimi decided taking care of Tuck was job enough.

The cleaning lady's name was Brenda Acosta. She wasn't so much a cleaning lady as she was a cleaning tycoon. She had a whole crew, a business she called "Diamond Shine" that sanitized the offices in the plant every night. On Thursday mornings, three of the women came to the Jackson house and cleaned all five thousand square feet in under two hours while Brenda sat outside in her bright red Lexus.

Mimi was still in the nursery. Everywhere she looked she saw Tuck, all the different versions of him that had existed in that one room. He'd been a blob at first, a snuggly little slug. Easy in some ways—immobile, content—harder in others—constant feeding, no long-term sleep. Mimi had enjoyed that version of her son, but felt as if she might break him at any moment. She liked Tuck at six months better. At six months, he would turn to the sound of his name. His eyes tracked her eyes, mimicked her expressions. Peek-a-boo was Tuck's favorite game. Mimi's too.

Lying flat on her back, Mimi pressed both palms to her eyes. When she pulled her hands away, her son was still gone. It didn't seem possible. Sure, she'd seen similar trag-edies on KNWA. A six-year-old drowned at the Horseshoe Bend Marina last year. The body was never found. There was even worse stuff online. Sometimes, real early in the morning before anyone else was awake, Mimi read blogs written by mothers who'd lost their kids to leukemia, neuroblastoma, Hodgkin's and non-Hodgkin's lymphoma. The doomscrolling was a protective measure, a spoonful of the world's harshest realities that, when taken regularly, allowed Mimi to realize just how lucky she'd been. Her son was healthy. Mimi's grandparents were still alive. All four of them. Stuff like this happened to other people, and it was sad—Mimi went through Kleenex box after Kleenex box reading all those cancer blogs—but what had befallen her now felt worse. There was no doctor there to answer her questions. No nurse with a tray full of Goldfish, a cold can of Sprite. Mimi couldn't talk to anyone about what had happened. All she could do was wait.

The tide inside her mind was rising again, swelling as she picked the coffee mug up and stumbled out the door. Her toes kept dragging behind her, scraping over the hardwoods. Her head felt funny, too. Sandy and dark. Like the hallway now, closing in on her.

Mimi made it to the kitchen before she fell. She caught herself on the island but her legs were already asleep. A thousand tiny needles tingled up her thighs. She set the empty mug down on the granite and poked at her knees but felt nothing. Absolutely nothing.

Shock, maybe? Was that what this was? Mimi wasn't sure, but the pinpricks kept coming, moving up her waist, spreading out over the back of her head. The sensation was strange yet comforting. Mimi watched her right hand unfurl across the counter, sending the coffee mug whirling to the floor. A half second later, she was on her back beside it, staring sideways at the khaki-colored liquid, a mess that would need cleaning when she awoke.

9.

The Dodge came to a stop under the Kum & Go's red-and-white sign. Edwin hooked his arm over the passenger seat. The infant was asleep on a pile of wadded towels on the floorboard. Static leaked through the speakers in the doors, the radio tuned to a fuzzy station. The child hadn't stirred. Not when Gabriela left the trailer, glancing back at Edwin with her hairnet on already. Not when he'd loaded the child into the car. Not when they'd pulled down the dirt road leading out of Wink-Land Trailer Park, rows upon rows of trailers where other struggling families were waking up and starting another long day.

Edwin dug into his back pocket for his wallet. He knew there wasn't any money, but he pulled the flap back anyway, staring down at a picture of Gabby from high school. Behind the picture were three quarters and a nickel. Was eighty cents enough to buy baby formula? Edwin wondered, then shook his head, remembering yesterday should've been his payday. It didn't matter if he'd been fired or not—Luke Jackson still owed him money.

Fifty grand.

Edwin smiled, picturing himself holding all that cash, feeling the weight of it as he remembered Luke Jackson standing in the plant lobby yesterday, saying, *"You're late, son. That's what you are."*

It wasn't the fact that he was two minutes late. That's not why Edwin lost his job. Luke fired him for the same reason he could've fired almost any worker at any moment. All those made-up numbers on the government-issued forms, the forged dates and times—they hung heavy like a guillotine's slanted blade over the plant. Who would show up to work tomorrow? Who wouldn't? That's what Mr. Jackson wanted his employees thinking. He wanted them on their toes, no thoughts of slacking off, not a single complacent bone in their bodies. Luke got away with it because most of the workers didn't know the rules, but Edwin did. He'd done his research at the library, the same computer stall where he'd sat and read up on what causes a woman to lose a child. Edwin could've filed a maltreatment claim with the APU—the Arkansas Poultry Union—like he'd done when Gabriela had the miscarriage. He could've filed another claim for the firing, but it would've taken months, maybe longer, and then what?

No, Edwin thought, turning away from the sleeping child and opening the driver-side door, carefully, trying not to make much noise. The path he'd chosen was the right one, the only way.

The hissing static seeped out of the car as Edwin started for the convenience store. The automatic glass doors slid open. He was still a few feet back, close enough to the parking lot to hear the purr of an engine he recognized. He turned in time to see a lowrider pulling into the parking space beside his Dodge, hip-hop music thumping out through rolled-down windows, loud enough to rattle the trunk.

An arm appeared, black and blue tattoos covering every inch of brown skin, the letters B-U-R-R stamped across the knuckles on the left hand. Chito Ortega had gotten the knuckle tats as a joke their first year out of high school. When he put his fists together, keeping his thumbs tucked under, all eight letters came together and spelled BURR-ITOS. It looked like a prison tattoo, all done up in that Old-English font the real cholos had etched across their backs, under their necks, somewhere with enough bare skin to display their street-gang affiliations, the words "Los Zetas" or "Mara Salvatrucha" scraped into their hides forever.

Chito wasn't a cholo, though. He was just a pothead.

Edwin could smell the bud drifting out of the rolled-down window from where he was standing, over thirty feet away. There'd been a window of time where Chito had almost become affiliated. A man by the name of Guillermo Torres, a little guy Chito could've sat on and killed, came into town a few years back looking to hire some muscle. Said he had a deal set up with a skinhead down the road in Taggard. Chito was ready to go, had his bags packed and everything, but then he backed out at the last minute. That was Chito for you. All talk, no action. A teddy bear with tattoos.

"Saucy, my friend. No chickens need plucking today?"

Edwin couldn't hear the static coming out of his Dodge anymore. He could barely hear his cousin over Snoop Dogg saying something softly about gin and juice.

"I'm kidding. *Geez*," Chito said. "But seriously, you

ready to come work for me? Your big cuz can hook you up, man."

Chito was older than Edwin by exactly one month. To look at him, though, all three hundred pounds of man stuffed in behind that steering wheel, the droopy eyes and the balding patch sweeping back across the top of his head—Chito could've passed for Edwin's uncle. He'd played football in high school and always blamed his receding hairline on the helmet. They'd grown up together, Chito the only kid Edwin ever trusted enough to invite over to the Econo Lodge. Chito was a cannonball master and could lift every weight in the fitness center.

Edwin raked his mustache with two fingers, trying to think of what to say, wondering if the child was awake now, his screams masked by the sound of Chito's thumping bass.

Chito said, "Hey, man. Look like you seen a ghost or something."

"I'm in a hurry," Edwin said. "I've got to go."

Chito cupped a hand behind his ear and said, "Hold up. I can't hear nothing."

Chito's hand disappeared from the driver-side window and Edwin knew what would happen next. What he didn't know was whether the child was awake. He had slept through "Ring of Fire," but this was Snoop Dogg bumping out of the subwoofers now, not Johnny Cash.

The music died off all at once and a harsh silence followed, the sounds of the gas station coming back in waves: the clicking pumps, the engines turning over, the patrons' voices. There were no cries coming from the floor of the Dodge Neon.

Edwin made a move for his car. He was almost there,

his hand reaching out for the driver-side door, when Chito honked the horn on his lowrider and "La Cucaracha" blared out across the parking lot. Chito opened his car door and said, "You shading out on me, Saucy?"

It wasn't until Chito was coming around the tail end of Edwin's Neon that the child began to cry.

BY THE TIME the chickens got to Gabriela, they did not look like chickens anymore. They didn't look like McNuggets yet, either. Something in between. A gelatinous glob of pink muscle that always reminded Gabby of toothpaste.

Gabby had arrived at work exactly one minute after eight. The first thing she did when she made it to her place in the factory line was check the long glass window that overlooked the plant. The lights were still off in Mr. Jackson's office. The next thing she did was separate the two loose flaps of breast meat from an already cut and deboned chicken coming down the line. She would repeat this motion—the gentle twist of both wrists followed by a forceful tug—forty-five times per minute for the rest of her ten-hour shift. At the end of the day, every day, over twenty thousand broilers would pass through Gabby's station.

Her wrists hurt, constantly. When she was at home, chopping onions or brushing her teeth, her wrists hurt. When she was working, they hurt even more. The plant was kept at a frigid forty degrees Fahrenheit to prevent bacteria growth. The cold made Gabby's joints ache and her teeth chatter despite wearing rubber rain boots, thermal underwear, jeans, a T-shirt, a sweatshirt, and a plastic Detmer poncho with an elastic cord in the middle, holding it all together. Safety glasses covered her eyes and a hairnet that looked more like a shower cap was draped over her head. Her hands were stuffed down inside two metal-mesh gloves. Gabby's job didn't require a knife, but there were sharp objects everywhere.

Edwin cut the left leg off the chickens all day. His station was on up the line a couple hundred feet, closer to the loading docks, where the chickens still looked more like chickens. Gabby's hands moved on their own, going through the motions as her eyes stared at the spot where Edwin had stood just two days before. There was another man there now. Younger. With fire left in his eyes and a knife in his hand.

Edwin had been excited about getting a job that required a knife. A promotion. That's why he'd grown the mustache. Like he was Zorro or something. A swordsman. But the cold and the blood and the antibacterial spray made it hard to hold anything properly, not to mention the metal-mesh gloves. After only one week at his new station, Edwin held his knife with both hands and made a simple, single cut that removed the broiler's left leg.

A dissected carcass scooted past Gabby before she had the chance to pull the breast meat off. Mr. Baker, the completely bald line supervisor whose head always reminded Gabby of a plucked chicken, barked from down the line, "Shit, Menchaca! Your boy toy gets canned and now you can't de-breast a goddamn broiler?" He made a mark on the employee-observation sheet attached to his clipboard. There was a point system for everything. Absences. Injuries. Bathroom breaks. Gabby never saw the results.

Nobody did. But if a worker lost too many points in one day, she went to see Mr. Jackson.

A light flickered on behind the window overlooking the plant. Gabby didn't notice, too busy trying not to think about Edwin and the child for fear of missing another chicken and getting another mark. Today was not the day to see Mr. Jackson.

A few minutes and a couple hundred chickens later, Gabby was finally finding her rhythm. The cold was bad, sure, but the ten long hours spent standing in the same spot repeating the same damn motion—that was worse. Brain numbing in a way that most people couldn't imagine. There was a balance required to survive. Gabby had learned this years ago. A worker who zoned out could lose a finger, or get fired in less than a month. One who worried too much, or thought too heavily about the motions, couldn't keep up. Gabby survived through compromise. She'd picture herself in her dream home, years from now with children running around everywhere, but her hands would keep working.

Gabby's dreamworld was slightly different today. The house a bit bigger. Three kids instead of two. She didn't dwell on the differences, or why they'd worked their way into her dream. It was just another way to pass the time.

FROM WHAT LUKE could remember, he had ten, maybe twenty grand in the 0.30 caliber ammo box on his desk. That's where he kept his dead-broiler stash. To the unsuspecting eye, the foot-tall metal box was only a decoration. Something Luke might've gotten from his father if Jim Jackson had fought in Vietnam. Truth was, Luke's daddy dodged the draft with a medical deferment, and Luke had gotten the box at a gun show down in Pope County. When people asked about it, he told them he kept his nest egg in there. Looked inspectors and employees straight in the eye when he said it and waited for them to laugh. Nobody ever sniffed around, and now it was time to cash in. Couple the dead-broiler stash with what Luke could take out of his personal checking account, and he might really be able to piece together the ransom.

Luke's office was a cold dark space without any natural light. He sauntered up to the long window overlooking the interior of the plant, all his workers down there wrapped in plastic, nothing moving but their arms and hands, performing the short, exacting motions that fed the world. Luke thought of his new office, the one across town in the Detmer Commercial Building. He tried imagining the view, rolling hills and clear blue skies, but couldn't see past the plant humming along beneath him. There was beauty in the process, the way a living, breathing chicken came clucking out of one of those modular bins and then—less than five minutes later—was reduced to drumsticks and thighs, ready-to-be-cooked-and-eaten parts of the original whole.

Luke flicked on the lights and got to work.

His fingers traced the ammo box's lid as he moved in behind his desk. His mind drifted to Ferg sprawled out in the backseat of his Ford and the phone call he still needed to make. Nina Ferguson was thick and soft in places where Mimi was hard. Luke had tried—Jesus Christ, he'd tried—to make it work with Mimi, but she was so different now. Even last night, in their bed, Mimi was different. She'd come at him with a desperation he hadn't felt from her before. Mimi even moaned in the end, real loud, trying to turn what they'd done into something it wasn't. That was the part Luke hated most. How Mimi always tried to make it seem like everything was okay. They weren't perfect. They weren't even all that happy, but after Tuck came along, what choice did Luke have? Six months was too long for any man to wait.

Luke took the ammo box by the handle and pulled it across his desk. He'd told enough people the can belonged to his father he almost believed his own fabricated history. The thought was enough to make him remember Tuck again. *Tuck*, his six-month-old son, asleep in another man's house. Luke's fingers spread wide over the cold metal as he recalled his hard-as-nails father, the lessons he'd learned from that man, the habits he'd picked up. What would Jim Jackson have done in a situation like this? He would've found the guy who took his kid and whooped his ass, Luke thought. No doubt about it.

Luke dragged a hand over his face, trying to wipe the memory away, the long nights when his daddy never came home, always out "working the fields." Luke would crawl into bed with his mother, and they'd nod off together. Maybe, if Luke called Ferg and told her what had really happened, she'd be done with him. Maybe then Tuck would turn out okay, different from his old man.

For the first time that day, Luke could see the situation clearly: Tuck was all that mattered. Tuck and the money. Luke flipped the latch on the ammo box. The metal handle rattled against the sidewall. The sharp sound was louder than he'd expected, like a cowbell clunking. Luke pulled the lid back, inch by inch, then peered inside. All thoughts of Tuck were replaced instantly by the shadows at the bottom of the empty box.

CHITO'S MOUTH HUNG open, lips stuck to his teeth, forming a taut circle as the baby boy's cries carried across the Kum & Go parking lot. Chito's jaw came unglued and started to move, bobbing up and down as he said, "Gabriela had a baby? *You* have a kid now, cousin, and you didn't tell me?"

Edwin walked around behind the car and looked in through the back window's heavily tinted glass, getting the same view as Chito. The tint made it hard to see anything more than movement, the child's chunky legs kicking, fists punching at nothing.

"I'm sorry," Edwin said and put his hand on Chito's back, guiding him toward the Chevelle. "It's a long story, but, yeah, I'm glad to see you."

"Yeah?"

"I need your help."

Chito crossed his arms and leaned back against his Chevelle.

"Listen to my kid, cousin," Edwin said, nodding over his shoulder. "He's starving."

"Where's Gabby?"

"You know where she is."

"Today is Saturday. You both work Saturdays."

"Ah, Chito, we both *worked* Saturdays. I'm looking for new work now."

Chito pushed off from his car, leaning forward and staring straight into his cousin's eyes. "I've asked you—for what, going on three years?—to come and join me in my business." Chito waved an open palm over the Chevelle. "I make good money."

Chito's right hand disappeared, digging in the back pocket of his skinny jeans. When his hand came forward again, it held his wallet open, showing Edwin what he'd shown him so many times before.

"You see this?" Chito said, fanning the green bills out in his hands. A couple hundred bucks. Maybe more.

"I see it."

"But you still won't come work for me. Just a couple deals. That's all." Chito flipped his wallet shut. "That plant, it's been killing you. Eating you up. Look how skinny you are."

"It's honest work."

"*Honest?* There ain't nothing honest about working for the man."

"What man?"

"*The man*, cousin. The big boss. The slimiest, richest bastards at the top of the American food chain. You been greasing their palms with your sweat."

Chito wasn't wrong. In fact, he'd just perfectly summed up why Edwin was in this mess now, the pressures that had forced him to steal the child.

"Me?" Chito said and slapped his meaty chest. "I work for myself. I make my own rules and don't have to bend for nobody. Fuck the man, man."

"Maybe some other time. Right now," Edwin said, "I just need your help."

People were starting to notice the screaming coming out of Edwin's Dodge, women's faces wrinkling behind the wheels of minivans.

Chito said, "What kinda help?"

Edwin glanced around the lot. "Can you go inside and buy a couple bottles of formula?"

"For your car?"

"For the kid. It's like food or something."

"*Baby* formula," Chito said. "Yeah. I got you, man."

The glass doors hissed as they opened and Chito lumbered his way inside. Edwin stood beside his car for a moment, listening to the baby cry. When he finally opened the back door, the cries were a physical force, a wall of sound. Edwin shut the door again, trying to come up with a way to get the formula from Chito without him seeing the kid's face. If Chito had a clue the kind of shit Edwin was in, there was no telling what he'd do. Probably something stupid, Edwin thought, and jerked the car door open again, sliding into the backseat as he reached for the boy.

Humming didn't work this time, so Edwin started to sing: "I went down, down, down . . ." By the second chorus the child was asleep. Edwin watched as the boy smacked his lips. Dreaming of his mother's milk? Edwin didn't know, but he could feel the hunger coursing through him, too. The hunger that drove all men to desperate places like the Kum & Go. Edwin's stomach grumbled as the glass doors opened and Chito came shuffling out, two milk jugs in each hand.

Edwin placed the kid on the floorboard and slid out of the backseat before Chito made it to the window. "They didn't have no formula. They said this isn't the place for that stuff." Chito lifted the milk jugs, looking at them for a moment like he was proud. "I got the two-percent, though. That way he don't end up like Uncle Chito."

Chito slapped his belly and passed the jugs to Edwin. They were cold and heavy. Something healthy for a boy to eat. Edwin kept standing there, waiting for Chito to turn and leave so he could begin feeding the child, but Chito wasn't budging, still an arm's length away, grinning like a giant baby.

"I can't pay you," Edwin said. "I told you, I—"

Chito waved it off. "I want to see him."

"The kid?"

"Yes, Edwin, your son. I want to see if he looks like you or Gabriela."

Chito began pushing past Edwin like he was back out on a football field. At barely 130 pounds, there was nothing Edwin could do to stop him. Chito cocked his head to one side, the way a dog does when it's confused.

"Maybe more like Gabby?" he said. "His nose? No, maybe not."

Edwin rushed around the front of the car and was back in the driver's seat, cranking the engine. "Thanks for the milk, cousin. Thank—"

The engine sputtered. Edwin jabbed the key forward again and this time there were only sharp clicks. The starter, Edwin thought, or maybe a dead battery. *Shit.*

"First you take my money," Chito said, knocking on the hood of his Chevelle, "and now you need a ride? You might have to work for me after all." Chito opened the door but didn't sit down, looking over his shoulder at Edwin. "I am only kidding, cousin. Get the boy and let's go."

Edwin's fingers were still wrapped tight around the key. The child stirred in the backseat, taking a deep breath as he woke, loading his cannon. Edwin reached into the backseat and draped the towels around the boy just as he began to scream.

Darting across the parking lot, Edwin looked like he'd just robbed the Kum & Go. Arms loaded down with towels, the four milk jugs, and the child. The boy's hands pawed at Edwin's chest as he ducked into the Chevelle and slammed the door behind him.

"You have the milk," Chito said, checking the rearview as he jerked the car into gear. "What are you waiting for? Feed him."

Edwin unscrewed the top off one of the jugs. It wobbled in his hand as he brought the rim closer to the still screaming child's mouth. The boy slapped at the plastic. Edwin set the milk jug down.

"I need a bottle."

Chito reversed the Chevelle out of the parking space, looking over his shoulder as he said, "Check the glove box. I think I've got one in there."

"You have a baby bottle in the glove box?"

Chito said, "A Mountain Dew bottle, maybe. You could poke a hole in the lid or something."

The Chevelle's engine roared, throwing Edwin against the seat. He had to fight to lean forward again as Chito pulled the vehicle back out into traffic. When Edwin's hands finally made it to the glove box, the child fell silent. The engine whined higher and higher as Edwin pulled the latch on the little door.

There was no bottle in the glove box. Not even a Mountain Dew bottle. But there was a gun. A snub-nosed pistol with rubber bands twisted all around the grip.

Chito said, "You see what I got in there, cousin?"

Edwin said nothing, unable to take his eyes off the gun.

"It ain't no bottle," Chito said, giving the Chevelle a little gas, "and that ain't your kid, neither."

10.

"You wanted to see me, Mr. Jackson?"

Terri stood in the doorway of Luke's office. The headset attached to her left ear bobbed as she gnawed away at the bubble gum. Luke stared at her. He couldn't recall her last name. "Yeah, come in," he said. "And shut the door behind you, please."

She was shorter than what Luke remembered, but maybe it was just that he rarely saw her standing up. *Mashburn*. That was it. Terri Mashburn.

The chair legs groaned as Terri took her seat. "Am I in trouble or something?"

Luke said, "Trouble?" and waited.

"Just never seen you so stressed."

"That's one way to put it."

"I can always tell. Just like when my husband, Barry, gets all riled up, he'll set his jaw kinda like you got yours set right now." Terri and Barry Mashburn, Luke thought, *perfect*. "That little muscle in your temple's going ninety to nothing. Is it the new job?"

"That has me worried? No . . ." What had Luke worried

was the corn-fed country girl sitting in front of him and whatever the hell she'd done with his money. "I'm thrilled about the promotion."

"Should be. Shit—" Terri put a hand to her mouth and grinned. "Sorry. But I's gonna have me a high-speed come apart if they gave that job to Steve Ferguson."

Luke leaned forward until Terri Mashburn stopped smacking her gum, so close he could smell the fruity "Watermelon-Mango" flavor on her breath. "I'm not worried about Steve, or the job. I'm worried about the money, Terri." He reached across the desk and tapped the empty ammo box. "You do know what I'm talking about, don't you?"

Terri straightened, for just a moment, and then she winked at Luke, or at least tried to, closing and opening both eyes at the same time. "Nope," she said. "I ain't got a clue what you're talking about."

"Yes, you do," Luke said, miffed, but still somewhat impressed that Terri had kept her trap shut. Detmer could use a hundred Terri Mashburns, especially on the line. "Just last week, we bought hot dogs for that church-league softball tournament. You got the cash out of the box for me. You're the only—"

"You seriously asking me about the money you told me to *never* talk about."

"Did I say that?"

"That's exactly what you said, Mr. Jackson." Terri plucked the gum from her mouth and started rolling it between her thumb and index finger. "That's why, when I got word you'd landed your dream job . . ." Terri paused, grinning as she chunked the gum in the trash can beside

Luke's desk. "I got rid of it. Didn't want them fancy suit-wearing sons of bitches messing up your shot at the big time."

"You got *rid* of it? What the hell did you do with all the money?"

Terri did her double blink again, but this time she wasn't trying to be cute. "I—I added it to this month's input?" Terri's voice cracked. "I thought it's what you'd want me to do."

Luke said, "How much?" and let his head fall forward into his hands, fingers flexing as they ran over his close-cropped hair. "How much was in the box?"

"A little under thirty grand. Nothing crazy."

"Nothing crazy? Terri, are you—" Luke stopped. The last thing he needed was his receptionist crying in the lobby all day or filing some sort of maltreatment suit. "You were just looking out for me, huh?"

"I got your back." Terri wiped her nose with her shirt-sleeve. "Always have, always will."

Luke stood and walked around his desk to the chair where his receptionist sat. He put a hand on her shoulder, inches away from her neck. A coral-colored earring dangled above his fingers. Luke stared at it, waiting for the heat inside him to cool. The earring was a bird of some sort, a flamingo, wearing sunglasses and holding a coconut cup with one foot.

"You did the right thing," Luke said and exhaled. "I appreciate it."

The flamingo danced as Terri looked up. "You mean it?"

Luke said, "Of course," and gave her shoulder a squeeze before turning for the door. Terri stood and started after

Luke. She lifted both arms and took hold of his waist before he could get away.

"I'm gonna miss you so damn much, boss." Now Terri was the one squeezing. With both her meaty biceps clamped around him, Luke could barely breathe. He managed to croak out, "Me too," then felt the woman's grip loosen. She leaned back and stared at him for a moment, the mascara smeared beneath her eyes like sad war paint, and then she was gone.

Luke waited for the office door to click shut before he doubled over. His hands went to his knees as he fought to catch his breath. A few moments later, Luke staggered back to the window. He peered down over the plant, trying not to think about the extra thirty grand Terri had dumped on the books, how everything he'd worked for—the promotion, the Executive Officer of Poultry position—was crumbling around him now.

Was it his fault? Had Luke's affair led to this? Or maybe it was the way he ran the plant? Had he cut too many corners? There was no handbook. No rules that really mattered except the bottom line. To run a plant effectively, one had to see all the different versions of the truth, all the white lies and altered data points. Being the boss of anything required as much. There were similarities between the lies Luke told his workers and the lies he'd told Mimi over the years. Both were for the greater good. People had to eat and immigrant workers needed jobs. Mimi ate fine, but she worried too much. Dreamed up ways things could go wrong, ways Luke would've never thought of even if he were trying to think up the absolute worst of the worst. Of all the scenarios

Mimi had imagined, she'd never come up with something as bad as what they were up against now.

Luke fanned his fingers out across the cool glass, too worried about the money and Tuck to feel anything, Mimi as far away from him now as the workers beneath his feet.

The supervisor had his clipboard out, writing up what looked to be a woman. It was hard to tell with all the ponchos and the hairnets. Yes. It was a woman. Luke could see her dark mane, wadded up in a bun behind her head. He leaned in, close enough his breath fogged the glass. When he wiped the condensation away, the supervisor was gone, but the woman was still there. The girlfriend of the guy he'd fired yesterday. What was her name?

MIMI'S BODY HAD fallen through the cracks and become a part of the floor. Her conscience drifted up like a ghost balloon but stopped when it hit the ceiling. Somewhere inside her mind she knew that she was dreaming, staring down at her kitchen, watching her son play atop the floor that had melded with her body.

Tuck.

He was right there, ten feet away, pushing up behind his favorite toy, a baby-blue Thomas the Tank Engine. The train's motor whined when Tuck got hold of it, stripping the gears as he yanked it back then let it go again. The train shot forward, taking the kitchen with it, pulling the cabinets like a curtain, revealing more vivid scenes: Tuck with his crop of golden hair catching sunlight in the field out front of their house; Tuck on his back, pawing at a pearl necklace dangling from Mimi's neck. The sounds he made, had just started to make, vowels, mostly.

The train was louder now, that high-pitched whine. Mimi felt it bump into her thigh and Tuck was gone. Just like that. She was in the kitchen again. Another bump, and Mimi opened her eyes to find her Roomba reversing course, starting off between the island and the oven.

The robot vacuum had made a mess of the coffee, smearing it everywhere without getting much of the liquid up. Mimi stared down at the swirls, searching the stains for an answer. Her head was still foggy as she rolled to her knees, her mouth dry. She stood and started toward the pantry. The shelves were lined with tiny glass jars of baby food. Tuck wasn't very good at eating them yet. His tongue got in the way, pushing the globs of carrots and squash around as he smiled. Mimi shut the pantry doors and headed for the fridge.

A bottle of ketchup. A half-empty jar of mayonnaise. Three cans of Diet Coke. There was another fridge in the garage, the one where Luke kept his beer. He was picky about what he drank. Only going for IPAs that came from local breweries, beers with strange names like Lost Forty Brewing's "Rockhound" or "Snake Party Double." Mimi didn't feel like a beer, but the jar of dill pickles in the door didn't look half bad.

Mimi ate half the jar sitting on the steps, surveying the growing pile of junk in their three-car garage. A mixture of what their lives had been like before Tuck and what their lives were now. Mountain bikes and tennis shoes that were never ridden or worn anymore. A baby jumper that was too big for a six-month-old, yet Mimi hadn't been able to pass up the Amazon deal she'd found late one night while Luke was still at work. She remembered the look on his face when the package arrived a couple mornings later. He almost looked sad. No, Mimi thought. *Disappointed.* That was the better word.

She crunched into another pickle, glancing down at her phone. *Call the police. Right now. Just do it.* Her thumb hovered over the glass until she remembered Luke's warning. What might happen to Tuck if they broke the rules.

A dull pain blossomed out from the base of Mimi's skull. It was different from the tingles that had started in her legs, but similar enough for her to fear she might go down again. As she waited for the sensation to pass, Mimi peered back around the garage. The piles of never-used junk by the green trash can were at least four feet tall, such a mess. Which was just what Mimi had been searching for all morning, wasn't it? All that junk was a problem she could solve.

Thirty minutes later, Mimi had the debris separated into three piles: throwaway junk, garage junk, and attic junk. She was sweating and no longer thinking about anything other than getting the garage in order, starting to feel a little better too. So good, in fact, she made a deal with herself: if she could get the garage completely clean before Luke got home, everything would work out.

It was silly, bargaining with fate, but Mimi liked the idea. The trash bag bulged as she lugged it toward the green receptacle beside Luke's beer fridge. Mimi had the lid up, jerking at the red drawstring, trying to swing it into the bin, when the bottom burst and the junk spilled everywhere. It was worse than before, but Mimi didn't notice.

Her eyes were fixed on the bottom of the green trash

can, the six beer bottles sitting in their cardboard holder with "Bud Light" printed across the side.

Luke hated Bud Light.

Mimi reached into the bin. Two of the bottle mouths had red smudges around the rims.

Mimi's phone began to buzz in her pocket. She didn't feel it, too focused on the lipstick stains and the six empty bottles of a beer Luke said he never drank.

THE HOUSE WOULD be a white one. Gabby had known this since she was a girl. A white house with a white fence on a road in a neighborhood that had real streets. No dirt road like at the trailer park, with dust that was all the time getting on your car and in your hair. An electric stove, or a gas one with a pilot light that worked. No more stinky propane. Three bedrooms would be plenty. What did people do with four bedrooms? Gabby wondered and tugged two loose flaps of meat from another carved-up chicken as it came down the line. Her wrists hurt, like always, but she was used to the pain. That was something people with four-bedroom houses would never know. Or if they had known it once, they had forgotten. Pain could be ignored.

What Gabby couldn't forget, though, was the pressure building just below her waist. A hot prick of light. The same way it had burned before, when she'd refused to wet herself even though the child that was growing inside her needed the water more than she did.

Gabby wasn't wearing a diaper today. There were no diapers left in the trailer. Yes, she had been paid on Friday. She could've gone to the store once her chores were done, but then Mr. Levon stopped by, and that changed everything. Edwin most of all. What she thought of him. The man she always believed him to be, gone, just like their rent money.

It was tricky, raising your hand while you were supposed to be stripping meat from chickens coming so fast down the line, but Gabby did it. And Mr. Baker grunted from inside the plant somewhere. She couldn't see him. She couldn't even hear him grunt over the sound of the automated machines whirring around her, but she knew Mr. Baker grunted when he saw her hand go up. He was always shouting, *"Got a hundred applications waiting in my office!"* and tugging the crotch of his pants. He used his words like the workers used their knives, carving out a place for fear in their hearts. Fear was the fuel that powered the plant. Mr. Baker was a disgusting man, but if Gabby wanted to go to the bathroom, he was the one who'd have to give her permission.

Mr. Baker was still a station over, watching the other workers and making marks on his clipboard. He would not come fast. Gabby knew this, and that made it okay. She could handle almost anything if she knew it was coming. What she didn't know was whether or not the man would let her go to the bathroom.

As she waited for Mr. Baker to make his way down the line, Gabby turned her attention to the chickens again, the birds that fed the world. Forty-five days. That was how long a broiler had to live. They were raised in structures without any windows and pumped full of steroids and antibiotics and so much food that if they were human children, they would weigh nearly two hundred pounds by the end of the forty-fifth day. Gabby had read this in one of the online articles Edwin found back when he was trying to come up with a reason to quit the plant. Saying he'd even stop eating chicken, if that's what it took. Edwin still ate chicken and Gabby did, too. What else was there?

"You raise your hand, Menchaca?" Mr. Baker's voice cut through the noise of the machines.

Gabby kept her eyes on the chickens coming down the line. "I have to go to the restroom."

Mr. Baker slapped his clipboard. "Here we go again."

"The alternate," Gabby said, taking her eyes off the chickens long enough to see the woman in the corner of the plant whose job it was to fill in for workers during their bathroom breaks. "She can cover my position. There's not any cutting involved. No knives."

Mr. Baker dragged one gloved finger along his recently shaved scalp. "You know how many other workers already asked to use the pisser today?" He paused, like he was waiting for Gabby to answer the question. She knew better. "Shit, if I let all you bean eaters go pee-pee every time you asked, wouldn't no work get done around here."

"Mr. *Baker*," Gabby said. "Please, just put my name on the list."

He grunted and began flipping through the pages clamped to his clipboard. Mr. Baker didn't have to wear a hairnet because he didn't have any hair. His bald head glistened as he said, "There, Menchaca." The pen in his hand scratched at the paper. "Your name's on the god-damn list. Happy?"

"How many?"

"Holy shit. Are you serious?"

Gabby was serious because she had to be. There were workers at the plant from Mexico, Ecuador, Laos, Haiti, Nepal, China, Arkansas, and even the Marshall Islands. So many languages crammed into one place that nobody spoke much at all. Just nods and points, eyes darting over the protective masks, saying things without saying anything at all. Of the hundred or so line workers, only a handful were white. Ten, fifteen, maybe less. These men and women were able to go to the bathroom whenever they pleased. That was why the alternate was standing instead of working. There were no white people who needed to urinate.

"How many until I can go?" Gabby said, fighting to keep her voice steady.

Mr. Baker slapped his clipboard again and laughed. Gabby kept waiting for him to say something, but there was only silence behind her now. A few chickens later, Gabby realized he was gone. The alternate still stood on the far wall by the vending machines, smiling at something on her phone.

Gabby's fingers shook as she pulled the chicken breasts from the bone, one after another, thinking *this* was the reason Edwin had done what he'd done. He would blame Mr. Levon, blame the rent and the money they didn't have, but the plant had scarred him. It scarred all of them, eventually. She was almost able to rationalize his stupidity as more broilers came down the line, a never-ending stream of bloodless, gutless bone and muscle. The pressure just below Gabby's belly button swelled like a tomato before it fell from the vine, a bright red ball of pressure.

Her problem was nothing new. Workers pissed their pants every shift. Sometimes multiple times a day, small puddles forming around rubber boots, and the line just kept moving, the chickens whose lives meant nothing somehow ruling supreme over the workers and their most basic needs.

There came a point where there was no holding it back. Most people—people who lived in four-bedroom houses, Gabby thought—never know this. They would never understand that there comes a point when you have no choice.

Gabby was almost there, all the muscles in her abdomen tight, focusing so hard on holding it in that a chicken slipped past her with the breast meat still attached.

"Menchaca!"

Gabby knew Mr. Baker would be waving the clipboard at her, giving her another mark and erasing her name from the bathroom list. She didn't want to see his ugly face, his shiny head. She just wanted to go pee. Gabby's muscles relaxed. She closed her eyes.

"Menchaca! Get your ass over here . . ."

Gabby's knees snapped together. She opened her eyes. Mr. Baker was still there, at the end of the line, waving his clipboard, but who was the man standing next to him?

Mr. Jackson?

Gabby spoke the name in her head, trying to guess why he'd come down from his office wearing a hard hat and safety goggles, pointing at Gabby while Mr. Baker nodded and grinned.

Yes, that's the one, Gabby could almost hear the line supervisor say to his boss, this man whose child Edwin had stolen only the night before. *That is the one you are looking for.*

11.

The bathroom door in Luke's office opened and Gabriela Menchaca stepped out, Edwin's girlfriend, the one he liked to use as an excuse. Gabby was probably a few years younger than Mimi, if Luke had to guess, but there was no way to tell from looking at her. Not now. Wrapped from head to toe in a plastic Detmer poncho, still wearing her safety glasses and hairnet. Luke wondered what she was hiding under there.

"Gets hot up here real quick if you're dressed for the plant, Ms. Menchaca," Luke said in his slow Southern drawl. "You can take the poncho and that other mess off."

"I'm fine."

She did not hesitate, and that surprised Luke. "You sure?" he said.

"I need to get back to work."

Luke wagged his finger. "You got spunk, huh? I like that," he said, thinking of the money he had to pay to get his son back. He'd fired Edwin Saucedo the morning of the abduction. Did it in front of the inspectors, trying to make a point, but Luke let workers go every week. None of them had ever stolen his kid before. Maybe this was all just one big mistake. Maybe his mind was playing tricks on him, trying to put a troublemaker like Edwin at the center of his own private mess. Maybe not, Luke thought, then narrowed his eyes on Gabby, ready to find out.

MIMI'S PHONE BUZZED a final time as she reached into the bottom of the trash can and brought up the six-pack of empty beer bottles. A stillness spread through her. She placed the beer on the garage's concrete floor and sat down, seeing Luke's face distorted in the brown glass. All the things he'd ever said to her under review. All the plans he'd made. The promises.

Maybe he'd been eating something red? Cherries? A popsicle? Mimi knew better. For the first time all day, she wasn't thinking about Tuck, and then she was, her son crawling back into her mind, taking the place of his father. If Mimi was going to worry, she should worry about Tuck and Tuck alone. Whatever the hell was smeared across those beer bottles could wait.

She pulled her cell phone up from the pocket of her sweatpants. It was time to call Luke. Ask him how things were going. Did he have the money yet? Yes, Mimi thought, glancing down at the screen. Stick to a problem she could solve.

Except, there was a new problem glaring back at Mimi now. The phone started buzzing again as the name "Gina Brashears" appeared across the top of the screen. Mimi moved her thumb over the red button and left it hovering there, ready to decline the call.

Her thumb came down on green. Then the phone was

pressed to her cheek, her mouth moving as she said, "Gina? Hey."

Mimi could barely hear Gina's voice on the other line, saying she was just calling to check in. "That was part of the deal, right? We're supposed to check on each other. Accountability partners, or whatever the hell you called it." Mimi nodded but said nothing. She could barely remember their night together at La Huerta, the way all the women had promised it wouldn't just be a onetime deal. How they'd keep in touch. It felt silly now.

Gina kept going on the other end of the line, her voice as far away as Thursday night. Mimi reached forward and picked up one of the beer bottles. She brought it in close to her face, studying the grainy red stuff smeared into the glass.

"Mimi? Hey? *Mimi*," Gina said on the phone, her voice finally breaking through. "You there? The hell's going on?"

Mimi's lips trembled, begging to talk to the woman, tell her something—anything—even if it wasn't the truth. Instead, Mimi brought the beer bottle to her mouth, wanting to taste what was left of her marriage. Her lips went tight around the rim, covering the red smudges Mimi knew were lipstick stains now.

A tiny drop of lukewarm beer streaked down the bottle's neck and into Mimi's mouth. It was stale, almost bitter, but hot enough to burn away Gina Brashear's raspy voice still coming out of the phone. Mimi kept holding the liquid in her mouth, sloshing it around and trying to feel something again, when the bottle flew from her hand, exploding against the garage wall in sparkling shards.

Mimi stood there a moment before she said, "Gina?"

and paused long enough to swallow the warm beer down. "I think Luke's having an affair."

LUKE PUSHED HIS chair back and crossed his legs. Gabby stood across from him on the other side of the desk, fingers wrapped tight around her thin left wrist.

"Please," Luke said and lifted a hand. "Sit down."

Gabby's fingers worked in deeper around her wrist. She shook her head.

"Might be a while. I got a couple questions I need to ask you about Edwin Saucedo." He watched her eyes for signs of fear. There was nothing, just a blank stare that reminded him of how chickens could sleep with one eye open when they had to, something about how their brains worked, a survival mechanism. "You know," Luke said, wondering if she'd been born with that look in her eyes or if it was something the plant had given her, "I had to let him go yesterday."

"Yes, you fired him for being two minutes late. But from what I could tell, Mr. Jackson, you were walking in the same time he was."

Luke cocked an eyebrow at her, thinking if she knew anything about his kid, if Edwin really had taken Tuck, Gabriela Menchaca had some nerve, talking to him like that.

"I really wish you'd take that poncho off and sit down," Luke said. "You've got to be burning up under there."

Gabby let go of her wrist. Her fingers found the poncho's elastic band. She pulled the scummy plastic over her head. Dark brown locks shook loose as she removed the hairnet. The baggy sweatshirt and the bulky jeans didn't matter; Luke could still see the shape of her. Different from Mimi, even Ferg.

"I take it I won't be working any more today?"

Her voice brought Luke back, shaking his head as he said, "Did I say that?"

"I don't want to put it all on again." Gabby pointed to the pile of plastic on the floor. "I told you—"

"You been telling me all sorts of stuff since you first walked in here," Luke said and flashed the smile he'd honed in bigwig board meetings over the years, a look that let them know he wasn't buying their shit. "And I've been listening. You got anything else to add before I move on?"

Gabby chewed her bottom lip a moment then pointed to the window behind Luke's desk. "We need bathroom breaks. The way it's set up now isn't fair."

Luke made a motion with his hands, telling Gabby to keep going.

"Sometimes, we can't go all day. That's ten hours, Mr. Jackson. We have to hold it."

"That's a long time."

"No shit." Gabby paused, like she couldn't believe she'd just taken such a tone with him, and Luke almost bought it. He'd been thinking maybe her plan was to come in and talk so tough he'd never believe she was scared, knowing her boyfriend was back home with the boss's baby. Now, though, Luke was starting to think maybe she was telling him the truth, all the stuff she wanted to say before she walked out of his plant for good.

Luke said, "Every employee is guaranteed an hour-long break. It's in the contract."

Gabby threw both hands in the air. "We get no breaks,

Mr. Jackson. And by *we*, I mean people who look like me. Most of the other workers can't even read the contract. Your line supervisors, they—"

"You sure you want to bring other employees into this?"

Gabby took a quick breath before continuing: "The supervisors don't allow certain workers the same breaks. Mr. Baker? He's the worst."

"Stanley Baker's a good man. He's been working here his whole life. Stan's from just down the road in Goshen. You know where that is?"

"My family," Gabby said and patted her chest, "my *people* are from—"

"—Celaya." Luke waited for Gabby's expression to change, something to signal he was on the right track. She cracked her knuckles and did not break his gaze. "Yeah, Celaya, Mexico," he said. "Nice little city, or I guess it used to be. From what I've heard, that's a pretty scary place to live now. Cartels running loose in the streets, drug wars and all that."

Luke gave her time to digest the fact that he'd done his homework. He knew about her, had her file sitting right there on the desk behind the empty ammo box. He hadn't gone for it yet, hadn't even looked over at it, but the file was still there, within reach.

"Don't believe everything you read on the internet, Mr. Jackson. Celaya has its problems, sure, but I don't think it's any more dangerous than this plant."

"You not see the sign out front? We haven't had an accident in—"

"That sign is a lie. Whenever somebody gets injured, you still make them come in. Make them sit in the infirmary so they're not counted absent. It doesn't matter if the tip of their left pinky is missing like Martín's was last month. No, that's fine, as long as another day gets added to that sign." A strand of dark hair had fallen down between Gabby's eyes, perfectly dividing her nose. "This plant hasn't gone one week without an accident," she said, "not since I've been here."

"Seven years, right?" Luke flashed his grin again and waited for Gabriela to get to the point, hoping if he gave her enough rope she'd hang herself.

"And now you're smiling at me?" she said. "You think this is funny? You don't know what I've lost, Mr. Jackson. What I've given to keep my job at this plant."

"If you hate it here so much, why don't you leave? Just move on back to Mexico?"

Gabby kept standing there, staring back at him for so long Luke could feel a new coldness creeping in around his heart, bringing back memories of the morning.

"I don't want to go anywhere," she said, finally. "This is my home. My first memories are of Arkansas. I've lived here since—"

Luke slid the manila folder out from behind the ammo box and flipped it open. The woman's loopy handwriting was everywhere. He could feel her eyes scanning the pages, knowing damn well what was missing. Luke wasn't worried about the false documents. He was still stuck on the empty crib. The phone call. The money he had to pay to get his son back. Luke could even hear Edwin's voice on the phone now, calling from that private number. Luke imagined him—or maybe Gabriela—sifting through the Walmart dumpster, picking up the different bags and tearing them open, hoping to find the money.

All the warm blood left in Luke's body rushed to his head as he stood and said, "You lost a child, Ms. Menchaca. Last year. Edwin filed a maltreatment claim." He flipped to a page in the back of the folder. The handwriting there was different, slanted, not nearly as neat. "Up until today, I didn't have a damn clue what that felt like."

Gabby's face finally cracked, going for a look of surprise but coming off scared as she said, "Something happened to your child?"

"Oh?" Luke said. "You heard?"

"No. Not like that. You just said—"

"*Yeah*," Luke said, cutting her off. "I think you did. I think you know all about the fifty grand Edwin said it would take for me to get my son back. What you dumb shits didn't know is that I don't have the money. Fifty grand? Who do you think I am?"

Gabby flinched as Luke stepped out from behind his desk and started past her.

"You—you . . ." she stammered, still facing the long glass window that looked down over the plant. "You don't have the money?"

"I don't need the money," Luke said and turned the lock on his office door. "I've got you."

12.

The gun was out of Chito's glove box now, lying on the makeshift plywood table in the trailer's living room. Edwin had the boy in his arms, feeding him a bottle, a real one with a little plastic baggie on the inside and everything. Chito walked through the front door carrying an economy-sized box of diapers. Edwin watched as the boy sucked the bottle dry, trying to make sense of all that had happened since the Kum & Go.

There wasn't much to it. Not after Edwin decided to tell Chito the truth, starting with the plant, explaining the poor conditions, the diapers, everything. "A diaper?" Chito had said, pulling the Chevelle to a stop under a red light. "Shit." Edwin moved on to his boss, Luke Jackson, saying the guy was a real prick. Never paid overtime, no time cards, and that was fine. No undocumented worker wants a paper trail. That's why it stung so bad when Luke fired Edwin for being two minutes late. "Two minutes?" Chito shook his head and revved the engine, waiting for the light to change.

"Yeah," Edwin said. "Two minutes." The kicker, the

thing Edwin knew he had to tell his cousin if he wanted that snub-nosed pistol to stay in the glove box, was the truth about Gabriela. He didn't tell Chito about the look in her eyes after the toilet flushed. He just told him about the child they'd lost, saying, "She didn't want to piss herself. That's why she stopped drinking the water. That's why—" The light turned green and Chito hit the gas, the Chevelle's Turbo-Fire 307 V8 drowning out the rest of Edwin's story. Chito had heard enough. He didn't even ask Edwin what his plan was for the kid. It was like he already knew, steering the Chevelle into an empty space in the back of the Walmart parking lot, no other cars around, and saying to Edwin before he got out: "This man has taken so much from you, cousin. From Gabriela. I understand what you are doing. Let me help." Chito was gone and back in less than ten minutes.

It had all happened so fast, Edwin almost couldn't believe it, but there he was, the child's eyes growing heavy as he drained what was left of the bottle. Edwin felt his own eyes close as he imagined Gabby at the plant, trying to keep her cool. She could do it. Gabby could do anything. Edwin had seen this in her early, back during high school, and held on tight. Why Gabby had stuck with a guy like him remained a mystery. She could've done better. There was no doubt in his mind, but it was like she saw in Edwin what he couldn't see in himself, the man he'd almost become before he took his place in line at the plant, settling in for seven long years of nothing. The man who had come up with his own plan, the man who wasn't going to take any more shit—maybe this was who he was really meant to be.

The child's head fit perfectly into the crook of Edwin's

elbow. Edwin kept his eyes closed, not wanting the moment to end. The only sounds in the trailer now were Chito's footsteps, thudding through the front door to the kitchen and back again, unloading the Chevelle and packing the baby stuff away.

A warmth started up through Edwin's arms, a glow coming off of the child spreading out and covering Edwin's body as he drifted toward something like sleep.

"You remember that time at the hotel . . ." Chito's voice called Edwin back. "That time at the Econo Lodge when I jumped off the balcony or whatever. Think it was like two, maybe three floors up. I don't know, I was pretty high."

Edwin remembered the great splash, how the water hit the windows and Mr. Khoury came out screaming. "Stoned out of your mind is more like it."

"Still got that scar on my big toe, too."

Edwin felt a *thunk* on the sofa beside him and opened his eyes to find Chito's sockless foot propped on the armrest, inches from his face.

"See it?"

Edwin saw it.

"Ma was *so* pissed. Thought she was gonna have to take me to the hospital," Chito said, "and you know how she feels about hospitals."

Edwin hadn't thought of Maria Ortega in years. He could still see the flickering candles she kept lit in her windowsills, still smell the sharp scent of chili and cinnamon that always made him sneeze. Maria was the third woman in Edwin's life, a bridge between his mother and Gabriela. Maria was pure magic. She could cast a spell on a boy, make him feel bigger than he really was, stronger too.

"She got it to stop bleeding with that stuff she keeps above the fridge," Chito said. "You know, that curandera shit she gets her sisters to send her from the market in Tepic."

Edwin had seen inside that cabinet before. He'd put a chair in front of the fridge, climbed up it, and found tobacco leaves, the yellow bottle of mezcal, the jars of mud, and what looked to an eight-year-old Edwin like tiny bones sticking up from the corners of a faded leather bag, jaw bones with some of the teeth still attached.

"Look at this one," Chito said, pointing to his elbow. "Sixteen stitches from a face mask my sophomore year."

Edwin smiled and nodded, but the wounds from the plant made Chito's football injuries look like child's play, which they were. Edwin had a burn on the small of his back from an exposed wire on the eviscerating machine. Left this crazy welt like a lightning bolt running up his left side, fanning out over his ribs. His fingers were shredded too, every knuckle nicked. The worst injuries were the ones that weren't visible, the constant ringing in his ears, the pain in both knees from standing all day, and his mind, his mind was not the same anymore. How could it be?

A phone rang somewhere inside the trailer.

The child's tiny eyelids fluttered, still lost in the dream-world, the place Edwin had left behind so long ago.

"Edwin?" Chito reached for the phone on the plywood table. His meaty paws dwarfed the device, muting the sound coming out of it.

Edwin said "Who is it?" holding tight to the sleeping child as Chito leaned forward and turned the screen so Edwin could see it.

GETTING GABBY OUT of the office and into his truck was harder than Luke had expected. She wasn't budging, not until Luke told her he'd call the cops. Call them and tell them to go over to Wink-Land Trailer Park, Lot 123. Take a peek around and see if they found a little white baby. Gabby tried acting like it wasn't any big deal, giving him her cold stare again. But when Luke got his phone out and started tapping at the screen, Gabby finally said, "Okay, fine. What do you want me to do?"

Luke wanted her to put the poncho and the hairnet back on and go down to the locker room. He wanted her to get changed out of her work clothes and meet him in the parking lot. If anybody asked, she would tell them to mind their own damn business. It was as good of an excuse as Luke could come up with, and it didn't matter. With Edwin getting canned the day before, most of the other workers, even the supervisors, wouldn't think twice about Gabby leaving work early; everyone expected her to go next.

Luke watched Gabby on the monitors in his office, moving from screen to screen. She followed his instructions, exactly, and none of the other workers said a word. Most of them didn't even look up, too busy plucking and cutting and freezing their asses off to notice.

Terri was the last hurdle Luke had to clear. He was careful about the timing, waiting until he could see Gabby on the stairwell camera. That's when he buzzed Terri into his office, telling her he was going to be out for the rest of the day and wanted her to field the calls from his desk.

"Your desk?" she'd said, smacking her gum then shrugging. "You got it, boss." The office door shut behind Luke as Gabby came out of the stairwell and into the lobby. A moment later, they were walking through the front doors together.

The parking lot was empty as they hustled toward Luke's truck. He kept his cell phone in his hand, using it like a gun to prod her along. All Luke had to do was make one call and the pathetic routine she and Edwin called their life would be over. Gabby knew it, and that's why she didn't give Luke any problems when he handed her the truck keys and told her to get in.

She was in the driver's seat now, sitting up straight with both hands on the wheel. She seemed smaller than she had in his office, her alluring frame reduced inside the Ford truck's extended cab. Even after Luke got in behind her, Gabby kept a foot on the brake, unsure of which way to go.

"Take 412 West," Luke said, reaching down beneath the backseat, "and keep your eyes on the road."

GABBY THOUGHT IT was his hand, the tip of one finger, sharp and bony, touching her shoulder. When he asked her for her phone, though, there was something in his voice that hadn't been there in his office, a slight vibrato like his teeth were chattering. Gabby dug her phone out of her sweatshirt's front pocket and passed it back between the seats, keeping her eyes on the road.

A semi blew past and rattled the Ford's cab. Gabby had an idea about what would happen next. As soon as Luke had started talking in his office, asking her questions that meant nothing to him, being patient while she explained the problems inside the plant—Gabby knew what was coming, a feeling she had in her gut, similar to the one she'd had before she'd flushed that toilet.

The cab was quiet enough that Gabby could hear Edwin's voice coming through the phone when he answered, saying her name like it was a question, sliding into a higher pitch at the end.

"I sound like Gabby to you?" Luke said.

Gabby pictured Edwin glancing at the screen, fingers going to his mustache as he checked the caller ID again.

Luke said, "You know who I am?" and waited, just long enough for Edwin to mumble something Gabby couldn't make out. "That's right. And you see whose phone I'm calling from?"

Another semi carrying a truckload of broilers roared down the auxiliary road, the cab shaking so hard, so loud, Gabby couldn't hear Edwin's response.

"Still giving me that tough-guy act?" Luke said. "Well, here, let's see if this don't change your mind."

It was the same feeling as before, something hard poking into her shoulder. Gabby didn't move. Then Luke poked her again, and this time Gabby turned. The first thing she saw was the phone, the glowing screen with a digital image of Edwin wearing his hairnet and safety glasses on upside down. Gabby remembered the day she'd taken it, seven years ago, their first shift together. She reached for the phone, already thinking of what she'd say to Edwin—how she'd say it—when she saw the rifle laid out across Luke's lap, the barrel pointing straight at her.

"Edwin! He has a—"

That was all she got out before Luke jabbed the muzzle into her side, jolting her back toward the steering wheel as he said into the phone, "Now, then, let me tell you what's gonna happen next, Mr. Saucedo."

Gabby's ears started to ring, a high, lonesome sound like the tornado sirens on Wednesdays at noon. It was the sound of things falling apart. The sound of their lives shattering. She should've known better than to go along with Edwin's stupid plan. She should've told him no. All the way back to Springdale High, the first time Edwin asked her if she wanted to go cruising in his cousin's Chevelle, that's what Gabby should've told him.

No.

She tried to guess what Edwin was saying on the other line. The excuses he was making, his voice so small, so weak. But there was only silence in the truck's cab. A long run of it. Long enough for Gabby to glance up at the rearview mirror and see Luke staring down at the phone.

"He hung up." Luke found Gabby's eyes in the rearview mirror. "I don't believe it. The bastard hung up on me."

THERE WERE SHARDS of glass all the way out to the driveway. Mimi had a dustpan in one hand, a broom in the other, sweeping the mess up. Her phone was still wedged between her shoulder and her ear, but she couldn't feel the device anymore. She didn't even remember that Gina was on the line, not until the woman said, "Well, what're you gonna do?"

Mimi let go of the dustpan and pushed her hair back from her eyes, remembering the last time she'd cleaned up broken glass. Just a little over a week ago. Tuck coughing like crazy and throwing the biggest fit of his six-month-old life. Mimi in the kitchen trying to get supper ready before Luke came home. Rushing around, not paying attention.

Her elbow had clipped a glass on the counter. It was like time slowed down, Mimi standing there, watching as it fell and the oven timer dinged, but she didn't hear it. Not until the glass hit the tile and exploded. That's when her world came rushing back. This whole day had felt like that. Like time had been frozen all the way up until that beer bottle hit the garage wall and went scattering everywhere, leaving Mimi to pick up the pieces.

"Two lipstick-stained beer bottles . . . That doesn't prove anything, right?" Mimi kept sweeping the concrete even though she didn't see any more glass.

"Where there's smoke there's fire, hon."

"I don't know what that means."

"You need to talk to your husband," Gina said. "That's what it means."

Mimi clipped the dustpan onto the broom, knowing she wouldn't have that conversation with Luke. Not now. Not without— She wouldn't even let herself think her son's name. Not until Luke rolled back down the driveway with the money.

"You hear me?" Gina said. "You need to talk to him. First thing when he gets home, catch him in the garage, or the driveway. Shit. Don't let him get out the damn truck."

"I can imagine how that would go."

"Just stick to what you know. Tell him you found some lipstick on his beer. That's it. Focus on the facts and keep it simple," Gina said. "Come to think of it, you don't have to tell him nothing, just show him the damn bottles soon as he pulls in. Walk up and say, 'Hi, baby,' holding that shit in your hand. Let the bottles do the talking for you."

"It's not that easy." Mimi looked through the open garage door to the pack of Bud Light still sitting on the concrete, the one remaining bottle with the red around the rim catching the sun and reflecting back in her eyes.

"Gets easier the more you do it," Gina said. "Just like anything else."

Mimi was halfway through the garage doors, going for the bottle, but Gina's words stopped her. "Wait. Are you saying Brett—"

"Ain't saying nothing more than what I already told you. That should be enough."

"Oh, Gina. I'm sorry."

"Don't be. I could've walked out on Brett's sorry ass a hundred times over."

"Why haven't you?"

"You seen the size of our house?" Gina laughed at her own joke for a second too long. "Besides, if I left Brett, I'd be letting him win."

"He wants a divorce?"

"He's *been* wanting one. But I ain't budging. Finally had Brett right where I wanted him after all these years. He was getting older, starting to calm down and stick around the house, but then he got his hands on a Viagra prescription and our golden years were gone. He went back to thinking with his little head. Shit, he ain't thinking. It's just more of the same."

Gina's monologue stirred something in Mimi. Just holding the beer bottle made her feel closer to Luke, closer to the truth. It was so careless. Not like him at all. Almost as if he'd wanted to get caught. Mimi slid a finger down the bottle's neck, the inside slick and smooth like nothing

in the woods and fields that surrounded her house. Everything out there was protected. Tree bark. Scales. Thick
furry hides. Bony antlers.

A dust cloud rose beyond the wild blackberry bushes
lining the dirt road. Mimi blinked. It was still there. It was
real. She couldn't see the vehicle for the bushes, only the
swirling cloud rising behind it. She could feel it, though.
She knew Luke's gray Ford would turn left past the blackberry bushes, and then it did.

The truck was headed for the house, still a quarter
mile up the road, when Mimi heard Gina's voice coming
through the phone, carrying on about Viagra and prenup-
tial agreements. "Gina?" Mimi said. "He's here."

"You got the bottle?"

Mimi had the bottle in her left hand, the phone in her
right, eyes scanning the ten or so acres out in front of the
house as Luke's Ford rumbled closer. "Yes," she said. "I
have it."

"That's my girl." Gina's voice calm, reassuring.
"Remember, you ain't got to say nothing. Just give him
your best no-bullshit eyes and lift that bottle up high where
he can see it. You ready?"

The truck was close enough now Mimi could see through
the front windshield to the driver's seat, the shape of the
person sitting behind the wheel becoming clearer with
every rotation of the truck's tires. The driver was smaller
than Luke. Much smaller. With long dark hair spilling out
everywhere.

A woman?

Mimi's eyes jumped to the empty passenger seat,
searching for Luke. It wasn't until the truck pulled off

the gravel and into the driveway that Mimi saw her husband sitting in the backseat holding his deer rifle with both hands. A small voice inside her head said, "Mimi? *Mimi?* Don't leave me hanging, girl. You ready or what?"

13.

The woman looked sick. That was Gabby's first thought when she saw Luke's wife, standing there in the driveway, holding one elbow, the other arm straight down by her side. The wife never moved. Didn't say a word when Mr. Jackson got out of his truck holding that rifle, then used it to lead Gabby into the house. He laid the gun out on the guest bed, pointing straight at her as he taped her wrists. Luke picked the rifle up again when it was time for Gabby to get into the closet. Scraping sounds followed. A lock clicked.

Even in the dark, Gabby could tell the closet was bigger than her bedroom in the trailer. There were no clothes hanging from the racks. The whole house was like that, just a bunch of empty space. Much too large for a family of three. A child as small as the one she'd held this morning, the closet could've been his bedroom.

It wasn't, though. Gabby was sure of that. The infant had a room of his own somewhere inside the gigantic house, a room Edwin had been in the night before. Gabby wouldn't let herself think about Edwin and what he'd done. Why he'd hung up on Mr. Jackson after he'd said Gabriela's name, after she'd seen the dark snout of that hunting rifle and shouted loud enough for Edwin to hear. She *knew* he had heard her, and still, he'd hung up. If Gabby thought about that for too long a pressure formed between her eyes.

All Mr. Jackson had said when they'd pulled up was: "That's my wife, the crazy-looking one in the driveway. Bet y'all will get along fine." Like it was a joke or something. This man with his child still missing and his wife standing barefoot in the driveway.

Gabby wouldn't let herself think about the woman either, or the pain Edwin had caused her, so she walked small circles instead. She made laps. That's how big the closet was. The walking helped her mind wind down. There was no way out of this situation. Not without Edwin. Surely, he would call back and offer Mr. Jackson some sort of new deal. Edwin was nothing without Gabriela. It had been that way since high school. But now, with Gabby locked in the closet of some crazy white man's house, she was the one who needed Edwin.

It was a strange feeling. Desperate and angry at the same time. All the years she'd invested in Edwin adding up to this, a fistful of resentment. Yes. That was the right word. That was it, exactly. *Resentment.* Gabby didn't like putting all her faith in him any more than she liked the closet, but what choice did she have? She sat down on the carpeted floor, tired of walking without getting anywhere, and that's when she heard a voice, two voices, drifting out of the vent in the wall. Mr. Jackson speaking to his wife with same tone he had used on Gabriela in his office less than an hour before.

"YOU DIDN'T GET the money?"

Luke rolled his eyes and plopped down on the bed. Mimi stood in the doorway. Afraid to come any closer. Not after he'd gotten out of the back of his truck toting that deer rifle, the barrel pointed straight at the Mexican woman, the one in the guest room closet now.

"The money doesn't matter," Luke said, placing the rifle on the bed beside him. "We've got the guy's girlfriend."

"You—you *know* who took Tuck?"

"I've got a damn good idea."

Mimi slapped the doorframe without meaning to, her hand moving faster than her mind, her mouth not far behind. "A good idea? *Luke?* You just kidnapped that woman. You led her into our house at gunpoint. What were you thinking?"

The way Luke looked at her, Mimi could tell he hadn't been thinking at all.

"If you knew who took our son—who still has him—we could've called the police."

Luke shook his head. "We've been over that already. Even if I sent the cops straight to the guy's trailer, there's no telling what he might do when they came knocking at his door."

For so much of Mimi's life she'd simply deferred to Luke. Her husband called the shots, made the tough choices. This was different. Mimi stared at his lips, imagining them pressed tight to a Bud Light bottle. She shook her head, and the image was gone.

"How do you know who did it?" she said. "How'd you figure it out?"

"I saw the woman working down on the line, causing

problems, giving my supervisor hell. Got me thinking about yesterday. Something that happened before the inspection."

Mimi waited for more, watching Luke undress like he did every day after work, ridding himself of the plant.

"I fired a line worker yesterday." Luke's fingers made their way down the buttons on his tan shirt. "Didn't think much of it. This guy was always coming in late and making excuses. Always breaking the rules."

A memory surfaced, a stark image of that white Dodge parked outside the plant when Mimi had rushed in to give Luke his satchel. The way it was parked, pulled up on the curb. Mimi put her hand on the doorframe again, bracing herself.

"Few months back, he even tried to stage a walkout." Luke laughed as he slid his shirt down over his shoulders. His arms were the same as they'd been in college, veins running up his forearms to his biceps, bulging under his paper-thin skin. Mimi tried not to look. She tried not to think about the places those hands had been. "He didn't get very far."

A new worry bubbled up inside of Mimi. She should've never left Tuck in the 4Runner when she'd gone into the plant. That's when the man must have seen him. He must have heard her baby boy crying and . . .

Mimi was so lost in the memory, she almost couldn't see Luke in his underwear now, stepping out of them as he said, "Then I remembered the guy had a girlfriend worked at the plant. Called her into my office, asked her a couple questions. That's all it took. I knew."

"She told you?"

"I called the guy on the drive over. Called him from her phone." Luke was naked now, standing in the middle of the room, the loaded hunting rifle on the bed beside him. Mimi's hand slid down the doorframe, taking hold of her other hand, pinching the meaty part of her palm.

"Knew it was him the moment he answered, the guy that had called earlier from the private number? I recognized his voice."

The way Luke spoke, it was as if he were getting the story straight in his head. What was he leaving out? Mimi pinched her palm again, harder this time.

A dresser drawer opened and Mimi blinked, watching as Luke took out a fresh pair of boxer briefs, the new kind he had started wearing a few months back. Bright patterns with a pouch in the front. *Saxx: Experience Life Changing Underwear.* Was that when it started? Did those fancy underwear Mimi had ordered for him somehow lead to the Bud Light bottles she'd found in the garage? Mimi ran the numbers, realizing Luke only wore his Saxx on weekends, all those long nights he never came home.

"You called him," Mimi said, fighting to keep her voice steady, trying to keep from saying something that wouldn't matter. "What did he say?"

Luke had the underwear on, his firm backside moving beneath the fabric as he started across the room. "He hung up on me." Luke said it like it meant nothing and disappeared through the bathroom door.

Mimi waited for more, thinking, for the first time, of the woman locked in the guest room. How had it felt staring down the barrel of Luke's rifle? What did she think after her man had hung up? Mimi pushed the questions away. They were just like the lipstick stains and the flashy underwear. They didn't matter. Not until Tuck was back home.

Luke emerged from the bathroom and said, "The sucker's gonna call back," dressed from head to toe in camouflage hunting gear. "I mean, that's what I'd do if somebody had you. I'd do whatever it took."

THE CHILD'S SCREAMS escaped from under the bedroom door. Edwin stood at the sink in the kitchen, watching the steam rise. The way Gabriela's voice had cracked, the way she'd screamed out for him—that's all Edwin heard now. Gabby's cries and the boy's cries, mixing together as one. He could no longer hold the child. Not anymore. Edwin stood and listened to the sound of running water, the sound of time passing. How much time, he didn't know.

The water was cool as Edwin turned from it and said, "I'm calling him back."

Chito nodded from the sofa, surrounded by a couple hundred dollars' worth of diapers and bottles and wipes, the same place he'd been sitting and listening to the child cry since Edwin hung up the phone. "You are doing the right thing, cousin. This is no good. He has Gabby. Call him back and tell him it's over."

A dull pain lingered in Edwin's bones, a hangover caused by regret. He should've told the man he could have his child back as soon as he heard Gabriela's voice. *Yes. Yes, Mr. Jackson. Whatever you want, Mr. Jackson.* That's what Edwin should've said, but he hadn't. And even now, looking down at the phone on the kitchen counter, he knew it would be a hard thing for him to say, to cower before this man again, just like he had done for the last seven years. To give him what he wanted when he had been so close.

What Edwin had to do would be far from perfect, but he would do it his way. He would at least talk to the man how he'd always wanted, using his own voice this time when he told him exactly how the new exchange would go down.

Edwin dialed Gabriela's number and Luke answered on the first ring. Edwin imagined the rich, powerful man pacing his bedroom with Gabby's phone in his hand. The thought brought words to his mouth, gave him the confidence to say, "Here is the deal, Luke. The *new* deal. Are you listening? I will only say it once."

LUKE LEFT THE bedroom with the Mexican woman's phone pressed to one ear. Mimi fell back on the bed. The rifle was right there, on the mattress beside her, so close she could touch it. The house was silent without the sounds of her son to fill it. The front door opened then closed, the sharp click like a gunshot shattering the stillness.

A moment later, Luke stormed past the master-bedroom window, pacing around on the front porch. He never could stand still when he talked. Didn't matter if he was speaking to a driver about a delayed shipment of chickens, or negotiating an exchange with the man who had stolen their son. The way he'd held that rifle, close down at his hip like a sheriff in an old Western movie, it had surprised Mimi at first. But eyeing him now, as he stepped down from the front porch and into the driveway, the low-hanging afternoon sun casting his shadow all the way back up to the house, Mimi was no longer surprised. Not after what she'd found.

She realized then that she'd never really known him. Even after nine years together, there was no way to truly know a man's heart, what went on behind his eyes, the thoughts that flashed through his mind as he drifted off to sleep in the very bed where Mimi was still sitting. The same place she had lain down beside him for so many years that they'd all blurred together and formed one long patch of darkness, the night that lay ahead of them now.

As Mimi watched Luke lean over the hood of his truck and put his elbows on it, a glimmer caught her eyes, something sparkling up from beneath Luke's feet. A piece of the busted bottle she'd missed. With Luke's boots so close to the glass, Mimi began to worry. Her mind raced past the phone call and whatever Luke was telling the man, to what she would say when he came back inside.

Would he realize what she'd found? Would it distract him from what he would have to do? The beer bottles swirled together with the ratty Dodge parked outside the plant, stirring the apprehension coiled tight around Mimi's heart, the fear that she'd somehow caused whatever was coming.

Luke pushed off the truck and stepped backward over the broken glass. Maybe he was so busy talking to the man he wouldn't even notice. Maybe they wouldn't have to talk about it. Not tonight. Not until all of this was over.

Mimi put her hands out beside her, preparing to stand and go to the window for a better look, but then her fingers brushed against the rifle barrel, the metal so slick and oily. Mimi jerked her hand to her chest as a soft ding echoed across the bedroom.

There it was again. An alert. A single electric chime. Mimi's eyes scanned the room for the source of the sound, landing on Luke's work pants lying crumpled on the floor in the corner. The front pocket glowed blue for a moment before the light faded.

Still on for tonight?

The phone was heavy and warm. There was a crack in the glass Mimi hadn't noticed before, a diagonal line that cut across the words on the screen. The text was from "Bob Simpson." Mimi didn't know any Bob Simpsons. That didn't mean anything, though. Luke had hundreds of work contacts in his phone, managers from all across the country, all the different people he had to deal with on a weekly basis. Even if it did mean something, it didn't mean anything, especially not now.

That's what Mimi's mind was telling her, but her thumbs were already tapping at the phone, heart racing as she entered Luke's passcode.

His texts filled the screen and Mimi exhaled, staring down into a completely blank history. There were no previous messages from Bob. Nothing. Just this one text about tonight. Deep down, in her heart vault, Mimi knew the truth about "Bob." Knew the connection between the text and the lipstick, but now was not the time to go digging up what had been buried for so long. A few taps of her thumbs and the message was gone. Bob Simpson erased from their lives just as easily as she'd entered it.

Mimi slid the phone back into the front left pocket of Luke's work pants. Had it been in the left pocket, or the right?

"Mimi?" Luke's voice was loud and clear like he was

back inside the house. And then he was there, standing in the doorway, still dressed in that ridiculous camouflage. For a moment, Mimi didn't recognize him. She almost screamed.

Instead, the work pants slipped from her fingers. They thumped when they hit the floor. Mimi stared down at the crumpled slacks, the bulge in the pocket. "Well," she said, steadying herself before lifting her eyes. "What'd he say?"

LUKE DIDN'T TELL Mimi what the guy had said. He just snatched his phone from his work pants pocket and started for the guest room. Mimi's footsteps were so soft, he had to turn and make sure she'd followed him. She had, but the woman he saw barely resembled his wife, the skinny arms, the sunken eyes. This was killing her. He had to be careful.

A bike lock hung from the handle on the closet door, one of those flexible, combination-style locks. The lock was looped around the shelf mounted to the wall. Luke stood before it, holding the Springfield under his left arm, trying to remember the code.

"It's so quiet," Mimi said. "It's like she's not even in there."

"I put her in there. What are you talking about?"

A pause, Mimi's voice drifting farther and farther away. "Back in college, I remember my psychology professor explaining this thought experiment. I can't remember the exact setup, but it had something to do with a cat."

Luke hadn't taken any psychology classes at the U of A, but he remembered that dumbass cat from high school physics.

"There's no way to tell if the cat's still in the box. Like once it's in there, once the lid is closed, there's no way to be sure."

"The way you worry, it's like a disease or something. You know it? Besides, you've got it all wrong. It's whether the cat is dead," Luke said and picked up the bike lock. "That's the problem."

"Have you thought about what that means for our son?"

Luke could feel the weight of Mimi's gaze on his back, all the danger in the world coming together and forming the worry that filled her heart.

Luke picked up the bike lock. "What's the combination?"

"Tuck's birthday."

He spun the lock's dial, trying to remember if Tuck was born on the fifth or the sixth of April.

"What'd the guy say, Luke?"

With all four numbers lined up, Luke gave the lock a swift tug. It didn't release. "He said no funny business. Something like that. The way he talks, it's hard to understand."

"You understood him perfectly when he said not to call the police."

Luke could hear Mimi breathing behind him, the gears in her mind turning, thinking about the situation like they were characters in a movie, imagining a SWAT team busting down the trailer door, the whole damn thing in the *Northwest Arkansas Democrat-Gazette* the next morning. Luke didn't need that. Not with his new job dangling out ahead of him, Mr. Detmer's words like a warning label stamped on his forehead: *Don't get caught with your hand in the cookie jar, son.* Detmer Foods prided itself on being a good Christian company where good Christian men earned an honest living. The fact that that "honest living" was earned on the backs of mostly undocumented workers was not in the Detmer marketing plan. Neither was an ugly affair that involved two plant managers and their wives.

Luke switched the six out for a five, ready to try the lock again.

"You make up your own rules," Mimi said. "You know that?"

"Jesus Christ." Luke let go of the lock and turned. "You really want to get into this right now? I've got an hour until I'm supposed to meet this guy at the plant."

"The plant?" Mimi stood in the doorway, slumped forward as her eyes scanned the room, never quite settling on anything.

"Yeah," Luke said. "I'm supposed to take the woman to the plant and make the trade. That's what the guy said. That's it."

Mimi steepled her fingers at her waist and shook her head. "I'd like to go, too. I want to hold him, our son, first thing."

"*Mimi . . .*" Luke saw the tears in her eyes but made no move for her. He did the same with Tuck sometimes, too. The boy would roll over and bump his head on something, start throwing a little hissy fit, and Luke wouldn't move. Just stand there until he went back to playing with his blocks or that blue train he always lugged around. It was a hard lesson, but necessary. There's not always someone there to catch you when you fall. Sometimes, there's nobody there at all. Luke's father had taught him that much.

"I can't stay here." The tear tracks had reached Mimi's lips. She didn't wipe them away. "I won't—" Her face went slack. Her eyes were still moving, though, zeroing in on the bike lock in his hands. "It's the sixth," she said. "Your son's birthday is April sixth."

Luke gave the lock a tug and felt it come loose. "*Fine*," he said, uncoiling the cable from the door. "You can come with me to the plant, but you've got to help."

"Help?" Mimi sniffed. "What can I do?"

The lock was caught on the door handle, tangled up bad enough Luke needed both hands. He slid the Springfield out from under his arm and extended it backward. "You can start by holding this."

14.

All Edwin could think about was Gabby, bound and gagged, locked in a cage somewhere, being held hostage because of his plan. She'd been right. It was stupid. So stupid. He wished for what they'd had already, a simple life full of pain and heartache, sure, but nothing like this. Even the plant was better than this.

In the time since he'd spoken to Luke Jackson, every second was a new kind of torture. The baby was still in the bedroom. He hadn't stopped crying. Who knew a child could scream for so long? Wretched thoughts arose in the spaces between each breath. Edwin hated himself for thinking such things. His plan might've been stupid, but it had also been innocent. He'd never intended to hurt the child, never meant to cause him any pain, but now? Now he couldn't get Gabby's cries out of his head and there was still time yet to go until the trade. Chito had left a few minutes before, saying, "The kid didn't do nothing to you, cousin. He's hungry. Just feed him." But Edwin hadn't gone back there. A scab had formed around his heart and he wanted someone else to feel it. When Luke

Jackson took his son into his arms again, Edwin wanted him to know there had been pain involved.

There was no escaping the time that remained until the meetup. Would the child scream for that long? Surely, he'd fall asleep at some point. Edwin searched the kitchen cabinets for cotton balls or wax. Something to plug his ears with. There were three pieces of Trident in the drawer where Gabby kept their receipts, everything a mess in there now. How long had it been since Edwin had turned their life upside down? He didn't know. With the alcohol gone from his blood, all that remained was a dry, fuzzy feeling in his mouth. No more thoughts of better days ahead. No more hope. Edwin didn't know what Gabriela would say when he saw her again. He did not know if she would stay or go.

Edwin stuck all three pieces of gum in his mouth and began to chew as the child continued to cry. The clock on the microwave blinked, another minute closer to the meetup, Gabriela out there somewhere, waiting for him.

It was wintergreen-flavored gum. Edwin was chewing so hard, so fast, he almost didn't hear it when the child cried out a final time. The silence that followed was so complete—the exact opposite of what had been before—Edwin couldn't help but notice. He didn't move, though. He didn't go to the bedroom and check to see if the boy had finally fallen asleep, or if something else had happened. Something worse. He just stood there, chewing the gum and enjoying the flavor, how crisp and cool it made his mouth feel.

Sometime later, Chito's footsteps shook the trailer and Edwin opened his eyes. He watched his cousin burst through the trailer door, saw his mouth moving, but Edwin could not hear his words. Not until he leaned forward and peeled the two pale wads from his ears. Holding both bean-shaped blobs in his palm, Edwin looked up and said, "What?"

"The hell is that in your hand?"

Edwin looked down, blinked. "Gum. Trident gum."

"Have you checked on him?"

"Who?"

"Fuck you, Edwin."

"I think he's asleep."

"You *think* he's asleep? What's wrong with you, man?"

Everything was wrong with Edwin. Nothing had gone the way it was supposed to. Once Edwin had Gabriela back, they'd be worse off than when they started. Jobless and on the run. Edwin knew tonight wouldn't be the end of this. Sooner or later, Luke Jackson would make him pay for what he'd done.

"I think I'm getting sick," Edwin said and meant it. His stomach was all gas and bubble knots. He couldn't remember the last time he'd eaten.

"Sick in the head." Chito jabbed two thick fingers into his bristly scalp. "You know where I went earlier, when I left?"

Edwin didn't know, didn't care.

"I went driving, man. Made it all the way over to Ma's house. I almost told her. Almost marched straight in there and told her what you'd done, what you were doing, sitting there while that kid kept screaming."

"Tía Maria?"

"Yeah, that's where I went, but I never got out the car.

She don't need this shit. She's getting old, man. This is your problem. You need to fix it."

Edwin raised the gum and stared sideways at the perfect molds of his ear canal. So strange, just like what Chito was telling him. *Chito* the bad boy, always looking to make a buck but now that they were in the thick of something real, he was ready to tuck tail and run. Edwin's mouth turned up at the corners, forming a small, impish grin.

"The fuck is wrong with you?" Chito cocked his giant head to the left. "Smiling like you gone full stupid or some shit. *Loco.* That's what you are, man. Fucking crazy."

Edwin didn't argue, but he did stop grinning. He couldn't feel his face.

"This guy has Gabby," Chito said. "*Gabby.* And you're just sitting there like it's nothing? Like you're not gonna do nothing about it?"

"Fuck the man, right?"

"What?"

"That's what you said, at the gas station, talking all that cholo shit about how you work for yourself, how I was greasing rich white men's hands. You said, 'Fuck the man.' Well, *that's* what I'm doing. That's what this is."

"Nah, cuz. Gabby ain't the man, and that ain't no man back there, either." Chito nodded toward the bedroom. "That's a kid."

It was a straight shot of the truth and it should've hit some sort of nerve, but Edwin still felt nothing.

"Here's what's gonna happen." Chito pressed his knuckles to his chin and cracked his neck, a gangster move. "I'm gonna get the baby. I'm gonna make sure he's all right, and then you're gonna give him back to his parents. I wash my hands of this."

Edwin said, "You're not coming with me?"

"I went back to the gas station and jumped your car. I'll jump it again, if I have to. After that, I'm done. It's one thing to make this Luke guy pay for what he's done to you and Gabby. It's another thing to be nasty to a kid for no reason," Chito said. "What if he's not breathing back there, man? Then what will you do?"

Edwin still couldn't believe the change his cousin had made over the last few hours, Chito morphing from a Mexican dope slinger with a gun in his glove box to some kind of softy, worrying about the child as if he were its mother.

"The kid is fine, cousin," Edwin said and smoothed his mustache down. "Go see for yourself."

Edwin listened as his cousin started for the bedroom, wondering if there was a chance the boy had starved or rolled off the bed. That sort of stuff never happened to a child like that, a white kid with two loving parents and a nursery the size of Edwin's trailer. No, he thought, the boy is fine. Edwin held tight to the idea that he was somehow helping the child, giving him a taste of another life, the hardscrabble existence Gabriela's child would've endured if it had ever made it this far.

The bedroom door whined as it opened but Edwin didn't notice. His mind was on the mound of diapers spread across the plywood table, remembering how he'd told Luke Jackson not to bring a gun. For years Edwin had followed Luke's rules, obeying every new mandate as if it were the law instead of just some lopsided system meant to keep the workers in the dark and fried chicken on every dinner table in America. They would be back at the plant soon, but there wouldn't be any line supervisors watching Edwin's every move. Not tonight. Tonight, there were no rules.

Silence hung thick through the trailer as Edwin lifted the diaper boxes and pushed his hands past packages of unopened baby wipes. The child's cries erupted from the bedroom just as Edwin's fingers found what they were searching for.

A moment later, Chito was back in the living room, holding the child up and out. "He was asleep, sound asleep. He's fine. Look."

"Maybe the crying helped him," Edwin said. "Like, he had to get it out, or something, you know?"

Chito scowled as he brought the child in to his chest. He was so busy bouncing the baby boy, bopping him on his button nose, he didn't notice Edwin slip the pistol out from under the mound of diapers and slide it into his waistband. There was no plan this time, but the gun would give him an advantage. For once in his life, Edwin would hold the power.

15.

The rifle had wicked, wasp curves and a bulky black scope bolted over the chamber. Mimi could feel the blue steel, cold against her inner thighs. She was in the back of Luke's truck. The rifle stirred the ocean inside her mind as she waited for her husband to bring their hostage out. Memories of Tuck arose. She could almost feel him in her lap again, heavier than the gun, but she couldn't see him. Not the way he looked now. Mimi tried to imagine what parts of Tuck had changed in the twenty-four hours since she'd seen him last. In six short months, new expressions had already been revealed in her son's face. His hair had grown longer. Some had fallen out.

Two shadows moved behind the entryway's expansive windows. Mimi realized she didn't even know the woman's name. She didn't want to know it. It wasn't until the front door opened and Luke stepped onto the porch that Mimi could see the duct tape across the woman's mouth, and another thick silver band wrapped tight around her wrists.

Shadows played over Luke's face as he opened the back door and pushed the woman into the seat beside Mimi.

The smell of the chicken plant filled the cab. The same stench Mimi scrubbed from her husband's clothes every day after work, except worse. Sharp enough it made Mimi turn away, pressing her face to the window's cool glass. She didn't want to see the woman. She didn't want to smell her or think about her life. She wanted her son in her arms again, and getting him back would take all her focus.

Mimi watched Luke through the window, coming around the front of the truck with the roll of tape in his hands. The driver-side door opened. The cab shook as he peered into the backseat and pointed at his wife. No, not at her, at the space between her legs. The rifle.

"Look alive, hon," Luke said and spun back to the wheel. "We're going to get our boy."

THE WHOLE DRIVE into town, Mr. Jackson's wife kept her face to the window. The rifle barrel was propped on her left leg, aimed in Gabby's general direction. The woman didn't even have her finger on the trigger. Something about her weakness made Gabby want to touch her, to feel her skin and see if it felt the same as hers. She wanted to look the woman in the eyes and tell her it was all happening. This was real.

The tape across Gabby's mouth itched. Mr. Jackson had muzzled her. The same way he kept his workers muzzled and masked at the plant so he'd never have to hear their voices. The woman beside her was the same way. She'd never listen to Gabby's story. She was a mother of a blue-eyed baby boy, the wife of a man with money and power. She had nothing in common with Gabriela.

The chicken plant felt different in the night, like some

monstrous river barge run aground. Lights flickered across the parking lot as Mr. Jackson pulled his Ford in through the front gates and started around toward the back lot, the place where the trucks reversed up to the bay doors to unload the broilers.

As they drove into the darkest corner, Gabby realized she was no different from the chickens. Not to Mr. Jackson. Not even to his wife. She was a means to an end. Something to be used up and thrown away. Edwin was different, though. On this night, Edwin was the most important thing in these people's lives. Gabby peered through the window, wondering how she would feel when she saw him again. What would she say?

Lights appeared from around the plant's front-facing wall, dull at first but getting brighter. Headlights. Two bright dots in all that darkness, revealing the plant's rusty bay doors as the Dodge Neon came to a stop halfway across the lot.

Edwin parked the car so the high beams shined straight into the truck's cab, as if he was trying to blind Mr. Jackson. Gabriela couldn't see anything, either. She didn't have to. Edwin was so close now she could feel him, the life they'd shared bonding them together in a way the Jacksons would never know.

LUKE DRUMMED HIS fingers over the steering wheel and waited for Edwin to switch off his damn high beams. The stretch of concrete between them spanned less than a hundred feet. A few car lengths. Nothing more. The parking lot stood empty and silent all the way around.

The music started a moment after the car's driver-side

door opened and a shadow spilled out. The car was far enough away Luke couldn't make out the tune. He cupped a hand over his eyes, shielding them against the light. Edwin was alone, just like he'd said, but where the hell was Tuck? And what was with that music?

"Let me see her," Edwin shouted, barely audible over the car stereo thumping along behind him. Luke remembered the way he'd sounded on the phone, and even before, all the different excuses the guy had doled out over the years.

Luke laughed because he couldn't think of what to say. It didn't matter. Edwin couldn't hear him, probably couldn't see him either, the way the headlights were clashing. "Cut the shit," Luke yelled and stepped out of the truck. "Give me my son."

"You're not the boss, Luke Jackson. Not tonight." Edwin kept moving forward, his hands still hidden behind his back, a silhouette in the headlight beams. "I'm the boss now, and you—"

A sharp cry cut Edwin short, loud enough to be heard over the song Luke hadn't been able to place but could recognize now, knowing in the same moment that the cry belonged to his son.

"He's alive and kicking," Edwin said and took another step forward. Close enough Luke could see his hand rising, his fingers curled around the handle of a pistol. "For the first time in your life, Luke Jackson," Edwin said, teeth glistening in the headlights, "you are going to listen to me."

MIMI COULDN'T QUIT staring at the gun in Edwin's hand, the one that was pointed straight at Luke. The way Luke wasn't moving, just standing there, staring at it, too.

Tuck's cries joined the chorus of the Johnny Cash song, forming a weeping rendition that made Mimi realize the rifle was still in her lap, her right index finger already around the trigger. She saw herself hoisting the gun and marching across the parking lot toward the Dodge, the same vehicle she'd seen parked outside the plant just yesterday, right back to where all of this had begun.

Mimi reached for the door handle. Fear was not a question anymore. Not in that moment. Only action. Tuck was right there. She would do whatever it took to get him back.

The woman's fingers were warm on Mimi's forearm, her soft touch bringing Mimi back into the truck's cab, back to reality. The woman didn't say anything. She just lifted her bound hands and pointed. What she was pointing at, Mimi didn't know. Didn't care. Not until she saw the dim lights at the far end of the lot, bright enough for Mimi to remove her finger from the trigger.

A car was pulling in behind Edwin, a sports car, some kind of foreign model, its headlights revealing the scene from a different angle. The car brought to mind the text message Mimi had deleted from Luke's phone earlier. The name "Bob Simpson" flashed through her brain until she heard the cries of her son.

Mimi looked up in time to see Edwin flee from the light. He ran on the balls of his feet, each step springy and light as if he were bouncing over a bed of hot coals, but there was no sound, no footfalls, not even any music anymore. There was only Tuck, screeching, each wail louder than the last, calling out to Mimi. She felt the rifle's safety click over, going from black to red, "safe" to "fire." The woman did not put her hand on Mimi this time. She did not make an attempt to stop her. It was too late anyway. Maybe the woman knew it. Maybe she knew more than Mimi had given her credit for. Mimi reengaged the rifle's safety as Tuck's cries were engulfed by the roar of the Dodge, tearing out of the lot.

The thought of what she'd almost just done—what she should've done?—spun webs through Mimi's mind as a single tear streaked her cheek. When Luke slammed the truck door, her hands turned to fists over the rifle's stock. Mimi stared past her husband to the sports car—an Audi she recognized now—that had come to a stop at the edge of the plant.

Luke swore as the car reversed, but Mimi didn't hear him. The ocean inside her mind had been replaced by a rushing river of rage, rising as Luke jerked the truck into drive and said, "What the hell just happened?"

16.

"*The ring of fire. The ring of fire . . .*"

Miles out of Springdale and the song was still playing. Edwin had it on repeat, trying to drown the cries of the child as he turned down a dirt road, unsure of where he was going or what he would do next. Tree limbs clawed at the Dodge, accusatory nubs pointing through the window to the child in Edwin's lap, mouth open, eyes closed, head flopping with every bend and curve. Edwin recognized the painful expression, but did not hear the sound coming out of the baby's mouth. It was the same at the plant. After enough hours on the line, you didn't feel the cold or your fingers cramping. After seven years, you felt nothing at all.

They were deep down a back road, lost in the hills, when the first raindrop splattered against the windshield. Silent lightning flashed through skinny trees, and then it began to pour. So hard the wipers couldn't keep up, smearing the water back and forth without clearing any of it away.

The back end of the Dodge fishtailed around a

dead-man's curve, almost sliding into the ditch before gaining traction again. Edwin's mouth moved in time with the Johnny Cash song—"*The taste of love is sweet when hearts like ours meet*"—the soundtrack to his life now, what was left of it.

Maybe this is the end, Edwin thought. The final scene before the credits roll. It would not surprise him. Not after those bright lights had pulled up behind him at the plant, some sort of fancy-looking car with a woman behind the wheel. Edwin could still see the mound of red hair outlining her pale face as he'd blown past her on his way out of the lot.

A devil, that's what she was. Some sort of demon sent to dismantle his life. Edwin was sick of it. Chito's pistol lay in the passenger seat. Every time the car sloshed around a curve, the gun scooted closer, butting up against Edwin's thigh. *No funny business. No guns.* Yes, he'd said all of that then brought Chito's pistol to the plant. He'd lied, to himself and Luke. He'd even lied to Gabriela. What difference did it make?

It mattered, Edwin told himself, squinting through the smeared windshield to a one-lane bridge up ahead, the creek beneath it so brown and swollen Edwin had to stop the car. His phone vibrated in the cup holder. Edwin turned the screen and saw exactly what he expected: Luke Jackson. What could either of them say now? Another meeting was pointless. The whole stupid thing, pointless.

Johnny Cash sang his final line and in the short run of silence that followed Edwin could finally hear the baby crying. "Please," Edwin said. "Stop that. Please, just stop." The kid didn't stop. Tiny fists punched the air. Stumpy legs kicked, hard enough that Edwin had to reach down and hold the boy's shoulders to keep him from rolling into the floor.

He held him like that, squeezing his shoulders, gently, so gently, as he waited for the song to start again. The car's cab had grown cold in the rain. Through the windshield, Edwin watched as the storm raged and the creek bulged. The water was well over the bridge now, rising like a river, higher with every drop, and the baby was still crying.

Edwin leaned forward, looking at the child upside down as he said, "What is it? What do you want?" The way he was sitting, the invertedness of it all, made it feel like he'd asked the question to himself. Maybe he had. What did Edwin want, really? What had he wanted all along?

WATCHING LUKE YANK the woman out of the truck by her hair, then use both hands to shove her into the closet again, made the river inside Mimi swell.

She didn't know why it stirred her in such a way. Did she want this woman to feel her pain? Or was Luke's violence making Mimi hate him even more? She wasn't sure. She'd spent the whole ride home in uncertainty, hating herself for how she'd looked away from the cries of her child right when he'd needed her most. Like maybe if Mimi had never taken her eyes off Edwin's vehicle—if she'd just kept staring and listening to Tuck's cries mingling with that goddamn country song—Nina Ferguson's Audi would've never come around the front of the plant.

Then what?

The guy had a gun, Mimi told herself and winced as the

closet door slammed shut, echoing through the house. There was no way for Mimi to know what Edwin had planned to do with the gun, but standing in her kitchen, the hunting rifle propped against the island, Mimi felt like the whole thing was her fault. Like she just kept repeating the same mistake, over and over again. Why had she rushed past the ratty Dodge in front of the plant yesterday morning? Why had she deleted that message from "Bob Simpson"?

It was always easier not to know, to ignore the problems, the pain. Was that why she'd passed out in the kitchen? Was it some sort of survival mechanism, her body taking the easy way out? Or was it something else?

Mimi watched Luke coming down the hallway, headed toward the kitchen, and decided the time for easy was over.

"Call him," she said and folded her arms as rain began pankling down on the roof.

Luke said, "I've already called him," stepping past her without so much as a pause. "I kept calling him, probably once a minute the whole drive home. You didn't see me?"

Mimi wasn't sure. She'd been lost for so long, drowning under the weight of her worries and fears.

"Call him again," Mimi said. "I want to watch you do it."

Luke pressed his phone to one ear and left it there for three, maybe four rings. "See? He won't answer."

"Fine." Mimi slapped the granite countertops then dug into her sweatpants pocket. Phone in hand, she said, "I'm calling the police."

"And what about the woman I just locked in our guest room?"

Mimi had forgotten about her. She kept forgetting about

her. She still didn't even know her name. Everything that happened at the plant—the headlights, the Johnny Cash song, the gun, and finally Ferg's fucking Audi—none of it had seemed to bother the woman. The few times Mimi had glanced over at her, the look in her eyes was always the same, a blank, expressionless gaze over the duct tape stretched tight across her mouth. Like she'd seen it all before. Or if she hadn't seen this particular scene, she'd witnessed something similar. Something worse.

Mimi said, "What are we going to do then?" her tone flat, as if she were reading lines off a card.

"I'm going after him." Luke started across the kitchen, moving fast.

Mimi let him make it to the front door before she said, "Hey, Luke?" and listened as his boots clicked to a stop on the tile. "Who the fuck is Bob Simpson?"

He just stood there.

"Pull up his contact info," she said. "Let me see the number. What if he was there? *He* . . ." Mimi let that final note ring out as she studied her husband, the blue eyes that reminded her so much of her son, the eyes that had lied to her. "What's wrong? Afraid I'll recognize the number?"

Luke didn't give her his phone. He marched back across the kitchen and took her phone. Ripped it right from her hands.

"You think you've got it tough?" A vein in Luke's forehead pulsed. "You've got it *made*, Mimi. You don't have a damn thing to worry about, but that's all you do."

Mimi laughed. She didn't recognize the sound that came up from her throat.

"Oh, you think that's funny?" Luke said, holding her

phone up in both hands. "I'm sick of trying to keep you in check, keep you from going off the deep end and taking our son with you."

"Our son is gone, Lucas. Gone. And you—"

Broken glass blew out across the granite as Luke slammed Mimi's phone down. He brought the phone down again, catching the countertop's edge. Then again, each blow more vicious than the last. When he was finally done, the phone was bent in half and Luke's hand was bleeding.

What he said next scared Mimi more than the destruction, how calm his voice sounded after such violence. He said, "Everything will be fine," then walked out of the kitchen and into their bedroom. Tiny bits of glass glittered up from the tile, stray shards caught in the grout. He was only gone a moment. Long enough to turn the bathroom sink on, then off, then his footsteps started up again. Luke paused his march through the kitchen just long enough to snatch the rifle from the island and Mimi's 4Runner keys from the counter. He didn't look at her when he repeated that same, senseless line from before: "Everything will be fine, Mimi."

"*Fine?*" she said, but Luke didn't hear her. He was already gone, walking across the driveway. Mimi waited to hear the truck door slam, or the low growl of the engine starting, but those four empty words just kept cycling through her mind, an impossible refrain:

Everything will be fine. Everything will be . . .

Mimi staggered into her room and collapsed onto the bed. It felt like before, like she was losing it, but different. This time the darkness didn't come on as fast. This time she was able to hold it down by gritting her teeth and fanning both hands out beside her. The mattress was softer than the kitchen floor. Mimi squeezed her eyes shut and whispered, "Everything will be fine," even though things were worse. Without her phone or her vehicle, she was stranded, way out in the middle of nowhere, a prisoner in her own house.

When her eyes blinked open again, she saw a late-model iPhone on the dresser, the cracks across the screen, the dents in the aluminum casing.

Mimi walked to the dresser. She held the phone cupped in both hands, a sacred, holy thing, and then she dialed 911. She stared down at the numbers, afraid to complete the call, worried maybe Luke had been right. This was why he'd broken her phone, wasn't it? To keep her from making another mistake.

As Mimi watched each number disappear from the screen, she realized who the phone belonged to. The screen went dark and Mimi saw her reflection in the glass, her own face mixed with the woman in the closet, calling to her.

Pictures of Tuck lined the hallway, snapshots spanning all six months of his brief existence. The photograph outside the guest room door was from the hospital, a few breaths after Tuck had been born, lying face down on Mimi's chest, still covered in the gunk of new life.

Mimi reached out for the bike lock wrapped around the closet door, but a small sound from within stopped her. A rustling. Mimi let her mind go to the woman, so close to her now she could hear her breathing. She remembered the feral look in the woman's eyes. What would she say when the tape peeled free of her mouth? What would her voice sound like?

Mimi told herself it didn't matter, not yet, and began tapping out a message on the woman's phone, a message for Edwin.

THE CHILD WASN'T crying anymore. He was asleep in Edwin's arms, content because Edwin had finally listened to what the boy was trying to tell him. He was hungry, starving after going so long without milk.

The bottle was in the passenger seat, right there the whole time, driving the kid crazy. It had a purple screw-on lid. The formula was this chalky white stuff Edwin had poured into tap water before they left the trailer. It was cold, but the boy didn't mind. His nose whistled as he drank. That's how hard he was sucking. The sound took Edwin away, back to the sofa in his trailer where he'd felt the child's power before things had gone to shit. The power was real, strong enough to condense Edwin's whole world down to the sound of the breath and the bottle, the boy's warm back on Edwin's chest, the smell of his hair, salty and sweet. The sound changed when the bottle ran dry, a sound like a snorkel makes, but the boy didn't care about that, either. He was asleep already, fingers curled under Edwin's chin, head turned sideways over his heart.

It was then that Edwin answered the question for himself. What did he want? What had he always wanted? He'd had it all along.

Edwin's cell phone vibrated in the cup holder. He didn't notice, too busy holding the child, trying to keep him warm. The boy was the key, something that would unlock Edwin's true potential. The phone vibrated again. This time he saw the faint blue flash. Edwin stared down at the phone and rocked the boy, singing a song his mother had sung to him that he had not remembered until that moment, a lullaby.

When the phone vibrated a third time, Edwin reached for it, carefully, trying not to wake the boy. The words on the cell phone screen did not make sense. Edwin brought the device closer to his face.

The message was from Gabriela, but that couldn't be true. Even if Gabby had sent that text, Luke Jackson had told her what to type. The phone felt stony and dangerous against his fingers. The urge to throw it out the window surged through him. Instead, he placed the device in the cup holder as it vibrated once more. Edwin backed the Neon away from the creek. The water rose around him as he spoke to the silent child in his arms, words that made no sense, not even to himself.

"When you wake you will be made new," Edwin said. "You will be Gabby's child. Do you understand?"

The child coughed in reply, then coughed again, a dry rasp that would grow drier, weaker as the night wore on. Edwin patted the top of the boy's head, wondering, briefly, if all babies made such sounds. A dim light flickered up from the cup holder and the question was gone. The Dodge's back tires spun, throwing mud and gravel before they finally caught and lurched forward. Edwin steered the vehicle away from the bridge, following the road that had brought them there, the road that would take them home.

17.

A blue line on Luke's phone lit the way, telling him where to go and how long it would take him to get there. The clock on the truck's dash read a quarter past two.

The Springfield in the passenger seat reminded Luke of the hunting trips he'd taken with his father, the few times he'd had the man all to himself. Luke's daddy liked to hunt squirrels. None of the other boys' fathers hunted squirrels, not in south Arkansas, a place where the racks of twelve-point bucks and mallard ducks hung from living-room walls, trophies to be admired, stories to be told. There were no such prizes in Luke's childhood home. He had found a picture of his father in his mother's closet once. The photograph displayed two boys, barely old enough to drive, with blood streaked sideways under their eyes. War paint. Something like those racks and mounts hanging from the walls in other homes.

The wind was so strong Luke had to keep both hands on the wheel. He couldn't see the road for the storm, the one raging against the windshield and the one brewing inside his mind, blowing up memories of his father. The picture he'd found that day and the story his mother had told him about the blood.

One of the boys in the picture was Jim Jackson, back when he was still Jimmy, back before he'd ever met Lynn Crenshaw or had a son named Luke. A dead deer lay behind the boys, splayed out across the hood of a Volkswagen Beetle. The Beetle belonged to the other boy. Lynn couldn't remember his name, but she could remember the look in her husband's eyes before he was her husband, the boy who'd pumped that pitiful doe with so much buckshot there wasn't enough meat left to eat.

Just blood.

The boys had done what boys are supposed to do in Arkansas and other places where hunting is a rite of passage, a skill passed down from father to son; they'd smeared the red across their cheeks. They'd tasted it. Jimmy became Jim that day, a quiet young man who would turn into a silent husband and a distant father. Lynn told her son the story, all of it, from the Beetle to the blood, then put the picture in the folder and placed it back on the shelf.

The truck eased off the highway and drifted past the plant. Luke glanced through the side window, remembering Ferg's headlights in the dark. Edwin had had a gun. A pistol. Who knew what he would've done? Ferg had saved Tuck with those headlights. Saved all of them, really. And if that meant Mimi knew he'd been sneaking around, so be it. Tuck was still alive because of the decisions Luke had made. Right or wrong. His son was still alive. Mimi would never understand it that way. Luke knew this and could almost sympathize with his father's distant but calculating ways. The same way he liked to hunt squirrels. "Don't let the bushy tails fool you, son," Luke remembered his father saying. "They're still rats."

A voice came out of Luke's cell phone: "*Turn left at Sycamore Drive. Your destination is on the right.*" He clicked the phone off with his thumb, keeping his eyes on the sign up ahead. WINK-LAND TRAILER PARK. The words flickered red through the storm. Luke pulled off the asphalt and onto a dirt road. The even-numbered trailers were on the left, odd on the right. Luke parked the truck, took the rifle up in his hands, and stepped into the rain, eyes scanning the numbers for 123.

Dim lights burned behind blankets draped over trailer windows. The muddy street stood empty. Luke felt the rain as he took slow, careful steps and held the butt of the rifle cupped in the palm of both hands, the barrel sticking straight up past his right ear, the same way his daddy had taught him to walk in the woods.

Luke was back there again, the dense thicket of oak and pine behind his childhood home in Arkadelphia, trying to step exactly where his father stepped, doing his best not to make a sound. Jim Jackson would only take a couple strides at a time, stopping every few feet and cocking his ear to the trees. It was damn hard to see a squirrel. They could go flat against a trunk, blend in with the branches and disappear. But the sound their claws made on the tree bark was unmistakable.

Luke paused, scanning the trailer park for any sign of Edwin. There was only darkness and rain. Hunting squirrels was one of the only things Luke had ever done with his father, but he'd never gotten the hang of it. Too slow. Too boring for a boy his age. The sunlight creeping through the trees in the early morning dawn, the world waking up all around him—Luke never noticed. He hated the long pauses between each step. Hated the way his father insisted on using .22 caliber rifles instead of shotguns like other boys Luke's age, blowing the bushy-tailed bastards out of the air as they hopped from limb to limb.

With time, Luke finally began to understand what his father had fostered in him, a particular kind of endurance that most men lacked. Walking through the storm, past trailers numbered 101 and 103, Luke tried to summon the gangly pines of his youth, but the disheveled trailers and the crudely customized cars remained. Luke was in uncharted waters now, his father's footsteps no longer guiding him.

Lot 123 sat at the end of the muddy road. A sagging barbwire fence marked the far edge of the trailer park. A light glowed behind a window near the front door. Luke brought the Springfield down from his shoulder, catching it in both hands. There were no streetlights in the trailer park. No light at all that Luke could see.

With the night and the storm to hide him, Luke hitched the waist of his camouflage pants and squatted behind a trash can. He closed his left eye then pressed his right to the scope. With the crosshairs over the window of number 123, Luke settled in and waited for the perfect shot, just like his father had taught him.

MIMI STILL HAD the woman's cell phone in her hand. She stared down at the blank screen, waiting for a response.

She'd kept the first message simple, trying to be brief like she imagined the woman would be, and then she'd hit send. She sent two more messages before finally deciding to dial his number. Edwin didn't answer—of course he didn't—and now there she was, still leaned up against the closet, waiting for the man to call back.

Mimi's eyelids drooped. It was late, but she wouldn't sleep. Not until Edwin called back. *He won't do it. You know what you have to do.* Mimi placed the palm of her right hand on the closet door, wondering if it was the woman's voice she'd heard. She thought of that cat again, the one from the thought experiment. The woman was still in there. There was no way she could've escaped, but without seeing her, Mimi couldn't be sure.

With the four numbers lined up along the dial, Mimi jerked the bike lock, thinking of what she would say to the woman. She thought about it for as long as it took her hand to turn the knob, and then the closet door was open.

The woman sat against the back wall with her legs straight out and her taped-together hands pressed down in her lap. Mimi squatted as she entered, keeping her distance before reaching for the silver strip of tape across the woman's mouth. She ripped the tape free, leaving the woman's lips a pouty shade of pale pink, distorted like she'd been crying. There were no tears in her eyes. She didn't even bring her hands to her mouth, but her lips were moving.

"What?" Mimi said, creeping toward the woman, close enough the smell of the chicken plant was almost unbearable. "What did you say?"

"My name," the woman said, "is Gabriela."

Mimi could taste the gooey chicken meat, that's how

strong the stench was, but Gabriela's eyes were stronger. Mimi could see the strength that resided there for the first time, the two black holes exposing a pain Mimi would never know, not even this new, braver version that had been born in Luke's absence. Mimi started to back away. Her heels caught the carpet. She tripped and landed on her backside, eye level with the woman now.

Gabriela's expression did not change. She didn't look away, as if she were daring Mimi to say whatever it was she had come to say.

"A–Amelia," Mimi mumbled. "My name is Amelia."

The woman offered no response. In the silence, Mimi heard the storm again, raging outside the guest room windows. The sound of the water stirred something in Mimi, connecting her to a river she couldn't see, Luke's voice inside her mind like thunder now, compelling her to speak: "Everything will be fine."

"No," Gabriela said and snorted. "It's too late for fine."

The woman's tone surprised Mimi. The fact that she was talking at all surprised her even more. Mimi remembered the distance she'd seen in Gabriela's eyes at the plant, the way she'd never looked surprised, not the least bit scared, as her boyfriend waved that pistol around and the headlights cast his shadow across the lot.

"You have my phone." The woman nodded to the device in Mimi's hand. "You called Edwin? Did he answer?"

The strip of duct tape dangled from Mimi's thigh, the piece that had been stuck on Gabriela's mouth. Mimi reached for the tape, deciding she liked the woman better when she was silent. The woman's eyes went to it without emotion, like she knew the tape would come again. With the silver strip inches from her mouth, Gabriela said, "No, he didn't. Edwin knew it wasn't me."

"I texted him first," Mimi said, still holding the tape out. "I told him I was you. I told him you would call."

Gabriela laughed. It didn't sound like the laugh of any woman Mimi had ever known. "When your husband called him earlier?" Gabriela said. "When we were driving back from the plant? He used my phone."

"So?"

"So, Edwin doesn't trust the phone. No matter what he sees come across the screen, he won't trust it."

Mimi shook her head. "There has to be some message you could send to let him know it's really you."

Gabriela opened her mouth like she was going to laugh again but lifted her arms instead, pointing back at Mimi with both hands, the same way she'd pointed at Nina Ferguson's Audi when it had pulled into the plant. "I'm sorry, Mrs. Jackson," Gabriela said, "but my hands are tied."

Mimi thought of Luke driving through the rain with his rifle. He was just as lost as Tuck. She stood and looked down on the woman, trying to rekindle her fire from before, but it was gone too. Mimi stuck the tape on Gabby's forehead and stepped out of the closet, pulling the door shut behind her. Gabby shouted, but Mimi didn't hear her. Didn't want to. She was already in the kitchen, digging through the drawer beside the sink.

THE TAPE ON Gabriela's forehead itched. She tried to focus all of her energy on it, knowing better than to hide from her problem. Hiding would not make it go away.

She knew Mrs. Jackson wanted something, and that was

the problem. The only reason *Amelia* had opened the closet door, the only reason she'd ever even looked at Gabby, was because she needed some sort of favor now. That's why Gabby had laughed in the woman's face, and just like the itch on her forehead, Amelia went away.

It was a waiting game, a contest Gabby knew she could win. As a child, Gabby had loved hide-and-seek. The trailer was so small, her mother allowed her and her sisters free rein of the entire park, just so long as they didn't cross the fence. Being inside the Jacksons' mansion, Gabby knew Mimi would never allow her son such freedom. Never. The boy would be lucky to ride a bike without training wheels by the time he turned thirteen. Gabby's mother had been too tired for such caution, too busy. As soon as Isabela Menchaca got home from the plant, she got supper going. Gabby's father would take the chicken livers he'd pocketed from the line down to Lake Springdale and string them through giant barbed hooks. Gabby went with him sometimes. She remembered the fresh blood on his knuckles covering the dried blood from the plant. When Gabby thought of him, she thought of his hands, his skin stained forever red. If the catfish were biting, he wouldn't come home for supper. Isabela didn't mind as long as he brought home a stringer full of channel cats. Free food was hard to beat. Just like Gabby in hide-and-seek. She'd never feared the darkness, not even as a girl. She'd welcomed it. The storm of her young life was finally stilled while her mother cooked and her father fished and her sisters scoured the trailer park. Most kids want to be found. Wait long enough, and they'll start chirping, giving themselves away. Not Gabby. Not even when her mother started calling for her and the smell of tamales wafted over the park. Still, Gabby waited. All children crave power; a child with nothing craves it even more. Hide-and-seek was a game Gabby could win, a rare moment where she was in charge.

Stuck inside the guest room closet, Gabby knew she wasn't in charge, but she was alone, her worries at bay for the moment. When the door finally opened again, Gabby saw that what she was up against now was so much more than just some childhood game. The worst kind of problem stood before her, one that she hadn't seen coming: Amelia with a butcher's knife in her left hand, Gabby's phone in her right, ducking down as she pushed her way into the closet.

Gabby kicked and connected good with the woman's thigh, hitting Amelia hard enough to make her gasp, but she did not stop. Amelia just kept coming. No matter how hard Gabby struggled, she was no match for this woman and her knife, not with her wrists bound together. Gabby closed her eyes again and let her body go slack. She'd been fighting all her life and was tired of it. Let there be peace in the end, Gabby thought, expecting the blade to be hot as it punctured her skin. Instead, there was only the sound of tape slicing, and then a voice, the woman, crouching over her, breathing heavy in Gabby's ear as she said, "It's Mimi. Just Mimi."

Gabby blinked her eyes open. "What?"

"My name. I don't know why I said Amelia earlier. My mother calls me that."

Gabby patted her chest, the place where she thought the knife would go in. She looked up. "What are you doing?"

The knife slipped from Mimi's fingers as she leaned forward and wrapped both arms around Gabby, hugging her without restraint, like a child.

Mimi whispered, "I don't know," her voice so soft that Gabby believed her.

AN HOUR PASSED and nothing stirred inside the trailer. No one came in or out. No movement behind the windows. Luke's shoulder ached. His hands were cold, his feet soaked, his whole body trembling as he stared down the rifle barrel and kept a slight pressure on the trigger. Luke wondered if he'd spent too many days sitting in his cushy leather office chair, going soft while the workers beneath him were hardened by the factory line. The frigid temperature, the constant stream of work—that's why Edwin had gotten the best of him so far. Edwin *had* to be cautious. Had to be careful, always glancing over his shoulder for the line supervisor, always thinking ahead. Just like those bushy-tailed tree rats Luke had grown up hunting.

The trash can rattled as Luke stood from behind it. He'd waited long enough.

There came a point, even with squirrels, where you had to go after them. Eventually, they'd hole up inside the trunk of some hollowed-out tree, and Luke would smile, watching as his father finally brought the rifle to his shoulder. He'd start at the bottom of the tree, working his way up the trunk, one shot at a time. It never took long before the squirrels got spooked and came darting out, claws scratching at tree limbs as they ran for their lives.

Luke knew better than to pump Edwin's trailer full of

.30-06 high-velocity rounds, but he was done waiting. It was time to flush the bastard out.

Mud squished beneath Luke's boot heels. A bug zapper hummed above the trailer's front door. The rain had grown cold as the night wore on. Luke's joints were stiff from the waiting but loosening with every step.

He held the Springfield down at his waist with the barrel pointed toward the trailer, trying to decide whether he should knock or kick the door open. The sound of his father's rifle echoed across his mind, plugging the hollow trees with holes until the squirrels came running. Luke's boot connected flush beside the door's brass knob. The frame splintered then gave way from the force.

Luke kept the gun at his waist, scanning the premises before he stepped inside. A mix of diapers and wipes covered the piece of plywood held up by a set of Detmer crates. A *table?* Luke's index finger traced the curve of the cool brass trigger. A faded Mexican flag hung above the couch. He cocked his ear, just like his father had done, waiting to hear their claws, the creatures that lived in this place, the rats that had bedded down and made this hollowed-out aluminum can their home.

Luke took two steps forward and reached for the door, shutting it behind him without turning around. His eyes went to the mountain of baby diapers, half-hoping Edwin would pop out from the kitchen with that peashooter in his hands. Luke imagined the sound the Springfield would make inside the confined space and sat down on the couch, trying to picture Tuck in this place. Trying to imagine these people taking care of his son, but instead he saw the squirrels lying bloodied beneath the branches, their tiny chests heaving, their eyes so big and black, staring up as Jim Jackson took them by their bushy tails and smacked them against a tree, or sometimes a rock. When he was done, Luke's father would turn to his son and tell him it was the only way to stop the pain. Luke had grown to endure the silence and the cold, but he'd never understood that final, brutal part of the hunt.

Not until now.

18.

The morning sun caught the clouds and spun them like cotton candy. Edwin knocked on the screen door. The child lay limp in the crook of his left arm, silent like he'd been for so long. Around them the world was waking up, birds chirping as a new day's light crept over the neighborhood's still damp streets.

The idea came to Edwin in the night, sometime after the rain had passed and the boy finally stopped coughing. Edwin just kept driving, up and down the rolling hills, over bridges with more bloated creeks rushing below. The boy pawed at his thighs between the coughs and the cries, but Edwin did not stop. He would not stop until he found a place suitable for the child, so strong after their stop beside the creek, or had it been a river? Something bigger than Edwin had thought at the time. When the boy finally tuckered out, Edwin moved him to the backseat. Laid him out flat back there and wrapped him in a towel. Quiet and still because that's how Edwin wanted him to be, a good little boy, so far from his parents and the things they had let him get away with before.

The Dodge was parked on the street behind Edwin, the same place it had been for the last few hours, the first few hours of their new life together. Edwin had driven back to the trailer park first, but something stopped him before he pulled onto the dirt road, a feeling in his gut like his mother used to get. Bad juju. The trailer wasn't good enough anyway. Then it came to him, the only place he could think of that was suitable for the boy.

Edwin knocked again. He hadn't slept during the night, maybe not the night before that, either. He couldn't remember, but the world was still alive with possibility. The house looked like all the other houses surrounding it, red brick with a screen door and two windows in the front. A strong, simple structure, strong and simple like the woman who lived inside.

When the door opened, Edwin's eyes were on the low-rider with the spindly chrome rims parked in the front drive, memories from the backseat flooding his mind.

"*Edwin?*" Chito rasped. "What are you—"

Chito cut himself short as Edwin lifted the limp child. The boy's head rolled forward. His dimpled chin touched his clavicle. Edwin couldn't understand the look on his cousin's face but felt his own lips parting. There were no words for the road that had brought them there, the muddy creek, the rain that had washed the boy clean.

"Oh, shit," Chito said and puffed out his cheeks. "Shit. *Shit.*"

"He's fine." Edwin took a step forward. "Just sleepy."

"Look at his face, man. Look at his fucking face."

Edwin turned the boy around like a doll. The child's eyes were closed, the lids veined and translucent like bat wings in the daylight. He'd been so good, for so long. He hadn't cried out in forever. How long had it been since he'd moved? The last thing Edwin remembered was a different sort of sound, a dry, rasping cough. It reminded him of Gabby, how she'd mistaken the boy for a barking dog.

Edwin said, "He's fine," again, but the words felt wrong, the same bad juju that had turned him away from the trailer park, the same feeling that had led him here. Somewhere deep inside of Edwin, his heart beat faster than it ever had before. He brought the boy into his chest, holding him tight over the spot that was throbbing now, and stepped past his cousin on his way inside the house.

A crucifix hung above the table in the kitchen. Everywhere were pictures of people Edwin recognized. Aunts and uncles whose faces he had forgotten until now. Surrounded by his family, Edwin's heart stilled. A voice came to him from the kitchen, a ghostly whisper, like the pictures on the walls had come to life and spoken his name.

"Edwin?"

A woman appeared, standing beneath the crucifix, propping herself up on the kitchen table. Maria Ortega, Chito's mother, Edwin's aunt on his mother's side. She spoke to her nephew in Spanish. Edwin watched the lines around Maria's mouth go from slack to tight, like the creases in a drawstring bag. She wore her hair long for a woman her age. A red paisley headband held the bulk of it back, gray tendrils snaking down over heavy shoulders.

"You hear her, man?" Chito said.

Edwin heard her, but he could only make out half of what she'd said. The line back to Mexico, the language that connected him to his mother, had been broken when

Carmen died. Her whole life had been spent trying to shape Edwin into a real American boy. All the toilets she'd scrubbed, every room she cleaned, it was all done in hope that there were brighter days ahead, so focused on the future she did not realize the hotel was erasing their past.

"She wants to know what's wrong with the kid."

Edwin brought a hand to his mustache. "Nothing's wrong with him. He's sleeping."

Maria stepped forward from the kitchen table and clapped her hands twice. In the few short hours since the creek, Edwin had grown accustomed to the child's warmth. His fingers pressed in tight against the boy's soft back, but then he let go, passing him to Maria Ortega because she was the reason he'd come to this place.

The child melted into Maria's arms, this woman who had raised Chito and his five older brothers, all of them broad in the shoulders like their mother. Six boys—men who now weighed well over two hundred pounds—had been pushed out of this woman and into the world. Maria slid a thermometer under the boy's armpit, stared at the display, and frowned. She carried him across the kitchen then pulled a bottle of mezcal down from above the stove. That special place Edwin had riffled through as a boy. The refrigerator opened and Maria took a single brown egg from a carton in the back, shutting the door with her foot as she started for the kitchen table.

When Maria placed the boy on the table, his arms flopped out at his sides, mimicking the crucifix hanging on the wall. His eyes remained closed but his lips parted, revealing two rows of slick pink gums and one splinter of white, the first slice of an incisor. Edwin was so focused on the child, watching his belly now, trying to see if it was moving, he barely noticed the mezcal splatter across the table. Edwin turned away, toward his cousin. Chito narrowed his eyes as Maria unzipped the child's discolored onesie and sprinkled more of the mezcal on his chest.

"Dios te salve, María." The woman moved in circles around the table, hands dancing as she prayed. "Llena eres de gracia, el Señor es contigo . . ."

There were scenes similar to the one playing out in Maria's kitchen lodged somewhere in the recesses of Edwin's memory. Stories he'd been told of reincarnation and healing rituals. *Curanderas.* The term drifted across Edwin's mind, the past swimming through his blood, Chito's and Maria's blood, connecting them to the boy. Edwin fought the urge to take the child's hand. He wanted to feel his fingers and see if they were cold like his mother's had been when he'd found her on the floor of their room in the Econo Lodge.

Maria brought the egg up from a fold in her dress and popped it into her mouth. When the shell was good and slimy, she retrieved the egg and touched it to the boy's chubby thighs, his arms, tracing the tiny bump of his button nose. The boy didn't move. Not even one wrinkled finger trembled as Maria danced the egg back down his chin to his sternum and finally came to a stop on his navel.

The old woman whispered, "Bendita tú eres entre todas las mujeres," and lifted both hands, holding them out beside her face as if she were trying to start a fire. The egg stood straight up on the child's belly button. Edwin pressed both fists to his eyes. The egg was still there. He couldn't believe it. Was this what he'd come for? He didn't know. He was here now and that's all that mattered, staring at the chicken egg, watching it, waiting for it to move.

And then it happened, a tiny jump, like a bony beak had just pecked from somewhere inside. There it was again. Edwin blinked and turned to Chito, hoping to see the same revelation in his cousin's eyes.

"Bendito es el fruto de tu vientre, *Jesús*."

Edwin spun in time to see Maria snatch the egg from the child's belly and crack it on the edge of a green plastic bowl filled with water. Where had it come from? Had it been there all along? The yolk slid from the shell into the bowl. Hands on her knees, Maria studied the round yellow glob as the stories of Edwin's youth unraveled in his mind. He knew what Maria was going to say before she said it. He knew what she'd seen because he had seen it too: the yolk was perfect, glowing like the new day's sun beside the child.

Edwin saw it all now.

He could remember the tales his mother had told him in the hotel beds before he'd forgotten her ways and most of her language, before he'd walked the halls of Springdale High with his hair spiked, wanting the other boys on the soccer team to call him anything other than Edwin, before the trailer and the plant, before so much had been taken from him all that remained was a shell.

The old woman took the child up in her arms and finished the prayer. Edwin understood her now in a way that went beyond words, watching as the boy's bright blue eyes finally opened, blinking his new life into focus, born again.

WHEN LUKE AWOKE in the trailer park with the Springfield laid out across his lap, he felt like a child. The same boy who used to fall asleep as the mornings wore on and the squirrels stayed hidden in their nests, or wherever the hell it was Edwin had hunkered down. As Luke stood from the sofa, he wondered what he would've done if Edwin had walked through that door.

His phone vibrated, a short pulse indicating a text. Luke slid the phone out. He had sixteen missed calls and twenty unread messages, every single one of them from "Bob Simpson."

He'd forgotten Ferg all over again, and that wasn't good. When Ferg "got her Irish up," as she liked to say, she became a ticking time bomb. A short fuse. An uncontrollable variable.

Luke began typing out a message. He made it five words in before he felt the shabby sofa brushing against his camo pants. He powered his phone down, wary of the device's location capabilities. He didn't need to tie himself to Edwin's trailer. No evidence. He needed out of there, quick.

Luckily, Luke knew right where to go.

THE CHILD SAT up, teetered for a moment, then fell back into Edwin's waiting hands. Chito and Maria laughed as they slapped the kitchen table, wiped clean of the mess from earlier. Edwin was having a hard time remembering what had happened, or if it had actually happened at all. Could an egg really stand straight up on a child's belly? Had the boy been breathing when Edwin brought him in? He was fine now, and so was Edwin. They'd both fallen into the rhythm of the house, the order Maria had established all those years ago after she'd brought her boys into the world.

The way the child smiled, sitting upright on the kitchen table, really putting on a show for the Ortegas, it was like he could feel the rhythm, the security a family could provide. Edwin was smiling too, watching the child coo and paw at his face. What sort of security had he known before? What had his old life looked like? With the hours Luke Jackson kept at the plant, Edwin knew he hadn't been around the boy much. There wasn't enough time.

The child began to wobble again but this time stuck his left hand down, catching himself before he fell. They all cheered. Edwin even clapped a few times, proud of the boy, proud that he'd brought him into this house and let Maria bring him back to life.

Edwin watched the old woman reach across the kitchen table, sitting the child upright again, and thought, No, that wasn't right. Maria hadn't brought the child back to life. She'd given him *new* life. It was the same with Edwin, except it wasn't Maria who had started Edwin's heart beating again. It wasn't any egg-cleansing ritual, either. It was the boy.

Maria spoke in Spanish, a few quick words, and then Chito said, "Yeah, what's his name?"

The question surprised Edwin. Maria hadn't wanted to know anything about why he'd brought this child with blond hair and blue eyes into her home. She'd just gotten straight to work. The sun had barely been up outside but Maria Ortega hadn't minded. She'd already had her headband on and did what had to be done.

"His name?" Edwin said.

Maria raised her chin, keeping her piercing black eyes on the boy.

Edwin turned away, unable to lie straight to Tía Maria's face. Tired of lying. So tired. Edwin had not slept in so long. The child hadn't slept much, either. But look at him, Edwin thought. What would Gabriela say? For so much of his life, Edwin had scanned the horizon, always looking ahead to the next big thing. A get-rich scheme he'd found on the internet. A new pair of pointy boots he could wear to the bars. Edwin hefted the boy from the table, realizing the life he'd been searching for wasn't waiting out ahead of him. Not anymore.

"His name," Edwin said, thinking of the egg again as he eyed the crucifix on the wall, "is Jesus."

"Jesús?"

"No." Edwin shook his head at his cousin. "Not like that."

Maria made the sign of the cross over her chest and stood from the table. Edwin expected her to walk away yet she remained, staring back at him. She didn't speak, not one single word, and that was fine. Edwin understood her confusion. Miracles were hard to explain.

THE FERGUSONS LIVED in a gated community on the south side of town. Down closer to Fayetteville. It had taken Luke almost half an hour to get there through the Sunday morning traffic. The guard at the gate gave Luke shit about his camo, asking what the hell he was hunting this time of year. Luke said, "Squirrels," and the guard let him through.

Steve Ferguson got the Fayetteville job right around the same time Luke became plant manager at Springdale.

Looking at the man's house on Hickory Hollow Lane—the fountain out front, the three stories, not to mention the four different sports cars parked in the driveway—there was a serious discrepancy in dough. Steve came from money. His trust funds had trust funds.

Luke steered his Ford in between the Audi and a BMW. The memories from the night felt further away with every step he took. Whatever stress he was dealing with back at the plant, Mimi's passive-aggressive jabs, even this latest nightmare scenario—all Luke's worries were gone as soon as he walked into Ferg's house.

He didn't even knock, just turned the knob and stepped inside. The house was quiet. Most of the lights off. Ferg's daughter, Lucy, stayed with Nina's parents almost every weekend. He noticed a portrait above the mantel, Steve Ferguson done up in swirling acrylics, cheesing hard like always. Luke felt Steve's eyes on him as he started down the hall, creeping toward the master bath. He didn't call out. It felt like a scene from a dirty movie. The burglar finds the sexy redhead stepping out of the shower and . . .

The sound of a toilet flushing shattered Luke's fantasy.

He was holding his breath, staring into the master, when the bathroom door swung open. There was a moment, a fraction of a second, where Ferg looked surprised, and then it was gone.

"I'm not so sure about you anymore, Luke Jackson." The sash around the middle of Ferg's leopard-print kimono was tied in a loose knot revealing a pale run of skin rising up between her breasts. "Won't answer my calls or return my texts. And now look at you, coming in my house unannounced. What if Steve had been here?"

"Steve's on a golf trip," Luke said. "Won't be back till tomorrow."

"So you remember that, but you somehow forgot about our date last night? No, that's not right. You didn't forget. You had other plans." Ferg sauntered toward the sink and turned on the faucet. "What are you wearing?"

Luke felt the camo T-shirt's damp fabric stretched tight across his chest. "Long story."

Ferg gave him a once-over in the mirror. Luke was so busy trying to read her, he didn't notice her still-wet fingers take hold of the sash around her waist. The kimono fell open and Ferg said, "You can tell it to me after. Just get your ass over here."

19.

Mimi stood at her bedroom window watching a new day take shape, barely aware of the woman still asleep in the king-sized bed behind her. Light crept into the room, burning away the shadows that had been there before. Mimi cupped a mug of black coffee under her chin. The rising steam warmed her face as she thought back on the night.

The way Gabriela had fought when she'd first spotted the knife. The sound of the blade slicing through the tape. Gabriela's whole body had gone slack in Mimi's arms after she told her her real name, the name women like Gina Brashears and Nina Ferguson called her.

Mimi.

The two syllables had stirred the silence in the closet. Stirred something inside Gabriela as she turned to Mimi and said, "Gabby. Just Gabby."

There was nothing more to it than that. No great plan. Mimi wasn't thinking about what Gabby might do when she was finally freed, how the knife had been right there, close enough for the wild-eyed woman to grab it. Mimi was just tired of seeing her tied up like that.

Gabby hadn't gone for the knife, though. She didn't even speak for the longest time. Red welts rose on her wrists. Her chest heaved. They were both breathing steadily when Mimi finally said, "How about a shower?" And Gabby pulled herself upright as Mimi stood, following her out of the closet and down the hall to the bathroom. The shelves in the shower were lined with rubber toys and foam letters, a yellow bottle of baby shampoo on a tray in the corner. Mimi went to work clearing the mess away. Gabby's hands pushed in beside hers, touching the toys Tuck had touched, being careful with them, careful with Mimi.

As the shower hissed and steam rose from beneath the crack in the bathroom door, Mimi rummaged through her closet. The water was still running when Mimi knelt and placed the pajamas—a lavish silk set Luke purchased from Nordstrom for their three-year anniversary—outside the bathroom door. She'd backed away then, trying not to smell the soap that reminded her so much of Tuck, but it was too late. She saw him in the bathtub with those foam letters stacked on his head. Three different colors: red, yellow, green. The letters that spelled the name he hadn't called her yet, but would, one day. It was a game she liked to play. See how many words she could spell out on his head as he lounged in the blue bath seat that perfectly matched his eyes.

Mimi went back to the living room and waited, wondering if her son even realized his mother was gone. Did he miss her yet? If she never saw him again, would he remember her at all? She was working hard at an answer when the bathroom door opened and a hand slipped through the crack. A few moments later, Gabby emerged, hair slicked straight back over her head, filling out the pajamas in ways Mimi never had, not even when she was pregnant. Mimi imagined the last of the chicken plant spiraling down the drain as Gabby followed her all the way to the king-sized bed where she had slept beside Luke ever since he decided to build their forever home. Mimi held the sheets back and watched Gabby crawl in. By the time Mimi made it to the door and reached for the light switch, Gabby's snores filled the room, the soft purr of a cat in a box, proving it's still there.

As the night passed, Mimi paced the house, never once closing her eyes. Of all the horrible things she'd ever dreamed up, this was the worst, but there she was, still putting one foot in front of the other. The fact that she wasn't sucking her thumb on the kitchen floor surprised her. The bad times she'd feared had finally descended on her life, but somehow the knowing made it easier. The stakes were clear.

Looking down at the woman in her bed now, Mimi still didn't know why she'd done all she'd done. It just felt right, like something, after she'd done nothing for so long.

Gabby's eyes blinked open, lost for a moment in the strange bed, the strange house. Then she looked up at Mimi with the same fire she'd carried through the night. Maybe that's what Mimi wanted. Maybe that's why she'd done what she'd done. She needed the woman's fire.

Mimi extended the coffee mug, telling herself she'd done the right thing by letting Gabby out. She'd made the right choice, and good choices were like bad choices—they led to more of the same.

Gabby sat straight up in the bed without stretching or yawning. As she reached for the mug, Mimi noticed something she'd missed in the night.

"Your hands . . ."

Her knuckles, actually. They were thicker than Luke's, gnarled like the pine knots in the trees surrounding the house.

"Ah," Gabby said and took the coffee. "A gift from your husband."

"He did that to you?"

Gabby laced her fingers around the mug. "In a way, yes. They've been like this since my second year at Detmer."

Mimi tried to imagine the hours the woman had spent inside the plant, but couldn't. She wished she hadn't brought it up, hadn't pointed out her disfiguration. "How'd you sleep?"

"Like a child."

Mimi could still smell the baby shampoo on Gabby's hair. "Why would you say that?"

Gabby slid from the bed and shuffled to the window. The stray hairs around her head caught the light and sparkled like a crown. "You think I'm stupid?" Gabby lifted the coffee mug then tugged at the hem of the silk pajamas. "I know you gave me these things for a reason. You didn't even *see* me before last night. What do you want, Mimi Jackson?"

There it was. The only question that mattered. Mimi had spent the night searching for an answer. Maybe she really was just tired of being stuck in the house, alone.

Or maybe it was as simple as wanting to make a tangible move that didn't involve her husband. Yes. That was it. She didn't trust Luke anymore, and if she didn't trust him, then what other choice did she have?

"I want my son back."

Gabby's laugh swirled the steam above her coffee. "And you want me to help you?"

Mimi nodded. That was what she wanted—what she needed more than anything—help.

"But how?" Gabby said. "How do you think I can help?"

"Tell me about him." Mimi took a pillow from the bed and squeezed it to her chest. "Tell me about Tuck. When you saw him, how was he?"

"Fine. No locks. No tape. Nothing like what was done to me."

"Gabby. I'm sor—"

"You're desperate. That's all. And I understand. I would be too, but I still don't see how I can help you."

Mimi pulled the battered iPhone up from her pocket and placed it carefully on top of the pillow. "You could call him, couldn't you?"

"Edwin? Of course," Gabby said, "but what would be in it for me?"

Mimi kept her head down, hiding her eyes. A muscle in her leg pulsed. "I'll make sure nothing happens to you or Edwin. No charges. Nothing. If you can convince him to bring my son here, bring him now, today, then we can all just walk away like nothing ever happened." Mimi waited, expecting the woman to laugh again.

"What about your husband? How can you be sure he won't go to the police when all of this is over?"

"Let me worry about Luke."

"If we're making a deal," Gabby said, "I need more than that."

"Luke's not going to call the police. Not even when all of this is over. He's about to get promoted."

"He won't be the plant manager?"

"They called Friday night. The same night . . ." Mimi's voice faded. She took a breath. "The bigwigs at Detmer called and said Luke was about to be the next Executive Officer of Poultry. They just had to wait on the board to make it official. That's why he doesn't want trouble. Luke doesn't want his name in the papers, especially not now."

"And this is why he took me?" Gabby said. "Instead of just getting the money and bringing it to the plant like Edwin told him to do?"

Headlights flashed through Mimi's mind, the memory of Nina Ferguson in her fancy little sports car, fucking everything up.

"That's part of it," Mimi said. "The truth is, we don't have the fifty grand."

"Your husband tried telling me the same thing, but I don't believe it." Gabby motioned through the window to the seven chicken houses, then waved an open palm back across the half-a-million-dollar home.

"Luke handles all our money. I don't even have access to our checking account." Mimi paused, realizing she'd never told another woman that before, then thinking, *Why not?* "Besides, all of this has happened over the weekend. The banks are closed. Whether Luke has it or not, it would've been hard for him to come up with that much money that fast."

"Luke needed more time. That's what you're saying? He needs time to get the money."

"The money isn't part of the deal." Mimi picked the cell phone up and tossed the pillow back against the headrest. "The deal is you get to go home, and I get my son back."

"That's the deal, huh?"

"You and Edwin get to start over like nothing happened. I can promise you that much. Luke wants all this to go away just as bad as we do."

"What if I can't get Edwin to answer my call?"

"Text him first."

"What would I say?"

"Something so he knows it's you." Mimi extended the phone, holding it out for Gabriela, and she took it. Gabby was still staring into the darkened screen when the sound of a horn honking shattered the silence they'd shared. Followed by another quick blast.

"Is it him?" Gabby said. "Your husband?"

Mimi rushed to the window and pried open the blinds. What she saw in the driveway was worse than she'd feared. The fact that she recognized all four of the vehicles did little to lessen the shock. The blinds popped together again as Mimi spun back toward the room.

"What?" Gabby said. "What is it?"

"You stay here. Hide in the bathroom, the shower. I don't care. Just don't come out."

Mimi was gone before Gabby could respond, patting her pockets for her phone, wanting to check the doorbell camera even though she already knew who awaited her on the front step. Then she remembered how Luke had destroyed her phone. Which, if Mimi had to guess, was exactly why Gina Brashears and the rest of the girls had come to visit. Gina hadn't heard from her. She was probably worried sick, and had come to check on Mimi like a good friend.

But why'd she bring Trish, Whitney, and Lilly?

That's what Mimi was thinking when she opened the door and felt her fake smile falter at the sight of the box in Gina Brashear's arms, a cardboard box the size of a mini-fridge. The rest of the women carried smaller containers, grinning from ear to ear as they marched straight for Mimi's front door.

20.

Gabby was sitting on the toilet in the Jacksons' master bath. She'd snuck in there as soon as Mimi rushed out. The bathroom was like the closet had been, too big to be real. Too fancy. The walk-in shower was as large as the scalding bath at the plant and had two heads mounted on the tiled wall, with another, wider one hanging down from the ceiling. Despite the chilly house, the toilet seat felt warm through the silk pajama bottoms.

Gabby laced her fingers around her phone. It wasn't the deal Mimi Jackson had offered her, that's not why she'd texted Edwin. It was the child, the one she'd held herself, small like she'd been once, like Edwin still was in many ways. The message she'd sent him seemed stupid now: *My heart is in the backseat of Chito's Chevelle.* She still hadn't called him. She was going to, but then she'd heard the voices coming from down the hall.

Whoever had come to the Jacksons' house had brought friends. The thought was enough to make Gabby stand. She went straight to the master window, the same blinds Mimi had peered through minutes before. She leaned forward, ready to finally see what was going on out there, when the phone began vibrating in her hand. The picture of Edwin at the plant lit up the screen.

"Gabriela?" he said. "Is it you?"

Gabby pulled the phone back from her ear and stared down at it, listening to the ragged sound of Edwin's breath. "Yes," she whispered. "It's me."

"I knew it. The Chevelle," Edwin said. "But listen, you won't believe it. You won't believe what . . ."

"Where are you?"

"It's a miracle."

Gabby slunk back from the window but the Jacksons' house had disappeared, replaced now by Edwin. All the times she'd washed his clothes, the long summer nights where they'd lain beside each other in their double bed, sweating, then shivering when winter came. Their life together a constant juggling between hot and cold, nothing like that warm toilet seat in Mimi's master bath.

"Edwin, please," Gabby said. "Answer me."

"That's what I'm trying to do, but this kid. I've been caring for him so long."

"Two days?"

"A lifetime."

"You mean it's been hard?"

"Hard?" Edwin said and paused. Gabby wasn't sure, but she thought she could hear other voices beyond his, distorted through the phone. "No. Not hard."

Gabby waited, and even the waiting felt strange. She was not used to waiting on Edwin for anything. This impulsive man she'd given her life to. Always bouncing from one idea to the next, finding articles on the internet and bringing them to Gabriela, ready to upend their whole world for something he knew nothing about.

"I've been talking to the woman," Gabby said. "Mr. Jackson's wife?"

Edwin grunted, like that meant nothing to him.

"She let me out. She cut the tape from my wrists." Gabby waited, giving Edwin a chance to respond, to say something. When he didn't, she said, "She's ready for all this to be over. Mimi said—"

"*Mimi?*"

"That's her name. Mr. Jackson's wife, her name is Mimi."

A sound came through the phone, but it didn't sound like Edwin. Darker, somehow. Deeper. "This Mimi," he said, "what else did she tell you?"

"She said they won't press charges. All you have to do is come here and make the trade. Me for the baby. That's it."

"And when does she want me to come there and make this trade?"

What did it matter when? This was a child they were talking about, a baby boy who could barely hold his own head up, much less crawl. Miracle? It was a *miracle* that they'd even been given a way out, a second chance. It had been a mistake to stay in Arkansas. Gabby had known that for years now. She should've gone back with her family to Celaya. Pride had kept her from making that call. Her mother still believed her daughter was living the American Dream. There was nothing like pride left in Gabby. All she wanted now was to be done with it. All of it.

"Gabriela?"

Edwin's voice came through clear, no longer slurring

Gabby's name like he had the last time she'd seen him, but he still scared her. Maybe more now than before. Sunlight through the blinds drew her back to the window. Edwin said her name again, but Gabby didn't respond. She was staring now at the four vehicles parked in the Jacksons' front drive.

"*Gabriela?* Speak to me. When do you want me to come there?"

A couple of the women were still on the porch, hugging Mimi as they filed past her into the house. Gabby leaned back and said into the phone, "She didn't say when. She had to step out."

"She left you?" Edwin said. "And gave you back your phone?"

The realization that she could run—that she should've *already* run—hit Gabby just as the blinds snapped shut. Why hadn't she run?

"She trusts me," Gabby said, answering her own question.

"She's using you."

"Then come for me now." The words left Gabby's mouth before she had time to think about what she'd said, before she remembered the four cars and the women still milling around in the driveway. "It's just women here," Gabby said, talking faster, coming up with the plan as she went along. "I can meet you in the first chicken house on the left. The one closest to the highway. You could—"

"*Tonight.*" Edwin's voice was cold, all those years in the plant adding up to this. "I'll come tonight."

"Why won't you come now? Mr. Jackson could be back tonight."

"Luke said he needed time to get the money, so I will give him time. They still owe us."

Of course, it was about the money. Everything was about money. That's why Gabby's parents had come to America, why they'd left her in that trailer, alone until Edwin moved in and stole the cash she'd given him to pay the rent. Money was like air. Those who had plenty didn't even know it was there, while those who had none struggled for every breath.

"This kid," Edwin said. "He's so . . . What's the word?"

Gabby said, "Edwin, *listen*," but she knew better. Edwin had never listened before, and he would not start now. She shook her head, noticing the buzz coming through the phone, the voices surrounding Edwin growing louder for a moment, speaking words she recognized from another life, those voices mixing with the chorus of the women inside the house now, too. Gabby pressed the phone in tight against her ear, trying to imagine where Edwin had taken the child.

"It's like he knows my voice, knows I'm here for him."

Gabby grimaced as Edwin made noises for the baby, sounds she'd never heard him make. "Edwin, please," Gabby said. "Just tell me what time you will come."

He began singing the chorus to that same haunting country song he'd crooned for the boy in the trailer. Edwin had never been much of a singer. "Maybe I should just come for you now. *Yeah* . . ." He kept the melody of the song going, each word timing up with the downbeats. "Yes, if I came for you now, we could set straight off for Puerto Vallarta."

Gabby was still at the bathroom window, staring out at the fancy vehicles without seeing them. She let herself imagine Edwin's fantasy for a moment, let herself believe they could actually make it all the way down to those rocky beaches on the western coast of Mexico near where he'd been born. It would've been nice, a change of scenery, but Edwin's dream was a twisted one.

"What do you think about that?" he was still saying. "Me, you, and Jesus."

"*Jesus?*"

"The boy, Gabriela. That's his name now. Sounds strong, you know?"

It sounded stupid, but there was no point telling Edwin that. The man on the phone wasn't the same man Gabby had lived with since high school. He wasn't even the same man who'd stolen from her or abducted the child. *Jesus.* The world beyond the bathroom window wavered in the midmorning heat. Gabby sat back down on the toilet, still trying to make sense of the ridiculous name.

"If I come for you now," Edwin said, "we could all go together."

"*Wait.* You're talking about keeping the kid?" Gabby stood again, so fast she saw stars. "Like, really keeping him?"

"As our own. Yes. That's why I've —"

"How can you say such a thing?"

"It's what we always wanted. A child. That's what Luke took from us. Luke and your new friend, Mimi. They stole that part of our lives, and without the money, we may never get another chance. We—"

"Mimi has the money." Gabby watched her free hand rise in the bathroom mirror, two trembling fingers touching her lips, struggling to hold them in place, to keep the words down. Gabby spoke around them. "That's why I called you, Edwin. She has money of her own. She keeps cash in her dresser drawer, beneath her panties. I saw it." The best lies were specific, outrageous even, too wild to be anything but true. "She's afraid of Luke. She doesn't trust him. That's why she has her own nest egg."

"Scared of her own husband?"

"Yes." Gabby did not hesitate. The best lies came straight from the heart. "Terrified of what he might do."

"And she'll give us all this money in exchange for Jesus?"

Gabby watched her head shake in the mirror, two quick jerks. "The child for the money. That's the deal. That's it."

Edwin made a low whirring sound, as if he were considering the proposition, weighing it against his ridiculous getaway plan.

"Ten o'clock," Gabby said. "Bring the kid here at ten. Then we'll be done with this. All of it."

"And you're sure she has the money?"

The sound of women laughing barreled down the hallway, rich women who drove cars that cost more than everything Edwin and Gabby had ever owned.

"Yes," Gabby said. "She has money. She will give it to us, and you will give her the child. No tricks this time. No problems, right?"

"What about Luke?"

"I told you. He's not here."

"But where will he be tonight, at ten o'clock?"

It was a good question, one Gabby hadn't considered until right then. She could still feel the spot where Luke had jabbed that rifle in her back, his smooth palms on her arms, his fingers gripping her hair. "Even if he's here," Gabby said and pressed down harder on her lips, feeling every word, every lie, "what difference would it make? He'll still get what he wants. He'll get his son back."

Edwin waited so long to respond Gabby's attention drifted to the sound of the women again, high heels clacking over hardwood floors, a cacophony of shrill, piercing laughter. She turned to the window and gazed out upon their cars, the size of them, how the sun caught and reflected off their perfectly clean hoods. Hundreds of thousands of dollars' worth of rubber and glass and steel, but the Jacksons couldn't pay the ransom?

"Okay," Edwin said, finally. Gabby could barely hear him, his voice so small compared to what she was up against now, the trap she'd set for herself, the impossible sum. "See you—"

Gabby ended the call, cutting him off midsentence. The tip of her nose was cold, her whole face numb. She needed out of there. She needed to get that money or things would go from bad to worse.

The closet door was open, just wide enough to catch Gabby's attention. She stepped in and sat down cross-legged on the carpeted floor. The closet was dark on the inside, the same kind of darkness as before, but different because Gabby was free now. Mimi had set her free.

The thought was enough to get Gabby to her feet again. The beginnings of an idea, a new wild plan, were taking shape as she stood and surveyed Mimi's wardrobe, skipping over the more expensive garments, past the silk and cashmere to the cotton. Yes. A plain blue polo shirt. That's what the women would expect her to wear.

THE WOMEN WERE huddled in one corner of the kitchen, blocking Mimi's view of the box Gina Brashears had lugged in from the backseat of her Denali. Gina was squatted in the middle of the group, trying to get the box open. It was all happening right in front of Mimi, but her mind was in the master bath. What was Gabby doing in there? What was she thinking? Styrofoam creaked and packing peanuts puffed out across the floor. Gina Brashears rose from the mess, holding the nearly three-foot-tall machine high above her head like a trophy. The women cheered as they broke their huddle, turning on Mimi with mischief in their eyes.

"Surprise!"

Mimi mouthed the word but could make no sense of it.

"Come on, Mimi," Gina said, placing the bulky contraption on the kitchen counter. "It's just a margarita machine."

Mimi said, "Oh." Something about the last chicken house, the one closest to the highway, drew her attention.

"Well?" Gina said. "You want a marg or not?"

There were chrome nobs and tiny switches all over the machine. A clear bowl filled with ice sat above the levers and nobs. Gina pushed a red button on the side and the ice began to rattle, hidden blades chopping away somewhere inside. While the blades spun, Mimi looked up from the machine to the other women in her kitchen—Lilly, Trish, and Whitney—all of them wide eyed with hands clasped under their chins, all of them wearing the exact same expression. What are they doing here? Mimi wondered, and then the machine chugged to a stop.

A green stream oozed out from a silver spigot and into

a bedazzled Solo cup. Mimi was trying to remember if it was Lilly Taylor or Trish Jameson who taught fourth-grade Sunday school at the First Baptist Church when the frosty cup found Mimi's fingers.

"Drink up," Gina said, "We're having an *affair*."

The other women nodded but their eyes remained fixed on the cup in Mimi's hand.

"An affair?" Mimi said, noticing a fuzzy white line running from the dirt road all the way back to the chicken house's door.

Gina said, "Call it what you want, hon, but I told the girls about them beer bottles. And if you're gonna get sour on me for spilling the beans, you can save it."

Chickens. *Broilers*. That's what Mimi saw through the window. They got loose sometimes. A worker left a door open. Storms peeled back the sheet metal, exposing all sorts of escape routes in the studs. It had rained last night, but . . .

Mimi thought of Gabby again, how she'd left her in the bedroom, unattended. What had she been thinking? She hadn't. She'd panicked as soon as she'd seen Gina's GMC in the driveway. What else could she have done? Taped Gabby to the toilet? Shoved her back in the closet? There was barely enough time for Mimi to make it to the living room before Gina knocked on the door. No, trust was her only option. She'd offered her trust, the last thing she had left to give.

"Oh, come *on*," Gina growled. "Every one of these girls knows what it feels like. They've all been through the exact same thing."

Mimi was at the door, fortifying herself against it as she

peered down the road. She fully expected to see Gabby running, a tiny speck in the distance, the only shot Mimi had at finding her son—gone.

"Mimi Jackson." Gina stomped her foot hard enough to shake the pictures on the wall. "You're the one that got us together last Thursday. You're the one—"

"Last Thursday?" Mimi said, still scanning the road, searching for something, for someone that was not there.

"The girls all pitched in," Gina said, thudding up behind Mimi now, "got you something nice. That's a Margaritaville margarita machine. The Jimmy Buffett brand. You know how much one them cost?" Gina squeezed Mimi's shoulder. "The money don't matter, sis. What matters is that you show these girls a little appreciation."

The chickens were scattered across the dirt road now, some of them marching their way up the front drive. It'd only be a matter of seconds before Gina saw the birds and asked what the hell was going on. Where was Luke? Where was *Tuck*? Mimi's mind raced, trying to come up with a story, but all she could see were the broilers. Of course, Gabby had opened the door on her way to the highway, Mimi thought. She'd set the broilers free.

Mimi turned to face Gina. The way the woman stared back at her, it was like Gina could see the thoughts flashing behind her eyes. Like she could feel the pain that went deeper than Luke and Nina Ferguson and those goddamn beer bottles. Mimi's mouth moved and the words that came out surprised her: "Where's Ferg?"

Gina coughed into her fist. "Well . . . I didn't think—"

"That's right. You didn't," Mimi said. "You *think* I wanted you to tell everybody my business? And a margarita machine?" Mimi pointed over Gina's shoulder to the hulking contraption on the counter. "What the hell am I supposed to do with that?"

Gina blinked twice before a small smile creased the folds of her face. "The first step's always the hardest. Keep going, hon. Get it out."

Lilly, Trish, and Whitney smiled, like just because their husbands had been sneaking around on them, they thought they really knew what was going on here. Their eyes crinkled in the corners, wrinkles worming through the masks the women painted on every morning.

The margarita burned cold in Mimi's hand, numbing her fingertips. She'd almost forgotten she was holding it. The urge to chug the frozen concoction—all of it, in one long slurp—rose in Mimi. Maybe with the tequila in her she could tell them what had really happened. She wanted to watch their plastic faces crack open. She wanted their tears to wash their makeup away. She wanted someone else to feel what she was feeling.

Mimi brought the cup to her lips and drank deeply. Gina said, "Easy now. Lord. You're gonna catch a brain freeze," but the other women didn't laugh. They weren't cheering anymore, either. Mimi had her eyes closed, but she could imagine the looks on their faces, the same expression that had been stamped across Mimi's face for the last six months. Mimi opened her eyes and tapped the bottom of the cup, trying to get the last of the margarita out. A green glob pulled free and started sliding along the plastic, inching its way toward Mimi's lips, but it never made it.

Not before a board on the front porch creaked and

Mimi cut her eyes over the cup's rim to the woman standing on the first step, just standing there, hands dangling by her sides, like she wasn't sure if she was invited to the party or not.

Gina turned to the front door. "You here to clean the house or something?"

And Gabriela Menchaca said, "Sí. I am here to clean house."

21.

Gabby was wearing a pair of Mimi's khakis. They were tight in the thighs but loose around the waist. As skinny as Mimi was, Gabby couldn't believe it. Maternity pants, maybe? The blue polo shirt fit fine, even better after Gabby tucked it in, filling up all that extra space around her waist. A black leather belt cinched down the rest. An apron or bandanna to tie around her head would've been a nice touch, but Gabby had found neither in Mimi's massive closet. She'd paused just long enough to look herself over in the mirror before crawling through the master bedroom window.

The chickens surprised her. Caught her eye as her feet touched down on the front porch. A line of white chickens, clucking around everywhere. Good for them, Gabby thought, listening as the big trucks downshifted on the highway. Not too far, only a couple miles, maybe, but then what? Where would she go? Back to Edwin and the mess he'd made? No, not until he'd given the child to Mimi and all of that was behind them. Maybe not even then. Edwin had started this. Not when he'd stolen the child. Before that. When he'd stolen from Gabby then lied to her about the rent. That was the beginning of the end.

Which is why the highway's call went unanswered. The Jacksons' house held dangers of its own, none more threatening than Luke Jackson and his rifle, but Luke wasn't home. It was just Mimi, having some sort of party with her friends. Gabby knew there was more to it than that, but whatever had caused the other women to come did not matter. They were there now, and Gabby needed to get close to them, close enough to figure out how to get the money Mimi said she didn't have.

Mimi was holding a red Solo cup when the front door swung open. The big woman took the bait immediately. A Mexican woman in a polo and ill-fitting pants? Of course she was there to scrub the toilets. The woman kept calling Gabby a "cleaning lady" without even looking at her, just like bald Mr. Baker never looked at her when he'd come around with his clipboard. Like he knew what he was doing was wrong but if he didn't look at Gabby, if he didn't see his reflection in her eyes, then it didn't make it real.

"Señora Jackson?" Gabby said. "Puedo limpiar hoy?" She waited, standing between the older woman and Mimi, trying to assume the role she'd been assigned by the world.

Mimi's gaze ticked up the slacks before landing on the blue polo. Gabby watched Mimi's eyes as she realized the clothes had come from her own closet. Gabby tried to read her reaction, but Mimi's face was blank, her lips a pale pink slash.

"I got the call." Gabby spoke in her choppiest accent, hoping Mimi wasn't like the other women, praying she'd hear the message beneath her words.

"The call?"

"Sí." Gabby nodded, once, twice. "The call."

Mimi said, "Yes, okay, señorita. You may clean today," and something flashed behind her eyes, a look Gabby had never seen from her before, like, for the first time in Mimi's life, she understood. "But I'd like for you to wait until after the party."

"After?" Gabby said, still playing up her accent because that's what the women expected. She wanted them to trust her. She needed to get close enough to listen, close enough to figure out how to get the money. "Yes. After is fine."

"Well?" Mimi said, still standing beside the other woman who would not look Gabby in the eyes. "Come in. The girls got me a margarita machine."

"Letting her drink on the job, too?" Gina said. "Lord have mercy, Mimi."

"Sometimes, yes," Gabby said and took a step up the porch. "Sometimes we drink and talk while I work. Nothing crazy. Just a couple glasses of wine."

The woman shuddered. "A couple glasses of wine, huh?"

"We are very close friends," Gabby said. "Isn't that right, Mrs. Jackson?"

There were chickens clucking all across the front yard. Gabby could hear them, but nobody else seemed to notice, especially not the big woman. She just kept staring down at Mimi, the same way Gabby was staring at her, waiting to hear her response.

After what felt like forever, Mimi finally said, "Sí," and turned for the door before the big one got going again. "Now come on, Gabriela. You can help serve the margaritas. Drink a few if you'd like, and I'll pay you for the extra work this morning. Deal?"

Gabby held down a grin as she started up the steps, following this woman whom she'd only met the night before. Then thinking, no, the Mimi Jackson she'd met yesterday was different from who she saw now, this winking woman talking about the one thing neither of them had—the only thing that mattered—money.

"YOU KNOW WHAT really grinds Brett's gears?" Gina Brashears said, halfway through her third margarita. "When I get hold of his guns. Especially that big one, the Browning BAR he uses on the weeklong trips up to Maine to hunt monster bucks. Brett damn near shits his pants."

"What do you do with it?" Trish Jameson asked, licking salt from the rim of her cup.

"I shoot the damn thing." Gina glanced around the room at each woman, getting their attention before she said, "And that's what *really* grinds Brett's gears . . . I shoot better than he does."

Mimi stood behind the island in the kitchen, holding her second margarita without drinking it, watching as Gabby weaved her way in and out of the women, never letting a single cup get half empty. Not even close. Mimi could feel the tequila working already, but there wasn't any use for it now. Not with Gabby standing in her living room, right there where Mimi could watch her. That "call" she'd mentioned. That's why Mimi had gone along with whatever game Gabby was playing, all dressed up in Mimi's clothes. Had she really talked to Edwin? If so, what had he told her? Was he the reason she was there?

"Luke got any guns?" Gina said, throwing her elbow over the sofa and turning to Mimi. The other women's heads rotated like birds on a wire. "You really wanna mess with him, you take his gun, hon."

Gabby stood behind the kitchen counter, the pitcher almost empty in her hands. Mimi could feel her glare above all the others, a woman who knew what it felt like to stare down the barrel of a gun.

"Yes, he has a gun," Mimi said. "A deer rifle, I think."

"Well, what're you waiting for?" Gina said. "Go get it."

Mimi's eyes were on Gabby as she said, "Luke took it with him."

Did it bother Gabriela? Luke out there, hunting her man? If so, her face didn't show it. Gabby brought the pitcher to her lips while the other women gossiped.

"Modern-gun season don't open till November," Gina Brashears said. "Was it a muzzle loader?"

Through the picture windows lining the back of the room, Mimi noticed the clear blue waters of the pool that had scared her since Tuck was born. Leaves drifted across the surface, the tips curled like burnt paper. Beyond the pool, the woods encroached, a thicket of skinny-trunked trees and vines growing closer with every month that passed.

"A muzzle loader?" Mimi said.

"Got a hammer you pull back and ramrod under the barrel."

"Yes. That sounds right."

"And you let him take Tuck?" This came from Whitney Blackburn, sitting cross-legged in the La-Z-Boy recliner where Luke fell asleep most nights. Lilly and Trish batted their lashes in agreement. Gina fought to keep her elbow hooked over the back of the couch.

"You think he asked my permission?" Mimi said, watching Gabby take another drink from the pitcher, a quick one.

"But Tuck's only six months old, Mimi. He could've—" Trish's words were cut short by the roar of the blender starting up again, the ice crunching and swirling. A few spins later, the sound died off and Gabby said, "My man is the same way, always doing stupid things, especially when it comes to money."

The women waited until Gina laughed and then they joined her. "Stupid ain't the half of it," Gina said, slapping her thighs. "And don't even get me started on money."

"In some ways, I would think money makes things more difficult."

Watching Gabby maneuver her way into the conversation, Mimi couldn't help but be impressed. She finally understood her angle too, the reason Gabby had come out of the closet wearing Mimi's clothes.

"Makes what more difficult?" Gina said.

Gabby touched her chin and looked up, a coy expression that Mimi couldn't imagine her making in real life. "Everything," Gabby said, nodding. "Yes, money complicates things, no?"

"Damn straight, especially when you've got to beg your husband for table scraps."

Gabby's finger fell from her chin. "I miss your meaning."

"Consider yourself lucky then." Gina glanced around the room. "Any dime I get out of Brett, I've got to pry from his greasy little paws. I bet you and your man are different, huh? Bet y'all share, keep all your shit above the table."

"Above the table?"

Gina rolled her eyes and Mimi knew the conversation was over. Gabby must have felt it, too, because she started the blender back up, trying to extend the exchange as she shouted over the noise: "Another round, señoritas?"

Gina snapped her fingers and the blender chugged to a stop. "You gonna have to drink that pitcher by yourself, *señorita*. It's one thing to miss church on Sunday morning. It's another thing entirely to skip out on lunch at the country club."

It reminded Mimi of high school, the way the women stood all at once, like the teacher had just dismissed class. Lilly, Trish, and Whitney brought their empties to the sink and began gathering their things. Gina guzzled what was left in her bedazzled Solo cup, dropped the homemade chalice into her purse, and fell in line behind the other women on their way to the door.

Mimi watched them go, filing through the foyer now in the same fashion they had entered, floating above it all, completely unaware of the situation at hand. Worried about all the wrong things, like making it to the country club at the same time as the church crowd. With Gabby standing behind her, already tossing the empties into the trash, Mimi saw the women from a different perspective. A herd of curious creatures, so far from the person Mimi had become in the last two days, this new woman splitting the old Mimi open at the seams, using all the energy she'd wasted worrying to think—really think—about the situation and all its complicated angles.

"Hey, Gina? You got a sec?"

The big-boned mother of three came to a stop as the other women waltzed through the door. "I got maybe sixty seconds," Gina said. "Just enough time for you to say thanks."

"Thanks?"

Gina's doughy face soured. "For the gift, hon. Gotta say it like you mean it, though."

Gabby had the water running now, washing the cups out one by one.

"I need to ask you something." Mimi motioned with her eyes until Gina got the picture and started back across the foyer, coming close enough that Mimi could smell the tequila on her breath. "Why'd you come out here?" Mimi said. "You could've given me that margarita machine tomorrow and nobody would've had to miss church."

"After I talked to you on the phone yesterday, I had a feeling," Gina said, "an itch I couldn't scratch."

"You wanted to see if Luke was still here. You wanted to see if I'd told him off."

Gina leaned back and squinted at the sink. "I know you didn't say nothing to him, hon. Not like I told you anyway."

"Yeah?" Mimi said. "And how do you know that?"

"Drove past Hickory Hollow Lane this morning," Gina said. "And you won't believe whose truck I saw parked right out front of that gaudy-ass mansion, sitting in broad daylight for the whole damn world to see."

Mimi's cheeks flushed as she pictured the gray Ford parked next to Steve Ferguson's stable of sports cars.

"*That's* why I called the girls up," Gina said. "Wanted

you to get the picture without me having to come right out and say it. But now I'm all kinds of confused." Gina tugged at the hem of her blouse, pulling it off of her belly. "You said Luke took his rifle with him?"

"He keeps it in the back of his truck."

"But that ain't all you said he took with him. You said—"

The water cut off and Gina's gaze shifted toward the sink. Mimi could hear Gabby's feet slapping against the hardwood floors. Then she was past them, already turning for the hall when Gina said, "Brenda Acosta's crew cleans my house. They do a damn good job, but I ain't never seen that woman working with Diamond Shine." Gina waited until Gabby disappeared around the corner. "You wanna tell me what's going on?"

Mimi could still hear Gabby's footsteps coming from the hallway, and then they were gone. Like she'd either stopped walking or turned off into one of the bedrooms with the carpeted floors. "I want to tell you," Mimi said, remembering the tape she'd cut from Gabby's wrists, "but I can't."

The sound of engines rolled in through the open front door. The other women steered their cars down the dirt road, headed to the country club, their lives no different than before. Mimi watched them go then turned back to Gina, the burly woman still standing there, like she wasn't budging until she'd gotten what she'd come for.

"Maybe it's a good thing Brett never put any chicken houses on our land."

"What?"

"Look." Gina pointed through the open door. "Your

broilers got loose. Trish damn near flattened a couple in her Yukon."

Mimi saw the chickens now, the same ones she'd noticed earlier, heads bobbing out in front of their bodies as they pecked at the dead grass on the side of the road.

"You call later," Gina said, stepping onto the front porch, "and let me know how Luke's little hunting trip went. Deal?"

Mimi exhaled as her friend started down the steps. "Thanks, Gina, for everything."

"There you go," Gina said and grinned. "Finally said it like you meant it."

22.

A phone rang. Luke could barely hear it, still caught in the afterglow. It felt like coming out from under a warm blanket, the distant chime peeling him back layer by layer until he was part of the world again, lying flat on his back in Nina Ferguson's king-sized bed. Silk sheets? He wasn't sure. They were shiny, felt good, but got sticky when they started sweating midway through round two. It was always better the second time, especially with Ferg. They only saw each other on the weekends. Five days spent building it up, waiting until Saturday when Luke would break out his fancy underwear—the striped kind with SAXX stamped across the elastic—and get lost down by the waters of Clear Creek.

The underwear were on the floor by the foot of the bed, right where Luke had tossed them after Ferg slipped out of that leopard-print kimono. He didn't last three minutes. Thirty minutes after that, they went at it again. Luke took it slow, finding his rhythm without fighting so hard to hold it in. Ferg did her thing, that crazy trick at the end that kept Luke coming back, and then a deep sleep washed over both of them like holy water on Sunday morning, a half hour before high noon.

The phone rang again, and this time Luke realized it was his cell, the ringtone that sounded like the analog phone from his mother's old house. Memories of Tuck flashed through his subconscious for some reason, the baby boy asleep in his father's arms. Luke liked his son best when he was asleep, and that's how he always remembered him, his tiny chest rising and falling, the quick patter of his breath. When the phone rang a third time, Tuck was gone.

Luke sat up and reached for the nightstand. He didn't notice Ferg's red hair fanned out over the pillow like the Ozark Mountains, all those leaves so full of color, a final burst of beauty before the cold winds tore them from their limbs. He didn't check the screen, just pressed the phone to his ear, still half asleep. He sat straight up when he heard the man's voice. The bedsheets fell from his chest to his waist as he stammered, "Mr. Detmer?" and cleared his throat. "Yes, *yes*. This is Luke Jackson. I'm sorry. No, sir, I wasn't asleep. I just, uh . . ." Ferg grunted and rolled over, flopping her hand into Luke's crotch. "The board meeting? Yes. Of course."

Luke listened to William H. Detmer as his eyes scanned the bedroom, afraid the old man was watching him somehow. A mirror hung from the wall opposite the bed. For the first time in a long time, Luke studied his reflection, a gateway to another world where he was in bed with his wife, his son by his side.

"You're pushing the meeting back?" Luke said. "Okay. Yes, sir. Tomorrow morning at eight. I'll be there. What do I need to wear?" Luke waited. "Mr. Detmer? Hello?"

He pulled the phone from his ear and stared into a blank screen. "*Shit.*"

Ferg gave a few lazy blinks as Luke plucked her hand from his crotch and rolled out of bed. "You think a man like Bill Detmer," she said, cutting her eyes at Luke, "would know better than to conduct business on a Sunday."

The mirror on the wall displayed the soft paunch sticking out from the bottom of Luke's midsection. He'd first noticed his new belly the week after Tuck was born, all those sleepless nights bleeding over into his days. Luke sought refuge in the plant, holing himself up in there, working longer hours than ever. He even slept there on occasion. His skin shone a pale, almost sickly shade of green, similar to the hue of the fluorescent bulbs in his office. Luke pinched the paunch and said, "The board meeting. They delayed the vote because—"

"—it's Sunday," Ferg yawned. "And they don't want the good people of Springdale to see their hundred-thousand-dollar trucks parked out front of the Detmer building and get the wrong idea." Ferg rolled her eyes and stretched. "Hey," she said. "You still owe me a story."

"A what?"

"A story. Whatever the hell it was you were doing at the chicken plant last night."

"Oh, that," Luke said and watched his mouth move in the mirror.

THE GUEST ROOM closet was open, the bike lock coiled like a snake on the floor. Gabby stood over it, staring into the darkness, trying to make sense of all she'd heard. The women were gone now, even the one with the hands like she'd worked on the line. *Gina*. She had come there for a reason, come to tell Mimi something important, to make her feel better. It wasn't about her child, though. The women still didn't know the boy was missing, and that was good.

Good for Gabby, and Edwin.

She recalled the mixed messages he'd given her. The strange tone in his voice, like he'd become a different sort of man in the hours that had passed since she'd last seen him. What kind of man? Gabby didn't know, but this was nothing new. Edwin lived for change. Never satisfied with what he had. Like how he'd tried to grow that ridiculous mustache. Gabby would come into the bathroom most mornings and find him combing the scraggly patch of hair, trimming it with scissors and saying into the mirror, "I like it. I really do." It was the same as when he'd dyed his hair, or shaved his head, or taken a whole week's worth of pay and bought a brand-new wardrobe from El Potrero Western Wear, going for the Mexican cowboy look.

Gabby tried to picture him now. The Edwin in her mind did not have a mustache, and that was fine. Gabby never liked it anyway.

Footsteps echoed up from the hallway.

"Gabby?" Mimi's voice came from behind. "What the hell was all of that about?"

"All of what?"

Mimi took hold of Gabby's shirtsleeve and yanked it. "You're wearing *my* clothes. You could've gotten us both in bad trouble back there."

"We're already in trouble." Gabby bent and picked the

bike lock up from the floor, feeling the weight of it in her hands. "I spoke with Edwin."

"I *knew* it," Mimi said. "When I saw you standing on the porch, wearing my clothes, you said you got 'the call,' or something."

"That's right. And after I spoke with Edwin, I had to come see you."

"*Tuck.*" The boy's name shot from his mother's mouth like a wet cough, loud enough to cut Gabby off. "What did Edwin say about Tuck? Is he okay? Is he . . ."

There were other voices inside Gabby's head, all the fragments of the conversations she'd overheard between Mimi and the women who would not look her in the eyes.

"He's fine," Gabby said then waited, expecting Mimi to become frantic and start asking her a hundred more questions.

The soft sound of Mimi's breath was all Gabby heard, and that surprised her. When she turned around, Mimi was sitting cross-legged on the carpeted floor.

"I should've told you Luke took the rifle." Mimi picked at the carpet as she spoke. "I wasn't trying to hide it from you. I wasn't thinking. I just—"

Gabby said, "The rifle?" running her palms along the length of the lock. "The rifle doesn't matter. Edwin is fine, too. Besides, your husband didn't go looking for Edwin, did he?"

A twitch above the left eye. That was the only reaction Gabby saw in Mimi, but it was something, enough to convince her of what she had to say next. "He's having an affair? That's why those women came to your house this morning? To comfort you?"

"That," Mimi said, picking at the carpet again, "is none of your business."

Gabby wrapped the bike lock around her left hand and clenched her fist.

"I don't want to talk about it, okay?" Mimi yanked at a stray string on the carpet and the stitching came loose, pulling up a line that ran all the way to the door. "I don't even want to think about it. I just want my son back."

Gabby set the lock down, right over the place where the carpet stitching had come loose, getting Mimi's attention before she got to the important part. "I'm here because Edwin still wants to make a deal." Gabby paused long enough to get the plan straight in her head, her plan and Edwin's plan, a mixture of the two, a way to make it work for both of them. "He wants everyone here by ten tonight, and that means *every*one, including Luke."

Mimi nodded, slowly, like she was working the details out in her mind. After a few seconds, she said, "Okay. Yeah. Ten o'clock, but what does Luke have to do with anything?"

Gabby squatted down eye level with the woman on the floor, no longer thinking of her by her name. Something had shifted inside her. Sometime after she saw the women's cars, the size of them. And then, there she was refilling the white women's cups with margaritas, thinking about how people in Celaya don't drink frozen margaritas. The variables were different, but the result was the same as the equation that had led to all of this, the figures she'd scribbled in her notebook, coming up with an estimate for their lost overtime pay. Luke Jackson owed them for the seven years they'd spent in the plant, and more, so much more than just that.

"Edwin still wants the money," Gabby said. "The money for your child. That's the deal."

"But we don't have it. I told you that."

"And I remembered. That's why I crashed your little party. All those women—your friends—they have money."

"My friends?" The guest room walls were bare, blank like Mimi's face. "They don't have anything to do with this. And there's no way Luke can get that much money. Not by ten o'clock on a Sunday night."

"That's what I said to Edwin. I wanted him to come and get me right then, while you were drinking margaritas. But Edwin's like Luke. He doesn't listen."

"You told him to come get you? I thought—"

"Of course." Gabby leaned forward and snatched the bike lock from the floor. "Your husband shoved his rifle in my back, Mimi. He stuffed me in that closet. *Locked* me in there with this." Gabby shook the bike lock until Mimi looked away. "And yes, I knew what you'd told me about the money. I tried to tell Edwin."

Mimi's head fell forward into her hands. Gabby watched her shoulders jerk but forced herself to stay focused on the money. Every extra minute she'd spent in the plant, all those hours adding up to days, *years*, of her life, lost. Now she could make them count for something.

"This woman your husband's seeing," Gabby said, ready now, recalling the conversation she'd heard as she waited in the hall. "She's rich?"

Mimi lifted her head up from her hands. "Her husband is rich. That's probably why she married him."

"And this husband, he's in the same boat you are. He doesn't know anything about what's going on?"

"You want me to call Steve Ferguson and ask him for fifty thousand dollars? Jesus, Gabby."

"No, no. I want you to call your husband," Gabby said, spinning the bike lock's dial until she had the numbers lined up, the date she'd heard Mimi say to Luke the night before when they were arguing outside the closet door. "Call him at this woman's house. That way he knows that you know."

"And then what?"

"Then you wait. With his big promotion coming up, I bet Luke will figure it out from there." Gabby gave both ends of the cable a swift jerk and the lock came free.

"How did you—"

Gabby said, "I've been listening," and pushed the lock back together until it clicked.

23.

Before Mimi called Luke she went to the bathroom, the same bathroom where she'd left Gabby only an hour before. Part of her wanted to call her husband and tell him off, tell him everything then hang up and leave him to figure out the rest. As much money as Luke made, there had to be some way he could get the fifty grand. Maybe Gabby was right. Maybe Ferg was the answer.

Maybe not.

Mimi needed a moment to herself, time enough to decide if she was really ready to burn her life down. Gabby had handed her the match, but a match without a spark is nothing. The fire that followed would erase all that had been before. Even after everything was over, even once she had Tuck back, her life—her family—would never be the same.

Mimi's reflection shadowed her in the bathroom mirror but she wouldn't look at herself. The bathroom was too big, just like the rest of the house. Mimi saw that now and sat down on the toilet's heated seat, wondering if building the house had been the start of their problems. Too much of anything is always bad. Too much time. Too many options. A life that was too easy turned hard real quick.

The vanity had two sinks. His and hers. Mimi stared down at the one with the toothpaste stains and the short black hairs around the drain. The place Luke stood each morning and brushed his teeth, shaved his face, getting himself ready for the plant. Mimi turned the water on. As she waited for it to warm, she noticed something she'd missed before—a scrim of light blue powder coating the countertop.

Steam rose from the sink as Mimi leaned forward, inspecting the residue. She extended both hands beneath the scalding water and scrubbed them clean. It wasn't until she reached for the small towel hanging from the loop to the right of the vanity that she noticed the orange plastic bottle tucked in behind it. The white cap had been screwed on crooked, sticking up at one edge. The bottle rattled as Mimi took it out from behind the towel. The blue pills concealed inside were the same color as the powder that remained on the countertop. Over half of her Xanax prescription was gone, the same prescription she'd just filled last week.

Mimi slipped the bottle into her pocket and finally looked up at herself in the mirror. Her hair was a mess, her lips chapped, but her eyes were open now, wide open.

LUKE STEPPED AWAY from the mirror and bent to pick up his underwear, buying himself some time to think of a story he could tell Ferg about the botched tradeoff at the plant. He had his left foot through the leg hole when the phone rang again. The sharp tone made the hair on the back of his neck stand straight up. Luke pushed his other leg through and stumbled for the phone, wondering what Mr. Detmer had forgotten to tell him.

"Shit," Ferg said, sliding out of bed and hopping over her kimono crumpled on the floor. "That's Steve's landline. I got to get this."

Luke said, "Steve has a house phone?" and watched as Ferg pranced across the bedroom and disappeared behind the double doors leading to the master bath.

"I missed it." Ferg stepped back into the bedroom with a clunky rotary phone in her hand, the cord dragging the ground behind her. "How about a *bathroom* phone?" She lifted the device for Luke's inspection. "Steve's got one of these bad boys in every room of the house. He'll only talk business on a landline. Doesn't want the government listening in on his calls."

"What's he got to hide?"

"Nothing, really. You know Steve."

Ferg had the phone on her hip now, leaning against the doorframe, standing there as if she were fully dressed. It was one of the things Luke liked most about her. Ferg had confidence and a nice body. Not great, but nice. It was the way Ferg carried herself that made her sexy. She liked to tell Luke she had what the kids called "swagger." Luke never thought that was the right word for it, but she sure had something.

"Steve's got more money than he knows what to do with," Luke said, spotting his hunting pants on the floor beside the nightstand. "If he had any grit at all, he'd be the one getting this promotion."

"What's he need a promotion for?"

"You're right," Luke said. "He doesn't need the promotion, just like he doesn't need all those damn phones around the house."

"It's kind of like those doofy Hawaiian shirts he wears to the plant on Fridays."

She stepped out from the bathroom doorway, as far as the phone cord would reach, and pointed to the closet. Luke's eyes followed her aim to the row of Tommy Bahama shirts hanging from the rack, some of them with price tags still attached.

"He wears those shirts for the workers," Ferg said. "So they'll trust him, or something. It's the same way with the landline. Steve has an old-school way of doing business. Or maybe it's new-school. That's the thing about Steve; it's hard to tell what he's thinking, but he's always thinking. Cautious like you wouldn't believe. Doesn't trust banks. Not for a second. Still likes to pay for stuff in cash. Who does that?"

"I know a lot of guys who pay in cash."

"Yeah, but how many of those guys keep stacks of it in their house? All rubber banded together in the back of his Marshall."

Luke tripped trying to get his left leg into his pants. He caught himself on the edge of the bed and pushed up again. "His Marshall?" Luke said, curious about the money but trying not to show it.

"Yeah," Ferg said, running her fingers along the sleeves of her husband's silky shirts. "You know the difference between you and Steve?" She paused, but not long enough for Luke to respond. "Steve doesn't give a shit, about anything, not even me. Or wait . . . I guess y'all have that in common."

"I care about—"

Ferg shook her head. "No, you don't. Not really, and that's fine. I mean, why would you?"

"Nina . . ."

Luke watched her take the tail of a Hawaiian shirt and dab the corners of both eyes. He couldn't believe it. She was crying. He took a step forward then stopped.

"I have a daughter, Luke. A kid," she said, still holding the shirt, staring down at the sailboats and pineapples printed on the fabric. "I forget about her some days. Like, after I drop her off at day care, I don't think about her again. I've even forgotten to pick her up a couple times." There were mascara stains on the trunk of a palm tree. Ferg dropped the shirt and let it fall back in line with the others. "What sort of mother does that?"

"I do the same thing all the time, especially when I'm at work." Luke peeked at his phone before sliding it into his pocket, thinking maybe he should call Mimi until he remembered he'd broken her phone. He hadn't thought once about her or Tuck since after he left Edwin's ratty trailer. That's why he'd come here, though, to forget. But now Ferg was having some sort of nervous breakdown, making him think about the way he treated his wife.

"I still worry, though," Ferg said. "That's the weird part. I'm scared I'm going to fuck something up, and that something is my daughter. I'm afraid if Lucy spends too much time around here, she'll wind up just like me."

Luke knew he should go to her, knew he should say something to help ease her mind, but this was Nina Ferguson. This was his mistress, not his wife.

"*Ferg* . . . Come on. Don't be so—"

"You should see Steve with her. He can't get enough of that girl. Treats her just like he treats me, like a princess. Buys her whatever she wants, whenever she wants it. And this is after he's been at the plant all day, or on a trip. Steve still finds the time."

Something about that last line made Luke clench his jaw. "If Steve's so great, what do you need me for?"

"*Need?*" Ferg said and turned on him. Her face was streaked with makeup Luke hadn't realized she'd been wearing. "Honey, I don't need you. Steve gives me everything I need. He doesn't hide anything from me, either."

"Well, since you don't *need* me," Luke said, hoping the squall had passed, "I'm gonna head on out."

A thump came from behind him. Loud enough to make Luke stop and turn, spotting the phone on the floor first, then Ferg with one finger to her mouth, tugging her bottom lip down. "I might not need you, Luke Jackson, but I still want you."

Watching the redhead stalk across the room, her face a mask of muted shades and creamy swirls, Luke truly saw Nina Ferguson for the first time. Saw straight through to the broken heart that drove her to men like himself, like Steve. All the money, all the sex in the world wouldn't fix Ferg. She just kept coming, one teetering step after another, a pitiful waltz, but she still looked good. Something about her sudden vulnerability made her even sexier, Luke thought. She was close enough to make his fingers tingle, preparing to touch her perfectly soft skin, ready to start all over, when the phone rang again.

The old rotary phone, rattling across the floor in front of the closet.

Ferg bent to pick it up, giving him a different view of the same old thing. She stayed bowed like that, pointing her ass straight at him as she cleared her throat, dragged a thumb beneath each eye, then said into the phone, "You've reached Steve Ferguson's landline. Steve's unavailable at the moment. Would you like to leave a—"

The way Ferg jerked up—forgoing the show—it caught Luke off guard. Like maybe she didn't like him staring so hard, or maybe this was just her way of keeping him guessing, keeping their relationship from going stale, a little weird phone play before they went for round three. But then Ferg pushed the receiver toward him, the base still on the floor, the cord stretched so tight it wasn't curly anymore.

Luke said, "For me?" noticing the way Ferg's fingers trembled, her eyes still red-rimmed but clear, all that raw emotion from before gone now, replaced only by fear.

WHEN MIMI RETURNED to the kitchen, she was holding the orange plastic pill bottle she'd found in the bathroom.

Gabby was on the sofa. She looked up. "Ready to call him?"

Mimi said, "I'm ready," and squeezed the pill bottle tighter.

Gabby extended the phone over the back of the sofa. Mimi took it, dialed Steve Ferguson's home number, and waited, thinking back to her first, and only, Mother's Day. How she'd spent every waking hour alone with Tuck. He'd just turned one month old, just started smiling when he saw his father's face, and then Luke was gone. Off on some sort of business trip in Laredo, Texas. Mimi spent the better part of that long weekend in May watching a nature documentary on Disney+ about moms of all different genuses and species. The lionesses were her favorite, how they disconnected themselves from the pride to give birth then stayed in the bush for weeks, hunting and raising their cubs all by themselves. The part that really got Mimi's attention was when she learned why the mothers went into this self-imposed exile. The male lions—the *fathers*—were a threat to the cubs. On rare occasions, they even killed their own offspring. Their own flesh and blood.

The answering machine picked up after six rings. Before she redialed the number, Mimi thought back to that nature documentary, how it had taught her something about Luke and every man who'd ever fathered a child. It wasn't natural for them to become daddies. Not at all. Loving, caring, present fathers were not the rule; they were the exception, an anomaly that went against thousands of years of evolution, all the hunting and fighting and fucking that had helped spread their genetic code for generations. When Luke got back from Laredo, Mimi went easy on him for a little while. He was an alpha, after all, rebelling against his own nature, trying to become this new person he was never meant to be. She wouldn't go easy on him now.

When Mimi finally called back, Ferg answered on the first ring.

"Cut the shit," Mimi said. "Let me talk to Luke." She tried to imagine the look on Nina Ferguson's face. She remembered the last time she'd seen the redhead, at La Huerta with the other women, when Ferg had informed the table of her surefire way to keep a husband from cheating. Gabby stirred on the sofa. Mimi looked down at her as her husband's voice replaced Ferg's on the phone.

"You drugged me," Mimi said, then screamed: "You *drugged* me, you son of a bitch!"

The plastic pill bottle hit the window above the sink. The realization that Luke had crushed up half her Xanax prescription, dumped it into a coffee mug, then fed it to her—less than an hour after she'd first realized her son was gone—that was it. The final straw. Fuck that Disney documentary. The rage was like rocket fuel. All the confidence Mimi had needed to make the call, and then some. Enough to carry her through the heated conversation. Enough for her to laugh as Luke tried to explain the poisoning as some sort of protective measure.

"It's wasn't like that, okay?" he said. "It was the only way to shut that little brain of yours off. You needed your medicine, needed rest. And if you would've called the cops, we might've never seen our son again."

Mimi laughed into the receiver, then told him everything Gabby had told her to say, relaying the details in a brisk tone, never once pausing long enough for Luke to respond. Mimi told Luke about the money last. She knew her husband, knew he'd try to tell her again how he couldn't get it, so she added: "I'm serious, Luke. Bring the money at ten, or I'm calling the police." And then she hung up.

Gabby was standing beside Mimi now. How long had she been there? Mimi didn't know. She just felt Gabby's fingers curling into her palm, prying the phone from her grip.

"Listen to you," Gabby said and tapped the darkened screen, "coming up with that bit about the police."

"I don't even know where that came from."

"That's the best way to talk, without thinking. Besides, what you said makes sense." Gabby took the pitcher out from under the margarita machine and drank what was left of it. "You call the cops, his little party's over. No more promotion. No more girlfriend. And a mother in your situation would call them, you know?"

Mimi eased herself into the leather sofa. She knew why she'd threatened Luke with the police; it was what she should've done from the start. She should've called them. But she hadn't, and then it was too late, and that's why her son was still missing. Guilt swarmed in the pit of Mimi's gut, overtaking the confidence from before.

"Maybe I should call them now," Mimi said, sitting back up on the sofa. "I should. I should just call—"

The plastic pitcher rattled as Gabby chunked it into the sink. "You call the cops and the whole deal is off. Edwin won't come here if the police are involved."

"But what if Luke can't get the money?"

"Then you'll have a choice to make," Gabby said and pushed off from the kitchen counter. "But there's no reason to worry about that yet. Your husband will get the money, and you'll get your son. What was it you said last night? *Everything will be fine.*"

Hearing Gabby speak Luke's words felt wrong, but the certainty in her voice calmed Mimi's nerves. She watched the woman walk around her kitchen, turning on the water in the sink, using the retractable nozzle to rinse the sticky mess out of the pitcher.

Mimi whispered, "How can you be sure?" thinking again of the lionesses lying low in the lemongrass, the cubs pouncing at her paws.

"Sure?" Gabby said and rotated her head, just far enough Mimi could see her lips moving. "There's no such thing."

24.

"You want to tell me what the fuck is going on?"

Luke didn't want to tell Ferg anything. He wanted to punch the wall, feel his knuckles crack open, warm blood between his fingers. What was Mimi thinking, calling him here, talking to him like that? Luke wanted to break something, something frail and beautiful. Instead, he placed the tips of two fingers on the inside of his right wrist and waited until his pulse steadied.

"*Lucas.*"

Ferg never called him that. He had to tell her something. Luke had come here to clear his mind, to get away from the shit storm brewing back at his place. But the winds had changed and now the whole deal stunk like a chicken house. The same way it happened at the farm. A cool, calm day could go straight to hell with the slightest breeze, blowing chicken shit and methane gas all over Luke's half-a-million-dollar home.

Ferg was barefoot but wearing leggings and a sports bra now, done playing sexy mistress, looking more like she was ready to go for a jog. Luke pictured her running away as she glared back at him, still waiting for him to answer her question. What could he say? My son was stolen by one of my employees? My wife called the guy, worked out some sort of deal where she pays him fifty thousand bucks I don't have? To admit such things would be admitting a weakness, an oversight on Luke's part. There had to be another way, a course of action that would allow him to get his son back, make it to the board meeting tomorrow, and nobody would have to know how close he'd been to failure.

Luke was still going over the details in his mind, trying to get everything straight, when Ferg stormed out of the bedroom. A moment later, the sound of ice cubes clinking into a glass found Luke's ears. That got him moving again, thinking as he traced her steps, still trying to come up with the right way to play this out without saying too much.

The kitchen was a lot like the one Luke had had built for Mimi, except it was bigger and not nearly as organized. A high-dollar Peloton bike stood in the far corner, a red one with a video screen attached. Who keeps an exercise bike in the kitchen? Luke thought and then remembered Steve's dumbass Hawaiian shirts. There was some sort of guitar amplifier in the same corner, too, black with gold knobs. No guitar around that Luke could see. The island had a built-in industrial stove, the grates still shiny and clean because Ferg never cooked. But there she stood with her back to Luke over by the sink, chopping away at a celery stalk. An open can of tomato juice sat beside her, along with a bottle of Louisiana Hot Sauce, a jar of olives, and a silver flask of what Luke guessed was Absolut Vodka, Ferg's favorite spirit.

"Yeah," Luke said. "I could use one of those right now."

The knife came down with a dull *thwap*, chopping the stalk in two. Ferg poured the vodka in next as she said, "Anything else, Your Highness?" then flicked the flask lid shut, stirring her Bloody Mary with the celery.

Luke stepped around her, going for the highball glasses in the cabinet next to the fridge.

"You're a piece of work," she said. "You know that?"

Luke imagined himself kicking the stationary bike, picking it up and tossing it out the window. He reached for her flask instead.

"A decent lay, or at least as good as I'm gonna find around here."

"You miss Florida so much," Luke said, pouring tomato juice into his glass then going heavy on the hot sauce, "why don't you go back?"

"I've got a good deal going here," she said, "or I guess I did, until about five fucking minutes ago."

Luke turned the flask over but nothing came out. "You're really out of vodka?"

He started for the liquor cabinet, had his fingers wrapped around the handle, ready to give it a pull when Ferg's voice stopped him.

"How'd she find out?" she said. "You told me she'd never find out."

Luke paused long enough to bring the vodka-less Bloody Mary to his lips. It tasted like shit. Without the vodka, what was the point? Luke realized he felt the same way about Ferg now. In all the months they'd spent together, she'd never, not once, shown any signs of weakness like she had in the bedroom. He'd never heard her complain, never seen her cry. He didn't like it. That wasn't part of their original arrangement. Luke set the glass on the counter, wiped his lips, and said, "I think we're done here."

"Your wife just called my house. My *house,* Luke."

"You mean Steve's?"

Ferg's head snapped up. She'd scrubbed the makeup out from under her eyes at some point. Luke barely recognized her. "I should slap your face," she said, her voice softer than it should've been.

Luke leaned over the island. "Go for it. Give me your best shot."

Ferg jerked one hand up, then brought it back down, grasping her drink, all ten fingers interlocked around the cocktail. She took a small sip. When she lowered the glass, tomato juice outlined her upper lip. "You're not worth the effort," she said. "Not anymore."

Luke tried to smile but couldn't make his lips work. His face felt like wax, like a mask he'd worn for so long it had become a part of him.

"You men," Ferg said and pushed back from the island, "you're all alike. You know that? Never satisfied with what you have." She was walking as she talked, making pointless laps around the kitchen. "I was perfectly happy with you and Steve. Never asked either of y'all any questions. Not even about the plant. That's why it worked for as long as it did. Nobody should have to know how the sausage is made. It just tastes good, and that was good enough for me. But now?"

She'd stopped directly in front of the cherry-red Peloton. Luke looked past the bike to the guitar amp with the golden knobs. There was a single word written across the black mesh that covered the speaker, a word Luke had missed when he'd first walked into the kitchen, a wavy white script like a treasure map's trail. Luke whispered the word without meaning to.

"What?" Ferg said. "What'd you say?"

Luke shook his head. "Nothing. Listen, I'm sorry. I just—"

"Get out," she said and raised one quivering finger. "Just get the fuck out, okay? I'll go for a walk or something, and when I get back, I want you gone."

She brushed past him toward the foyer, pausing just long enough to slip on her sneakers before yanking open the front door.

"Okay," Luke said, still eyeing the guitar amp. "Take your time."

25.

Mimi paced the house, going from room to room, moving furniture around, dusting the dustless cabinets and shelves. Gabby knew what she was doing. It was the same thing she did sometimes when Edwin stayed out late. Even the smallest task could provide a sense of relief. That's why Gabby had a skillet warming on the stovetop, a can of black beans open on the counter beside it. The beans had taken forever to find. As large as the house was, there wasn't much food. Gabby scrounged around in the spice cabinet, searching for some cumin, maybe some cilantro too, but all she'd come away with was garlic. The cooking oil was in the refrigerator for some reason. Along with a lime wedge in a Tupperware bowl. That was it, all she had to work with.

Despite the lack of ingredients, the kitchen was starting to smell like home. Gabby's stomach rumbled. She knew Mimi had to be hungry too, starving. Or maybe she always skipped lunch. She was so skinny. So different from Mr. Jackson with his toned chest and square jaw. Gabby wondered what Mimi would do when Luke came with the money. How would this fragile, mousy woman handle that exchange? Gabby didn't know and she didn't want to worry about it, either. Luke had to get the money first. He'd do just what Mimi had told him; he'd get the cash from his mistress. What would he do when he brought it there tonight? Gabby wasn't so sure about that.

"I'm going for a walk," Mimi said.

Mimi already had the front door open, stepping outside, before Gabby looked up from the stove. "Are you sure that's the best idea?"

"I can't keep waiting around in here. Those beans . . . The smell's making me sick."

The door shut and Gabby was struck by how much Mimi trusted her. Mimi had never once questioned the fifty thousand dollars. Her innocence made Gabby pause and think about what she was doing. She was getting this woman her son back, that's what she was doing. Why shouldn't she be paid for her time? The strange tone in Edwin's voice kept replaying in Gabby's mind. The way he'd waved that pistol around. Would he really pull the trigger? If it came to it, was Edwin that sort of man?

Gabby stirred the beans and watched Mimi through the window, her profile getting smaller and more distorted with every step. After three more turns of the wooden spoon, all Gabby could see was a blond ponytail bobbing at the end of the road. Edwin would soon be on that same road, gritting his teeth behind the steering wheel. There was no car seat in the Neon. Where would he put the child? Where had he put him when he'd driven to the plant? Where had he gone after that? It couldn't have been the trailer. Gabby had heard voices, soft whispers behind Edwin's flat tone, bringing up the ghosts of their past until she was in the backseat of a '77 Chevelle, cruising the strip and trying to talk to Edwin like the cheerleaders at Springdale High, losing her accent and her youth with every turn. There was only one place Edwin could've gone. It surprised Gabby that she hadn't thought of it sooner, but what surprised her even more was that Edwin had taken the risk.

Gabby told her phone to "Call Chito" as she added pepper to the beans. He answered on the third ring, saying, "*Gabriela,*" his voice like a song she hadn't heard in years.

"Are you alone?" Gabby said, still staring down the road. Even the ponytail was gone now. Gabby set the spoon beside the stove and started toward the window. "Chito?" she said. "Can you hear me?"

"Sorry, yes. I had to step outside. I'm alone now. Where are you?"

The chicken houses whirred in the distance.

"It doesn't matter," Gabby said. "I need you to do something for me."

"Doesn't matter? Do you know what Edwin has—"

"I know he has your pistol." Gabby waited, giving Chito a moment before she said, "Do you know what that means for you? A wannabe cholo with a record? If this gets out—"

"He stole it, Gabby. I swear. I was trying to help him with the kid."

"Oh, I'm sure the police will understand."

"I didn't think he was serious! You know how Edwin is, always gets these ideas he never goes through with. But then he stole my gun, and—"

"Take it back." The second the words left her mouth,

Gabby spotted Mimi outside the chicken house closest to the highway, bent at the waist, swinging both arms over the ground like a crazy person. It wasn't until Gabby noticed the white specks at her feet that she realized what Mimi was doing. She was trying to corral the broilers back through the chicken house door, and not having much luck. After a few more futile swipes, Mimi slapped at the air and started up the road again.

"Do you hear me?" Gabby said. "Just get it back."

"What about the kid?"

"Is he okay?"

"He is now," Chito said. "Ma is taking good care of him, but when Edwin first brought the boy in . . ."

Chito's words died away, leaving Gabby to imagine the rest, watching as Mimi stepped onto the paved driveway.

"I don't want no part of this, Gabby. That's what I'm saying. I mean, what's Edwin going to do with the kid?"

"He's going to give him back." The scent of burning beans pulled Gabby's attention to the stove. "He's going to leave your house soon and everything will be fine."

"You're not worried?"

The front doorknob turned, and Gabby's eyes went to it as she said into the phone, "Get the pistol, Chito, and I won't have anything to worry about."

The door opened before Gabby had a chance to hear Chito's reply.

"Did I hear you talking? While I was outside," Mimi said, neck splotchy, hair frazzled, "I thought I could hear your voice."

Gabby was back at the stove, standing right where she'd been when Mimi left. "No," she said, forearms flexing as she stirred the molten mess at the bottom of the pot. "I was just singing. I like to sing when I work sometimes."

The tip of Mimi's nose twitched like a rabbit, scanning the air for danger. "Okay," she said. "I just hope you sing better than you cook."

LUKE WAITED UNTIL he heard the front door close before he made a move for the guitar amp.

The word was right there. The same word Ferg had mentioned earlier when she was talking about her husband's money. *"How many of those guys keep stacks of it in their house? All rubber banded together in the back of his—"*

"Marshall," Luke spoke the word aloud as he spun the blocky guitar amp. It was lighter than he expected, less substantial than he'd hoped, or maybe it was just the casters. The four chrome wheels squeaked as they rolled. Luke saw the amplifier's rear cabinet before he got it turned all the way around. It wasn't much, just an open space with red and black wires dangling down into darkness. Luke held his breath and reached in.

He pushed his arm in deeper, all the way past his elbow. Then he felt it, the soft, cottony texture of old money. Stacks of it.

Each bundle of hundred-dollar bills was wrapped in a rubber band, just like Ferg had said. They weren't very thick, though. About half an inch. Some a little less. Luke was thumbing through a stack, trying to guess how many hundreds were packed in there, when the front door opened.

He should've known Ferg wouldn't stay gone long. Just

until the first drop of sweat darkened her sports bra. There was no time to count. Barely enough time to spin the amp back around and grab four more stacks, three in his right hand, two in his left, before Ferg's voice filled the foyer.

The last thing Luke heard before he slipped out the kitchen's exterior door—the one that led to the garage and the truck he'd thankfully parked right out close to the road—was the low, rattling hiss of a woman scorned.

26.

The flimsy door thwacked shut behind Edwin. The child in his arms squirmed, like he was ready to go, excited to leave this place. That's how Edwin felt, too, all the way up until he saw Maria Ortega staring down at him from behind the screen.

Edwin gave her a nod, backing away as he said, "Gracias." His feet never stopped moving, carrying him down the front walkway, stepping over the jagged cracks splintering the concrete, weeds sprouting up in between. Edwin thought of his mother and the superstitions she had passed on to him. A woman who saw black cats and upended saltshakers as signs of trouble to come. He could still feel her tugging at his elbow like she'd done when he was a boy, jerking him over cracks in the sidewalk as she walked him down to the bus stop early in the morning before school, afraid one misstep would send the life she'd worked so hard for spiraling down to el infierno.

The boy's blue eyes gave him hope. They seemed brighter somehow, more focused than they'd been before. Like all that had happened had sharpened him. The child yawned and rubbed his face with a fist. Edwin bounced him some more, humming the tune to the song he liked so much, so lost in the simplicity of the moment he almost missed his cousin, all three hundred pounds of him, ducked down on the far side of his Dodge Neon.

"It's time for me to go, Chito. I've already told your mother goodbye," Edwin said and kept humming the Johnny Cash song. He didn't want the boy crying while he said his farewells. It seemed like a bad omen.

Chito stood and jabbed both hands down in the pockets of his puffy, insulated jacket. "You lied to her, cousin."

"What lie?"

"Telling my mother this child's name is Jesus. Where did that come from?"

"Ah, I see," Edwin said and shifted the boy from one hip to the other.

"No, you don't *see* nothing. You don't say nothing, either. After all we did to help you?" Chito shook his blocky head two times, quick, like he'd been out here rehearsing his lines, preparing for this moment. "It's time you took that boy home, cousin. Just take him back."

"I didn't lie when I told her the child's name." The boy babbled and smiled, alive with energy now. "*Jesus Saucedo*. That sounds powerful. I've been called so many names. You remember how the guys on the team used to call me Saucy?"

Chito leaned back from the car, still keeping one hand shoved down in his jacket pocket. "I hear you, but I don't understand you, man. Not anymore."

"This child, what will the world call him? That's what I've been thinking. Look at him, cousin. Look at his eyes and see how happy he is. He wasn't like this when I found him."

"When you brought him here, he was almost—"

"Look at him now."

"Yeah, he looks good." Sweat stains blossomed across the front of Chito's blue and red Cruz Azul T-shirt, the down jacket much too warm for this early in October. "And that's why you need to take him back. Just take him back and all this will be over."

"Listen to my cousin." Edwin had his head turned, as if he were speaking to the child. "The dealer. The cholo."

"I know you and Gabby—"

"You know *nothing*." The boy's bottom lip curled, startled by Edwin's harsh tone. Edwin felt his own face mimicking the child's and hated himself for the softness. There'd been enough of that already, a whole lifetime's worth. From this point forward, Edwin would make his own rules. He would be the man, the father, he'd always wanted to be.

"Take it easy, Edwin. Just chill out. Okay?"

The boy began to whimper. Edwin's lips trembled under his mustache. "I'm leaving now," he said. "I've thanked your mother, but I have nothing else to say to you."

Chito stepped around the front of the car as Edwin jerked the driver-side door open, bringing the crying child into his lap as he sat down behind the wheel. He turned the key and the engine sputtered. He turned it again, staring through the windshield at Chito in his jacket. The child's cries reached a fever pitch as the engine finally turned over and the stereo clicked on. Edwin had the car in reverse, backing out into the street, when he saw his cousin's feet, both of them planted firmly atop a jagged crack in the driveway. Johnny Cash's voice drifted out through the speakers, putting words to the fear Edwin's mother had planted inside him so long ago. The ring of fire. *El infierno.*

IT WAS ALMOST like the truck was driving itself. Luke barely had to touch the wheel and it'd turn, spinning up another switchback curve. He'd gone straight for the hills after leaving the Ferguson mansion, wanting to get as far away from that place as fast as possible. It was getting late, a quarter till six, the sun almost down, what was left of it reflected in the burnt-orange leaves. The golden hour. That last burst of beauty before the dark. The truck turned at the top and started down the hill again, headed toward town.

Luke thought back to the morning they'd found the empty crib, how he'd handled Mimi then and there hadn't been any problems. The coffee was for her own good. Was that really what had made her call him? Was that why she'd *threatened* him? That wasn't the Mimi Luke knew. That wasn't the woman he'd married, the mother of his child. No. Someone else had told her to make that call.

Gabriela Menchaca was feisty like Ferg. Luke knew that much the moment she'd walked into his office. Gabby was a hot tamale, pure wildcat. Could she have gotten to his wife? It was a mistake leaving the two of them together in the house, alone. Luke saw that now. Maybe what had happened was some sort of backward-ass Stockholm syndrome. Gabby could've told Mimi all kinds of lies about the plant, the same sort of lies she could tell the news. Then what? Luke could kiss the promotion goodbye. There was also the problem of the money he'd taken from Steve

Ferguson. Luke probably should've counted it by now, but it felt so pointless. So stupid. What the hell would Edwin and Gabby do with that much dough?

At the bottom of the hill, the Ford eased off the highway and came to a stop under a red light. A car pulled up on the passenger side, a lowrider with the top down, blaring out the same Mexican shit music Luke heard every afternoon at the plant. The driver bobbed his head along with the beat, hair so slick and greasy it shined. Luke looked over his shoulder at the man and saw Edwin. There for a moment, then gone.

Luke tried to picture himself handing all that money over to Edwin in exchange for his son. Even if he did, that wouldn't be the end of it. There would still be loose ends, ways Edwin and Gabby could come back to bite Luke in the ass. Nothing like this ever happened at the plant. Not a chance. When Detmer Foods fired somebody, they were gone, deleted from the system, erased, along with any evidence of maltreatment. Everything nice and clean like the factory line's disinfectant sprays and scalding baths.

But somehow, Edwin was still out there with Luke's son. Edwin had nothing to lose. That was his biggest advantage, the only reason he'd been able to stay one step ahead of Luke thus far. There had to be something, though. Some lever Luke could pull, some knob he could twist, that would put his world back in order.

The lowrider revved its engine as the light turned green, back tires spinning before it sped away. Luke took his time, hands low on the wheel at four and eight, easing out from under the light. He didn't want to go too fast or rush into anything. He had time to kill.

SOMETHING ABOUT THE trailer seemed different in the dark. Edwin held tight to the child in his lap and checked his phone for the time. Almost nine. Enough time to gather their things and prepare for the road ahead. They were finally going home. All three of them. Even if they got the money, Edwin wouldn't give up the child. He couldn't. Not after all they'd been through.

The idea had come to Edwin during his stay at the Ortegas'. An image of his new little family on a road trip headed south, all the way down to Puerto Vallarta, the tourist-trap town near where he'd been born. They could make it there. After all of this was over, Edwin and Gabby would know their way around rich white people. They could find a job at a resort, or maybe a restaurant. No more blood and guts. Get on the other side of the business. A blond-haired, blue-eyed boy wouldn't seem so out of place with all those tourists around.

Edwin jabbed the gearshift into park and studied his trailer. The lone window burned bright against the night. "You remember this place?" Edwin lifted the boy from his lap, wondering for the first time how much the child would recall from these early days. What would Edwin tell him when he grew older and realized he was different, when the other kids asked him why he'd come to Mexico? It wouldn't be easy. Edwin knew this. He'd lived it, growing up in a country where kids asked him the same sort of questions. The answers his mother had given him, the stories she'd told him, her hopes and dreams, that's what Edwin had clung to, and it would be the same for his boy. He'd think of something.

The window still had Edwin's attention. It wasn't like

him to leave a light on. Gabby was always on him about the electric bill and wasting money. There was something else, though. Something Edwin could feel, the same way his mother got the pressure in her joints before it rained. The sky beyond the trailer swirled, another storm brewing. Edwin's knees throbbed, all the years he'd spent standing in line at the plant, his old pains trying to tell him something new. The boy jerked in Edwin's hands. His miniature body tensed like he could feel what was coming, too. Edwin reached over the child and spun the volume knob. The boy's body relaxed, recognizing the familiar tune.

The song had become ingrained in Edwin. He'd heard it before, sure, but now it was a part of him. It marked the start of his new life, the one he would share with the boy. Maybe that's what he felt. Maybe that was all. There was nothing different about this place. The trailer was the same; it was Edwin who had changed.

Edwin sat the child in the passenger seat and watched his bottom lip curl. Before he stepped out of the vehicle, Edwin gave the volume knob a couple more turns. The music was loud enough he could still hear the mariachi horns even after he shut the door. It was raining now like it'd been at the creek. Had it ever stopped? Edwin walked into the storm without shielding his face or his eyes, the smell of dead leaves rising. The blue glow from the bug zapper mixed with the orange coming through the window, calling to him, lighting his way.

Edwin had both feet on the first step when he noticed the door, the way the frame was cracked, the wood splintered, tiny shards sticking out like broken bones. Lightning flashed, revealing a muddy footprint outlined above the doorknob. By the time the thunder finally rumbled in the distance, Edwin was standing back beside his car again, opening the passenger-side door, the music mixing with the storm, the same tired song as before.

The boy didn't fuss as the rain pelted his hair. He almost seemed to like it. Edwin reached over his head and opened the glove box. A small bulb flickered on. The boy pawed at Edwin as he rummaged through stacks of napkins, pushed past the tattered owner's manual, but could not find the pistol.

Another flash of silent lightning and Edwin remained hunched inside his car, waiting to hear the low growl of thunder, trying to decide if it was worth it. He had the boy. He'd have Gabby and the money soon enough. What else did he need? All that remained in the trailer were memories from a life that was no more.

The thunder boomed low across the trailer park, closer this time, loud enough Edwin's eyes fell to the boy, smiling back up at him as the rain came down harder now, parting his golden hair. When was the last time he'd eaten? Edwin thought. Or had his diaper changed?

Edwin shut the car door and started back for the trailer, remembering the couple hundred dollars' worth of baby formula, all those diapers and wipes piled on top of his plywood table, enough to last the trip to Puerto Vallarta.

Standing before the bottom step again, Edwin told himself the busted trailer door didn't mean anything. It wasn't the first time someone had broken in. What would they take, anyway? Still, he felt exposed without the pistol. He realized now what must've happened—Chito in his puffy jacket sniffing around in his mother's driveway.

So be it.

Edwin skipped the second step, both feet stopping on the third as he lifted a hand toward the door, his whole life a storm spinning around him. He waited, hoping for lightning again, a strike so close it carried the thunder with it, an omen he could see and hear at the same time, something like his mother's superstitions telling him which way to go. But there was only the rain, the long steady rush of it, pushing Edwin's hand down as his fingers found the knob.

27.

The two women sat together on the front porch steps, watching as thunderheads replaced the mountains and blocked out the moon. Mimi saw the storm coming but did not move. She could feel Gabby sitting beside her, fidgeting a little every time a new bolt of lightning flashed blue in the distance.

"All this waiting . . ." Gabby said then stopped to clear her throat, shaking off the rust of such a long silence. "This is the worst."

Mimi nodded.

"Do you want to talk about it?" Gabby said.

"What?"

"All of it. None of it. I don't care. Just something."

Mimi watched the wind sweep a plastic Walmart sack across her driveway. "None of it," she said, finally.

"Okay. Nothing it is." Gabby tapped her chin. "When you were little, what did you want to be?"

Mimi hadn't thought of that question in forever. Growing up, it was all she could think about. A doctor. A lawyer. A schoolteacher. Kindergarten, maybe? All the regular jobs. She was majoring in education when she'd met Luke Jackson. He told her she'd never have to work another day in her life, and he was right, but somewhere along the way Mimi had stopped thinking about what she wanted at all.

"You go first," Mimi said. "What did you want to be?"

"A chicken plucker, what else?"

"Be serious."

"I don't know. I was in these honors English classes in high school. I thought I was going to college." Gabby laughed again but her heart wasn't in it. "I like to cook. So something to do with that, maybe?"

"Judging by those beans you burnt, I'd say you better keep thinking."

Gabby rolled her eyes. "Your turn."

Even though Mimi had known the question was coming, she still had to take a moment to come up with an answer. "I guess, more than anything, I just wanted to be a mom, but now . . ." Her mouth went dry. Her insides burned tight and hot. "Now I feel like I wanted it too bad, or something. Does that make sense? I feel like my worrying led to all this."

Gabby waited, shaking her head as each second passed. Then she stood. "I'd like to show you something."

Mimi stared past her to the storm blowing up from the south.

"Come on. Let's take a walk," Gabby said. "It's better than sitting here and talking about nothing."

"But it's about to storm."

"It's always about to storm somewhere, anywhere. You know?"

Gabby extended a hand. Mimi stared at it a moment, noticing the woman's knuckles again. Misshapen and round, like five swollen buckeyes. Mimi reached up and felt the raw strength in Gabby's grip. A moment later, they were moving, venturing off the gravel driveway and into the brittle grass, the world around them preparing for the cold that seemed to come later and later each year. Mimi wasn't thinking of a final destination. It was just nice to be moving again, a way to clear her head before the wind began to howl.

They were halfway to the chicken houses when Mimi caught that old familiar stench, the chemical aftertaste that always made her lungs clench. *"It'll be fun to have a few chickens around, something to keep us busy."* Those had been Luke's exact words, and Mimi had believed him. Even as she watched the bulldozers and the backhoes tearing away their land, she'd believed him. Luke took Mimi inside the chicken houses the day after they were done, before there were any chickens in the coop. Mimi had been amazed by the size, imagining the place filled with tiny yellow birds, maybe even bringing Tuck in one day to watch them grow. Then the trucks arrived and the smell overtook their property, erasing any misconceptions Mimi had had about Luke's plan.

Gabby stopped when she came to the side door. Mimi could already hear the tweets and clucks coming through the sheet metal walls. Thousands of them.

"I think the workers wear masks," Mimi said.

Gabby opened the door. The smell rushed out, stronger than ever. Mimi brought her elbow to her face.

"I—" Mimi coughed as her eyes began to water. "I can't go in there."

Gabby said, "Yes, you can," and stepped through the door.

Mimi stood alone outside the chicken house and thought of Luke and the orange plastic pill bottle she'd found in the master bath. It was a miracle she wasn't in the hospital. What would he do when he got there tonight? Mimi didn't want to think about that. Not yet. She yanked open the chicken house door and hustled to catch up with Gabby but didn't make it far.

The hot stink was so strong Mimi doubled over, coughing as more tears came, clouding her vision. The chickens moved in waves, blurry for a moment until Mimi blinked them into focus. Gabby was up ahead of her, holding a long stick, a repurposed broom handle, maybe? Every time Gabby moved, the chickens fanned out around her feet, a wake of mangy white feathers.

"Forty-five days." Gabby's voice fluttered behind the chorus of chirps, the whirling fans churning the musty air. "That's how long they live."

The tears in Mimi's eyes ran down her cheeks and her vision cleared, focusing on the stick in Gabby's hand, noticing the two nails hammered into the tip of it.

"You said it was your worrying that led to this?" Gabby tapped the stick on the ground. "So, I want to tell you my story. I want you to hear what I worried about."

Mimi opened her lips to speak but the thick air filled her mouth, a taste like sawdust. She coughed and nodded, then coughed some more.

"But if I tell you," Gabby said and moved ahead of Mimi, the length of the chicken house spanning out before her, the eight fans churning at the end like the bottom of a blender, "you have to listen. Really listen."

"I'm listening," Mimi managed.

Gabby used the stick like a cane as she started walking again, staying in the narrow lane between the feeding tubes. The broilers scurried all around her. Mimi took a few quick steps, trying to catch up, straining to hear her voice amid the whirr and churn of the chicken house.

"See those little nozzles?" Gabby said and pointed at the spigots with the stick. "Did Luke tell you what he feeds the chickens? The same ones that end up in the fajitas at La Huerta?"

"I don't see what this has to do with anything. What time is it?"

"The chickens are part of my story." Gabby stopped and waved the stick over the birds' heads. They didn't move away this time, like they trusted her now. "For seven years, broilers have been my life."

Mimi kept standing there, waiting for Gabby to start walking again. Instead, the stick came down. The nail tacked to the end tore through the air and caught the back leg of one of the chickens.

"Gabby!" Mimi shrieked. "What are you—"

"I'm telling you my story." Gabby dragged the wounded bird through the sawdust. Even with its leg bent backward and the strange-looking claw Mimi had never noticed before folded in on itself, the bird still didn't make a sound. Like it hadn't felt anything, eyes wide open, blinking as Gabby brought it into her arms.

"You see how she stays quiet? Even when I wounded her, she didn't squawk. She didn't make a sound."

Mimi remembered Gabby with the tape across her mouth, her dark eyes empty above the silver strip.

"When you don't have a voice, what's the point?" Gabby stroked the chicken's head with two fingers. A thin red line dripped onto her forearm. "This is what's called a 'cull.'"

Mimi spoke the word but didn't understand it.

"A cull is a broiler that's of no use. Did you notice this one limping before I"—Gabby mimed swinging the stick, then lowered the wounded bird headfirst toward the ground. The broiler's blank eyes seemed to widen as Gabby's heel pressed its beak into the sawdust. When Gabby removed her foot and brought the chicken back to her chest, there was no longer any fear left in those glowing orange eyes. No pain. Nothing.

Mimi clamped one hand over her mouth. "You—you—"

"Let me show you," Gabby said and spread the chicken's feathers with her fingers to reveal the breast. "Every day, for ten hours, this is what I do. Can you imagine?"

A sharp snap kept Mimi from answering, the bird's wings cracking. Gabby had most of the feathers plucked from the chicken's chest, the two wings lying at her feet, when she held the dead bird out for Mimi.

"Take it."

The place where Gabby had pulled the feathers away shined slick and pink. Mimi touched the spot and thought of Tuck. It was still warm.

"This was my job," Gabby said, pointing. "I pulled the breast from the bone. Six days a week. And that would've been fine. No problem. I can handle hard work. Even the cold."

"The cold?"

"Forty degrees. So bacteria doesn't grow. Makes your fingers hurt, bad, but that's not why Edwin stole your son."

It was so hot inside the chicken house. Mimi could feel nothing except the heat.

"They don't even let us go to the bathroom." Gabby lifted the stick, pointing the tip into the wad of chickens. "The other workers wet themselves."

Mimi followed Gabby's aim and saw another dead chicken lying in the sawdust, pink claws trampling its flattened body as the other birds made their way toward the spigots.

"But I wouldn't do it. I wouldn't let him take that from me."

"What did you do?" Mimi said.

Gabby started walking toward the fans at the end of the house. Mimi followed, still clutching the dead chicken, afraid to drop it for fear of the other birds' spurs.

The fans were so loud, Mimi could barely hear Gabby as she said, "I didn't drink, and because I wouldn't drink— because I wouldn't let your husband and his plant treat me like that bird in your hands—I lost something. Something I thought I wanted but wasn't sure and that made it even worse. The guilt, you know? Like what you were saying on the porch. Like I caused it." Gabby's words were chopped by the whirling fans. "But when I look back on it, I see God has a sense of humor. You know why?"

"No . . . I don't. What did you lose?"

"I lost a child," Gabby said, turning to face Mimi, "after exactly forty-five days."

Tears welled up in Mimi's eyes, tears from her heart, not the musty conditions inside the chicken house. Her fingers trembled around the carcass, all the warmth gone from it now.

"It's simple, really," Gabby said, lifting her hands and performing a tearing motion. "You just pull the meat from the bone. I want you to feel it, then imagine doing it for ten hours with a child growing inside you, crying out for the water you won't drink."

A black-and-white image slid across Mimi's mind, the first ultrasound where she'd seen Tuck. Just a blob, really. More like a raw chicken breast than the child he would become. Mimi knew what Gabby wanted her to do, but she also knew what she was holding was more than just a culled broiler. All the pieces of Gabriela's story coalesced in Mimi's mind, coming together to form the picture of a child who was never born.

Mimi turned and ran back down the corridor. The chickens parted, forming a path out ahead of her. She noticed more dead birds on the open ground, but she did not stop. Not until she reached the door and pushed it open, gulping in the fresh air as she dropped to the ground.

It was raining, a full-on storm with lightning and thunder. Mimi could barely feel the gusts walloping the sheet metal roof. She held the bird with one hand and patted the damp dirt with the other. When her fingers found a flat rock, she picked it up and began to dig. She was still digging when the door swung open behind her.

Mimi looked up at Gabby, a quick, harried glance, then returned to her work.

The hole was deep enough for the mangled bird to lie flat. Deep enough Mimi was able to fill the rest of the mud in and cover its contorted features. When she was finally done, Mimi placed both hands on her knees but she did not stand. She was still lost in the frigid plant, still trying to imagine all those broilers coming down the line. The very same birds that would soon be fed to the slaughtering machine, Luke's machine, the one that had taken Gabby's child.

CHICKEN BLOOD AND mud speckled their hands, their fingers. The two women were back on the porch again. It was getting late, close to ten. The rain was stronger now, just like their bond. As wretched as the chicken house had been, Mimi understood the importance of it. Why Gabby had decided to tell her that story before the men arrived. Gabby needed Mimi to trust her, and she did.

"I'm afraid Edwin thinks your son will heal the pain from the child we lost," Gabby said without taking a breath between her words. "The way he talked to me on the phone, I knew, and I should've told—"

"You're telling me now."

"But you don't understand, even after what I just showed you. You can't understand what we've been through."

Mimi said, "I can," and stood, forcing herself to remember the pain she'd tried to forget for so long. The heartbreak she'd suffered before Tuck was born. The new life that grew inside her and died before she even had the chance to give it a name.

"You lost a child, too?"

Mimi nodded. It was all she could do.

"How did it feel?"

Mimi breathed in and let her mind drift into the pain. "Exactly like when I woke up Friday morning," she said, staring straight back at Gabby, "and realized Tuck was gone."

Silence filled the space between them, a new silence louder than the storm, the hurt the two women shared out in the open.

"It took two times?"

"Yes," Mimi said. "Maybe it'll be the same for you." She lifted a finger, moved it halfway through the space between them, but stopped short of touching Gabby's skin. "This is what I want you to tell Edwin tonight, when he brings my son back. Tell him you're ready to try again."

"What if I'm not?"

Mimi hadn't considered that, but after what Gabby had shown her, she understood. It would be hard, almost impossible, to raise a child while working in the plant. Gabby wanted something better. And after what she'd been through, she deserved it.

"Tell him you are," Mimi said. "Just for tonight, just long enough to put all of this behind us."

Gabby nodded. "Maybe with the money, I'll be ready. I mean—"

Mimi's fingers found Gabby's wrist and squeezed. The money scared her. It'd been so long since she'd heard from Luke. All those hours of silence. Where had he been? What had he been doing? Was he really going to play by Mimi's rules?

Gabby turned her hand over and pressed her palm into Mimi's. Their fingers laced. "A part of me feels like I should say thank you."

"No," Mimi said. "That's not—"

"Another part, a bigger part, feels like this money was ours already."

"What?"

"Your husband, he owed us at least this much. Probably more," Gabby said. "For the extra hours we worked at the plant. So much overtime. He never paid us, though. I added it all up one night. I was just curious. I showed Edwin." Gabby bit her bottom lip. Her fingers tightened. "I'm sorry, Mimi. I feel like I—"

"No," Mimi said. "*I'm* sorry. Luke's sorry. Everybody at Detmer . . ."

Gabby shook her head until Mimi stopped. Then her mouth began to move, lips on the cusp of forming words when a chime cut the moment short. Gabby leaned up on her side as her hand slid into her back pocket, retrieving her phone.

"It's him," Gabby said and turned the screen so Mimi could see the text. "Edwin. He says he's on his way."

Mimi thought again of Luke's silence. She checked the phone for the time. A quarter till ten.

"I can't believe this is really happening," Gabby said. "I'm not ready."

"I didn't think I was ready, either. But I was, I am," Mimi said as the phone screen went dark. "We have to be."

28.

The rain fell like a thousand tiny voices, mingling with the words rushing through Gabby's mind: *Once we have the money, we can leave. We can start over, Edwin. I'm ready to try again.* Her lips moved, repeating the words until they didn't sound right anymore. Maybe they'd never sounded right. All the way back to their senior year, the year they'd moved in together. Had Gabby loved him then? Yes. Of course. But Edwin was different now, so different from the boy she'd first shared her bed with. Time slowed down in the midst of the storm, the same way it did at the plant as Gabby fended off the broilers and worked her way through to the end of her shift. Now, though, she was waiting for Edwin, waiting to see his eyes again. It would only take one look and Gabby would know whether she would need the words, those lines that didn't sound right in her head.

Gabby glanced to her left. Mimi was still there beside her, the two women connected by the rain. Mimi's blond hair cut slick, lines down her face like scars. Gabby turned back to the road as the headlights appeared, burning through the storm like two yellow eyes—Edwin's eyes—watching her from a distance.

The wind slapped the rain sideways against Gabby's face, but she did not feel it. She just kept repeating the words she'd say to Edwin when she saw him again, the promise of a new life if only he'd take it. Gabby squinted and saw the shape of the Dodge through the storm, a squatty, bug-shaped vehicle that was always giving Edwin fits. It had not failed him tonight. It had brought him back to her.

The car stopped at the far edge of the driveway, right before the concrete started. Headlights flashed. Two quick strobes, a signal. There were no other lights down the road, no sign of Luke.

"It's fine." Mimi nodded twice, once to herself, then again as she turned to face Gabby. "Go to him."

"But . . ."

"No, this is better, I think." Mimi spoke without taking her eyes off the car. "Yeah. It'll be good for you to talk to Edwin before Luke gets here."

Gabby whispered, "Okay," so softly she couldn't hear her own voice over the storm. When she stepped out from under the awning, the rain stung her face, every inch of bare skin. Of all the things she'd confessed to Mimi, she hadn't said anything about Edwin wanting to keep the child. It was too much. Too crazy to even consider. Still, she walked on, each step a struggle, a matter of will.

The tinted side window came down, black liquid glass revealing more blackness inside. Gabby waited a moment before bending to it, going over her lines a final time. Just tell him what he wants to hear, Gabby thought and ducked down, bringing her face even with the window before she said, "I am ready, Edwin. Ready to try—"

The emptiness in Edwin's eyes washed her words away, two hollow orbs staring up at Gabby, past her, and off into the world beyond.

THE LOOK ON Gabby's face reminded Luke of Edwin the moment after he'd opened the trailer door and stepped into his trap. Jim Jackson would've been proud. All those years later and his son had finally learned to wait, sitting on that stale sofa like a statue for two hours straight. Barely breathing with his finger curled around the trigger, the barrel aimed straight at the door, just like it was pointed out the car window at Gabriela Menchaca now.

Luke said, "Get in the back," and tried bouncing Tuck with his legs, but the boy just kept squirming. Tuck didn't have a clue about what his daddy was doing. What he'd done. How Luke had come so far there wasn't any going back. That was something the line workers never understood. Guys like Luke didn't get to the top by accident. Sacrifices were made. Hours upon hours, *worked*. Luke Jackson, the son of a southern Arkansas soybean farmer, was set to be one of Detmer Foods's highest paid employees come Monday morning, and he'd earned it. He'd made the tough choices. He'd scraped and clawed. That was the difference between Luke and a guy like Edwin Saucedo. Luke was willing to work for his dream.

The way Luke had it figured, Mimi would never have to know. Secrets were the secret to a happy marriage. Luke's singular maxim rang truer than ever. Once all of this was over, the things he'd kept from Mimi—the hard truths only he could stomach—would allow them to start over again. A man with a title like "Executive Officer of Poultry" needed a family, not a divorce.

Mimi stood a few steps out past the front porch's awning, getting wet for no reason. Even that close, she still wouldn't be able to see Luke through the Dodge's tinted windows. For all she knew, he was still on his way. And as soon as Gabby crawled into the backseat, Luke would get the hell out of there. Make it look like Edwin and Gabby had made a run for it. Let the authorities find the car and two dead Mexicans down by the waters of Clear Creek. Luke knew just the spot.

"I'm not telling you again," Luke said, jabbing the Springfield at Gabby's chest. "Get in the fucking car."

She didn't move, but Tuck just kept thrashing around, wriggling in Luke's lap like he'd been for the whole drive out to the farm.

"You hear me?" Luke said and pushed the rifle's barrel up past Edwin's nose, close enough he could see the dark red blood congealed in the dead man's mustache. Memories of his father slapping those wounded squirrels against the trunks of tall oak trees wriggled through Luke's mind as his finger found the trigger. He was going to have to shoot the woman and leave her there. Maybe Mimi would think Edwin did it. *Yeah.* As long as she never saw Luke, it wouldn't matter. All he had to do was hand Mimi her son and all sins would be forgiven. No questions asked. He pictured himself driving back up Monday morning, hell, maybe even later that night after he'd disposed of the bodies and dropped the money back off at Ferg's.

The money.

That's what had given Luke the idea in the first place. He simply couldn't imagine handing all that cold, hard cash over to a couple of Mexicans. But now? Maybe now it was just the bait he needed.

Luke popped open the glove box and said, "You see this?" as he grabbed a banded stack of hundreds. "This is what you wanted, right? This is why you stole my kid, mindfucked my wife. Come on. Get in the car, Menchaca, and I'll give it to you."

Gabby didn't get in the car. She didn't move anything except her lips, knotting them into an expression Luke had never seen before. Not from his mother. Not from Mimi. Gabby was different from any woman he'd ever known. The sound of her laughter filled the space between them. A wild, defiant cackle that did not match the tears streaming down her cheeks.

It caught Luke off guard, condensed his whole world down to this woman with terror in her eyes. He was really going to have to shoot the bitch. Right there in the driveway. He eased off on the trigger, just like his father had taught him to do, expecting the Springfield to buck. Instead the weight in his lap rolled forward.

The most basic of all human instincts coursed through Luke's blood as he let go of the rifle with one hand and lunged down beneath the steering wheel, trying to grab his son.

Luke caught Tuck by the back of his onesie before he hit the floorboard. The rescue move only took a second—a fraction of a second—but when Luke's eyes jerked back to the open window they found only the storm, the rain clanging against the sheet-metal chicken houses like rounds of machine-gun fire.

Tuck finally broke his silence as Luke stepped out of the car and shouldered the Springfield, tracking Gabby's shadow as she sprinted for the house. He couldn't hear the cries of his son or see the storm still swirling in the sky. Luke was aware only of what he saw through the rifle's scope, the crosshairs hovering over the woman's back as she ran. Legs churning, arms pumping, Gabby screamed, "He killed him! He killed Ed—" and then she was gone, replaced by a woman Luke almost didn't recognize, running headfirst into the crosshairs.

MOST PEOPLE THINK love and hate are opposites. Not Mimi. Not in that moment. The second she heard Tuck's cries, she understood that the distance between is twisted, more circular than straight. As she came closer to Luke—close enough to see his eyes, the same pale blue as her son's—Mimi found herself at the place where the two ends meet. And then she was past him. She did not stop. Even when Gabby called out for her, Mimi kept moving.

Her chest was heaving by the time she reached the open door, Gabriela Menchaca nothing more than a memory as she finally slid to a stop on the gravel. Using Gabby's phone as a light, Mimi ducked down beside the car, searching the darkened cab for her son.

Blood dripped from the passenger seat to the center console, pooling in the cup holders below. Mimi was so focused on finding Tuck, she didn't notice the blood, not even the dead man slumped in the passenger seat. The flood was upon her, everything she'd fought so hard to avoid surrounding her now, and then she heard it.

The same song as before.

Mimi spun the volume knob on the car stereo until the music died away. The last time she'd seen Tuck that song had been playing. It was gone now, leaving only the dead man she could not see and a brief window of silence before two raspy coughs rose up from the floor.

Mimi jerked the phone toward the sound, revealing everything inside her that had come together to make her son, all those pieces she'd lost, staring up at her from the floorboard.

She reached down and brought Tuck into her chest. The tears on his cheeks mixed with the rainwater dripping from his mother's hair. This was the moment she'd been waiting for, praying for, but it was short-lived. Mimi couldn't ignore the scene transpiring through the rain-slicked windshield: Luke's profile outlined in the headlights' glare, the rifle barrel jutting from his body, the muzzle pointed straight down at Gabby's chest.

The glass made it feel like television, a barrier between Mimi and the outside world, the real world, where women like Gabriela Menchaca never got the best of men like Luke Jackson. Mimi reached for the volume knob on the stereo again, turning that old country song all the way up, loud enough Tuck wouldn't have to hear what was about to happen, what always happened when somebody got in Luke's way.

29.

Gabby felt Luke behind her but she would not turn to face him. Instead, she stared through the rain to the rusty Dodge, her mind playing tricks with what little time she had left, whizzing back to when Edwin had first brought the car home.

"It's a steal," he'd said, trying to convince her of something he knew wasn't true. There were holes in the muffler, all four tires bald, but it had carried them the five or so miles from the trailer to the plant, six days a week for seven years, all those carefree nights spent cruising the strip in the backseat of Chito's Chevelle nothing more than a memory they'd shared, a lucid dream that was over now, their lives cut short because Edwin had made another bad deal.

Edwin, Gabby thought and squeezed her eyes shut. She felt the tears now, warmer than the rain, still salty by the time they reached her lips. The tears tasted like Edwin after a long shift. The memory of him surged inside her, strong enough to give her hope that the man she'd seen slumped inside the Dodge hadn't been Edwin at all. Maybe he was still alive. Maybe he'd come for her.

When Gabby opened her eyes, the scene she found did not match what she'd imagined. Luke stood where Edwin should've been, the rifle still clenched in his hands, aimed down at her. Gabby regretted sacrificing the cull earlier. There were other ways she could've made her point. Then again, she had saved it from the shackles, the rub bars, the blade. She thought of her mother in Celaya. *Isabela*. How long would it take the news of her death to travel that far? Would her family pay to ship her body back to Mexico? Could they? She was still thinking of her mother when she heard the music, the mariachi horns growing louder, like a train whistle blaring, sounding the alarm, clearing a path for the two tons of metal roaring across the driveway.

The Dodge's front bumper struck Luke behind the thighs, bending him back into an acute angle over the hood as it plowed forward. A flash of red and white erupted, the rifle firing into the night, and then it was gone, sucked beneath the car's undercarriage along with the man who held it.

The car jerked to a stop a few inches from Gabby's feet. She stared into the headlights and blinked. Then blinked again, tapping her chest with both hands as the song mixed with the storm.

I fell for you like a child . . .

Gabby spun on her knees, unable to comprehend what she saw lying beneath the Dodge's dented grille. Luke's eyes were still open, staring up at the sky as the rain came down, but all the life had gone out of them.

Oh, but the fire went wild.

Gabby was scooting backward down the driveway, small bits of loose rock jabbing into her palms, when she heard a faint click. The driver-side door opened, a few inches, just enough space for Gabby to hope that Edwin would emerge and save her like he'd promised he would back at Springdale High.

Instead, a cry to match the horror in Gabby's heart erupted from the Dodge's cab, a guttural wail. Different from the child's—stronger, louder—yet the same because the boy was crying, too, a wretched howl barely audible over the shrieks of his mother.

Through the crack in the door, Gabby could finally see Mimi, head back, eyes clamped, both hands covering her ears. The boy wobbled in her lap, fighting to keep his balance.

"I-I—" Mimi bellowed between sobs. "*Luke!*"

Mimi's whole body contracted, like the weight of what she'd done might split her in two. Gabby wanted to run to her, but her legs wouldn't move. Her arms wouldn't work. The rain fell and pooled beneath her, cutting small streams through the gravel.

Gabby fought each drop as she stood and pushed through the storm until she was back beside Mimi again, this woman who'd chosen Gabby's life over her own husband's. Mimi didn't look up. She didn't stop screaming, but the boy did. He saw Gabriela standing there and reached for her.

The second Gabby took Tuck into her arms, the shrieking stopped. Mimi slapped at her thighs. The boy's head was warm despite the rain as Gabby passed him back to his mother. Mimi brought him in to her chest and began rocking. The way she moved was broken, quick spasms in the cramped space. Gabby wondered if the child could feel it. Years from now, when thunder clapped and lightning struck, would he remember this night?

"Go inside," Gabby said, then said it again, like Edwin always did when he wasn't certain of something but wanted to be. "Please. Just take him inside."

"But—" Mimi blinked, coming back into the moment. Her eyes moved toward the headlights. They only made it halfway before Gabby said, "I will take care of this. All of it."

"*No*. You can't . . ."

"Yes. For him." Gabby touched a warm spot near her elbow, the place where the child's head had been. "I'll do it for him."

She watched Mimi's mouth move then raised one hand. Gabby didn't want to hear it. She couldn't allow herself to think of any other way.

"None of this ever happened. I was never here. When it's done," Gabby said, "we can never see each other again."

Mimi didn't speak. She didn't nod. She didn't have to.

"Take your son home." Gabby turned and pointed. The porch light flickered beyond the deluge, but it was still there. "Put him in his crib where he belongs."

Mimi's voice called Gabby's eyes back from the light. She watched the woman's mouth moving, forming words that touched that hole in Gabby's gut, the pain that remained off to one side where her child had been for a moment, a scar that would never heal.

"No, not the crib. Not tonight." Mimi took one short step toward the light. "Tonight, he'll sleep with me."

Gabby watched her walk away until she heard the front door close, a punctuation mark at the end of Mimi's story, but not Gabriela's. No matter how close they'd gotten over the last twenty-four hours—regardless of the pain they shared—their stories were not the same. There was no one coming for Gabby. Her only way out was the car still parked in the drive.

She looked past the Dodge to the road, trying to keep more tears from falling, telling herself that if Edwin had come for her in the day none of this would've happened. He could've handed Mimi her son, gotten Gabby—and then what? They would've been back in the trailer and Mr. Levon would've come knocking again, asking for money they did not have.

Gabby squatted down eye level with the cab. Edwin was still slumped in the passenger seat, but that's not how Gabby saw him. She saw him in the back, laughing at one of Chito's stupid jokes, holding Gabriela like he'd held her before they ever worked their first shift. Back when there'd been time enough to dream. Gabby reached out and touched his hand, so cold, so different from the child she'd held only minutes before. She was still holding his hand when she spotted something she'd missed before, something that changed everything.

Gabby knew that their life together would've never been enough for Edwin, but through his mistakes, he'd given her a chance at something better.

There was blood on the stack of wrinkled bills in Edwin's lap. Past his knees, the glove box door gaped, revealing four more stacks held together with rubber bands, each one promising a new life in shades of red and green, a new dream that started like any other. Staring down at all that money, Gabby realized something she'd always felt but never fully understood until right then: for every American Dream there is a corresponding nightmare. Every fortune, even a small one, is built on the back of some great sin.

What came next would not be easy. There was still more work to be done, always more, a whole night's worth of cleaning and lifting, then driving to some new place she hadn't decided on yet. Gabby was cold. It was late. Her wrists hurt just thinking about it, but she had learned long ago how to ignore the pain. The dead man beneath the car had taught her that much.

30.

Over a year later—eighteen months since the headlights, the rifle, the storm—Tuck waddled his way through a restaurant's double doors. He had a Spider-Man backpack strapped over his shoulders; Mimi a few steps behind him, sporting a blunt cut, parted straight down the middle, the ends the same length on all sides. She kept her distance, giving Tuck enough space to explore. He was two years old now, and so full of curiosity he made his mother smile constantly. She'd let his hair grow long, longer than hers. It fluttered behind his ears as he ran circles around the restaurant's lobby.

Mimi gave the hostess a *boys-will-be-boys* look and said, "Table for two, please. No, wait. Make that one and a half."

"Will he need a high chair?"

"He'll need one," Mimi said, watching her son stick out his tongue at the sugar skulls beaming down from the stucco-adobe walls, "but I'll give him a chance to be a big boy first."

The hostess nodded and ducked beneath the booth,

affording Mimi time to watch Tuck, down on all fours now, crawling beneath the archway that led to the dining area.

"Table or a booth?" the hostess said, two laminated menus in her hands, along with one quartered sheet of paper and a pack of crayons tucked into the fold.

"Just keep us as far away from other people as possible."

"That won't be a problem." The hostess started through the archway, explaining to Mimi how Sunday afternoons were usually slow after the church crowd cleared out.

Mimi snapped her fingers and Tuck fell in line behind his mother as they entered the dining area. It was beautiful. Nothing like Mimi had expected, so far from La Huerta's cheesy décor it was almost sad.

Chavela was the hottest new Mexican restaurant in eastern Oklahoma for a reason. Candles spaced out every ten feet or so gave off a soft glow even in the afternoon light, flickering against the exposed ironwork lining the ceiling. Colorful ceramics sat on shelves in the back corner of the room. A tile mural hung directly above the hacienda-style table where the hostess had come to a stop. She was placing the menus in front of the straight-back chairs when Mimi said, "I'll have a margarita."

"And for your son?"

"Tuck?" Mimi said. "Tell the woman what you'd like to drink, please."

The boy glanced up through his shock of golden hair, trying to get his backpack straps hooked over the chair. When he finally did, he blew the hair from his eyes and said, "Ma-ga-*wita*."

The hostess laughed, waiting for Mimi to correct her son's order. Mimi paused long enough for the silence to become uncomfortable, and then she added, "A *virgin* margarita, of course."

The hostess turned away as Mimi took the menu and began scanning the entrées. Her eyes jumped from dish to dish, finding words she didn't recognize: flautas, non-dairy horchata, and elote. The words she did know were even stranger: soy, mushroom, hibiscus, and cactus. *Cactus?* Tuck was scribbling away on the child's menu when the waiter appeared, a thirtysomething Mexican male with a clean face and boyish features.

"I must be reading this wrong." Mimi jabbed a finger at the menu. "Where are the chicken fajitas?"

The waiter placed the margarita glasses on the table and slid one Mimi's way, saying, "Ah, señora, this is a *vegan* restaurant."

With the long-stemmed glass to her lips, Mimi took a sip and scrunched her brow. "You call *this* a margarita?"

"We don't use the mix. Everything in Chavela is auténtico." He smiled. "You know this word?"

Mimi thumped the glass back down on the table hard enough the lime-green liquid sloshed over the rim. "No chicken fajitas and margaritas that taste like lime juice? *Authentic?* I thought this place was supposed to be *good?*" Mimi paused and took another long swig. She needed something in her system to keep up her act. "You seriously don't have anything with meat in it? My son's allergic to soy."

The waiter placed both hands on his waist. "Apologies, señora. Would you like to speak with the manager?"

"The manager?" Mimi snapped. "I'd like to speak to the *owner*."

"Yes, of course."

Mimi brought the glass to her lips again, finishing what was left of her drink without another word. The waiter's heels clacked across the concrete floors before he disappeared into the kitchen. Mimi's head felt fuzzy. She pushed a stray strand of hair behind Tuck's right ear as he sipped his lime juice, worrying about his teeth because she hadn't worried about much in so long. Not after what they'd been through. But she wanted to see this place with her own eyes. The vegan restaurant in Tulsa that everyone in northwest Arkansas kept talking about, the two-hour drive west a small price to pay for "authentic" Mexican cuisine.

When the kitchen doors flapped open again, Mimi stayed turned toward Tuck, the part in her hair hiding her eyes, listening as another set of footsteps started her way, softer than the waiter's had been.

"There's a problem?"

With her head still down, Mimi could see the owner's feet, long toes stuffed into a faded pair of Birkenstock sandals.

"Maybe." Mimi turned and let her hair fall from her face as she stared up into the woman's dark brown eyes. "Sit down and let's talk about it."

The look on Gabby's face, it was like she'd been waiting for this day to come, but now that it was here, she didn't know what to do. She sat in the open chair, the one without a menu or drink in front of it, and said, "Your son, he's allergic to soy?"

"No, but he's terrified of storms."

Gabby leaned back and crossed her legs. She hadn't cut her hair like Mimi, or made any other drastic changes, she just looked good, sitting there with an apron tied tight around her waist, the white V-neck T-shirt and jeans going well with her sandals, completing the laid-back-boss-who-isn't-afraid-to-work vibe.

"I'm sorry to hear about the storms, but our tofu tacos might be a good option for him."

Mimi said, "Tofu? You're serious."

"Yes, with black beans. I think you'll be surprised." Gabby pushed back from the table. "Will there be anything else?"

It stunned Mimi, caught her off guard, the way Gabby didn't seem to care, but *she* cared. Mimi still couldn't believe Gabby had pulled it off. They'd really gotten away with it. And now, here she was, over a year later, a restaurant owner, pushing back from the table like she was about to just get up and walk away.

"I know this wasn't part of the deal," Mimi whispered, fending off memories from the storm, how Gabby had hefted her husband's body into the Dodge and driven away, "but I couldn't help it. I needed to see you to believe it was real."

"I don't know you," Gabby hissed. "You don't know me. *That* was the deal."

"Where'd you get the money to open up a place like this?"

"A small business loan. Your waiter? He filed for it. He's a friend." Gabby's fingers fanned out across her thighs. "We're still paying it off. Wait . . . What am I saying?" Gabby grimaced and Mimi noticed wrinkles around her eyes that hadn't been there when they'd first met. "It's time for you to go."

Mimi nodded, gearing up for the hard part, the one thing she had left to do in order to put the past behind her.

"The report said they found Edwin in the front seat of his Dodge." Tuck's crayon scraped to a stop on the paper. Mimi heard it, but didn't turn. This was what she'd come to say: "Luke was there, too, laid out in the back lot of the chicken plant, not twenty feet from where they found Edwin. The only spot on the whole grounds where there weren't any cameras."

Gabriela raised her chin. "I have to get back to work."

Mimi waited, watching Gabby watching her. "That's it, huh? That's all you have to say?"

"There was another woman involved," Gabby said, an edge to her tone now. "Did you read that in the report, too?"

Mimi bit her bottom lip, hard.

"Your husband had a lover, and Edwin, well, he found out and saw an opportunity. He'd just been fired from the plant, so he blackmails his old boss." Gabby scanned the dining area again, still empty. "That's the word they used on the local news. 'Blackmail.' Remember?"

"It was a good story, but that's not what caught my attention," Mimi said. "The reporters kept harping on the fifty thousand bucks. It was the way they put a price on it that bothered me."

"Like it was too much, or not enough?"

Mimi looked over at Tuck. "They got everything else wrong—the whole story mixed up—but somehow, they nailed the *exact* amount of money? Fifty thousand dollars.

That's the part I couldn't figure out." Mimi smiled down at her son before turning to Gabby. "Not until the Springdale PD brought me in for questioning, and I realized what you did."

"*Me?* What did I do?"

"You left it," Mimi said, "the fifty grand the police found in the glove box of Edwin's car. You *had* to leave it, or else there wouldn't have been a motive."

"Open-shut case." Gabby slapped her thighs and stood. "I hope your son enjoys the tacos."

Mimi looked up and could see Gabriela's eyes in headlights again, Luke standing there, aiming the rifle at her chest. She blinked and Gabby was closer, down on her knees in the rain, then upright, lugging her husband's body across the gravel drive. There were no words for what she'd done—what they'd both done—for each other. And Gabby was right, Mimi shouldn't have come to Chavela. After she'd collected Luke's life insurance payout, she didn't need anything or anyone. Not anymore. She knew all that before she left Springdale, when her 4Runner crossed the Oklahoma state line, she'd known it, but there she was. There they both were, together.

Mimi stood and began dropping broken crayons into Tuck's backpack. When the mess was cleared away, she said, "It was nice to see you, Gabriela. The restaurant is beautiful." Mimi took Tuck by the wrist and started for the door.

"Why'd you come here?"

Mimi stopped beneath the archway but didn't turn. "I wanted to see you."

"You said that already."

"I needed to see you."

"You said that, too."

Tuck tugged at Mimi's hand, yanking her toward the doors the same way the memory of Gabriela Menchaca had pulled at her heartstrings for the last eighteen months, knowing what that woman had done—what she'd given up—so that their lives could go on.

Mimi sighed as she gave in to Tuck's wrenching, letting him pull her toward the exit. They only made it a couple of feet before Gabby said, "His backpack. You forgot his—My God. *Amelia*. What is this?"

"It's yours."

"No, no . . ."

"*Yes*, Gabby, you said it yourself. That's exactly what my husband owed you."

Mimi let go of Tuck's hand and watched him run, each teetering step a brand-new adventure, zigzagging this way and that, his whole life out in front of him. Mimi wished she could see Gabby's expression, the backpack hanging heavy from her fingertips, but she didn't dare turn around. The restaurant's front doors were right there, a busy city street beyond the glass, a whole new world of danger. Though so much had changed, one thing remained: Mimi still couldn't take her eyes off her son. Not yet. Maybe never.

ACKNOWLEDGMENTS

Much love and many thanks to:

Peter Lovesey, whose generosity jumpstarted my career.

Juliet Grames, who saw what this book could be and endured the many, many drafts it took me to get it there.

Bronwen Hruska, the boss lady who makes the whole thing go but who's so chill you'd never know, not until it matters.

Paul Oliver, who's got the magic touch, and hair he won't let me braid.

Taz Urnov, for the early, honest read.

Nick Whitney, for coming through in the clutch.

Rachel Kowal, for the little things and always responding to my emails.

Lily DeTaeye, for logistics and the soulful tunes.

Janine Agro, the best damn art director in the biz.

David Hale Smith, for getting this book out the door.

Michael Sutton, who not only read this draft when

it was still bad and told me so, but also worked hard to wrangle the "Ring of Fire" lyrics. Love you, brother.

Alex "Tater" Taylor, for calling me on my bullshit.

Josh Wilson, for the late game read and the Hemingway hat.

Robin Kirby, for knowing the difference between Junior Auxiliary and Junior League.

Jayme Lemons, a true Arkansawyer who's helped with so much more than just this book.

Graham Gordy, the man in the alligator shoes.

Michael Koryta, for showing me the ropes, time and again.

Josh Getzler, for taking a chance

Arkansas Tech University, especially Dr. Emily Hoffman and Dr. Jeffrey Cass, who gave me the job that completed the dream.

Arkansas, my home state, for showing this small-town boy big love.

My first block students, who told me a part of this story.

Emmy and Fin, for being six-months old once, but never again.

Dad, for the Beetle and the blood.

Mom, who gave me life and still tells me to "be careful."

Mal, my rock, my person, my muse, who revealed this book to me one layer at a time then arranged our life so I could write it. There are no words, Queen, but here I am, still trying.